Wisdom of the Grandfathers

To Kathy, Travis, and
Enjoy
keep loving history
Kathy Lynn

Also by Kathy Lynn "Sonseeahray"

Water on a Flat Rock
The Locust Thorn
When the Morning Stars Sang...

Wisdom of the Grandfathers

Kathy Lynn "Sonseeahray"

Denton Texas

This is a work of fiction. Names, characters, places, and incidents are products of the author's imagination or are used fictitiously and are not to be construed as real. Any resemblance to actual events, locales, organizations, or persons, living or dead, is entirely coincidental.

Roots & Branches
An imprint of AWOC.COM Publishing
P.O. Box 2819
Denton, TX 76202

© 2008 by Kathy Copeland
All Rights Reserved.

Cover image of Cherokee Mounted Rifle soldier courtesy of Reverend Jimmie Lee Robins, pastor and General in the 1st Cherokee Mounted Rifles reenactment group

No part of this publication may be reproduced, stored in a retrieval system, or transmitted in any form or by any means, electronic, mechanical, recording or otherwise, without written permission, except in the case of brief quotations embodied in critical articles and reviews.

Manufactured in the United States of America

ISBN: 978-0-937660-12-6

Visit the author's website: **http://www.anniesbook.com**

For Ben Joseph Tripodi.

Acknowledgements

I have always enjoyed learning about the Civil War and writing this particular book has been a dream of mine for several years. I couldn't have written it if it wasn't for a few very special people who have made it a wonderful experience for me.

Debbie Aylesworth, thank you for your wisdom, your humor and your good nature. No one can have a greater friend.

Most of all, thank you and much love to Joe, Mother and Chelsea.

God bless you all.

TENNESSEE MAN INJURED IN WRECK ON HWY. 72

Benton County Morning News,
October 7, 2001
Bentonville, Arkansas

A 27-year-old Tennessee man was critically injured yesterday when a pickup failed to stop at a stop sign on Highway 72 early Saturday morning. The Benton County Sheriff's Department reports that Travis Coker was ejected from the car although it appears that he was wearing the seatbelt.

Deputy John Luna, with the Sheriff's Department, said that Travis Coker, of Cowan, Tennessee was driving southbound on Highway 72 in a rented 2001 BMW M3 convertible. Norvis Sand, age 55, of Little Flock was driving his pickup westbound on Sugar Creek Road and pulled out in front of Coker's vehicle.

Law enforcement is continuing to investigate the accident and state that no charges have yet been filed. Coker was taken to Saint Mary's Hospital, where he remains in a coma.

PROLOGUE
June 7, 2002

The sun had come up and Travis Coker was sitting by an upstairs window that was foggy with the breath of a life gone by. Yesterday morning after leaving for town he inexplicably had returned home, gone into an unused upstairs bedroom, locked the door behind him and refused to come out even when Melody had cried.

Now he sat there, shaking with the cold even though it was June. Melody would have been shocked at his appearance: a heavy sweater pulled over his wrinkled designer shirt, a woolen scarf wrapped twice around his neck. The thermostat on the electric blanket he was wrapped in was set as high as it would go. And yet he was cold.

He thought that he had come to terms with the past. The whole thing had been a dream—after all he was home.

But yesterday morning, on his drive to Heavenly Red's, he had swerved his Hummer into the ditch at the sight of a large battered gelding, mane and tail full of burrs, calmly grazing in the ditch just a mile down the road.

Bolliver.

Chapter One
September 27, 2001

Silver-streaked clouds shimmered against a sapphire sky as the white jet plunged on and on into the emptiness. Travis Coker sighed, stretched, and leaned back into the cramped seat, closed his eyes and vainly attempted to sleep.

Home. The very word was filled with memories and meaning. His family sitting around the old brick fireplace; Travis' face warmed by the flickering, snapping flames as he listened to his mother read a story.

Lying on the comfy brown sofa in the den reading a good book, and listening to the steady beat of rain against the roof.

Studying at his desk under the large picture window, glancing up and seeing the green fields glistening in the sun.

Climbing the giant old oak's gnarled limbs until he reached the perfect fork near the top. Travis Joel Coker, master of all he surveyed.

The pictures faded back down the dusty road of time, and the steady hum of jet engines brought him back to reality. Travis was never one to sleep on an airplane. Goodness no, for he was usually fiddling with his PDA, or reviewing notes for a meeting, or furiously typing away on his laptop. Standard fare for what his dad called a "Yuppie." Travis smiled at that. One time he had actually looked up the official meaning of the word and found out that his dad was right; for he, Travis Joel Coker, at age 27 was indeed a "self-reliant, financially secure, and usually self-centered individual." He was on the executive fast track at Hicks-Bahr, a privately-held company that was the market leader in eight of the eleven product categories in which it competed. He had been hired as a marketing intern upon earning his Master Degree from the University of Tennessee, and found the work stimulating, exciting and pressure packed.

As a junior executive in the marketing department, his performance was reviewed monthly and rated on a relative basis against other junior marketing executives. On the first day of each month an email was sent to senior and junior marketing executives ranking the juniors from first to last based on their previous month's performance. Too many months on the bottom half of the list meant intense scrutiny from the senior marketing committee and the very real possibility of being fired from the high-paying job.

The bottom half of the monthly e-mail list was a nasty place for a Hicks-Bahr junior marketing executive. Travis had found himself there two times shortly after being hired, but quickly pulled himself above the line and since had been moving quickly to the top.

As a result, his immediate supervisor, Art Cuthbert, had taken a shine to Travis and had taken him unofficially under his wing. Cuthbert was in his late fifties, was short and thin, wore half-lens tortoiseshell glasses, and dressed immaculately in high-dollar suits.

Melody, Travis's college sweetheart and bride of four years, didn't always appreciate the fact that Hicks-Bahr required long hours in the office and a certain amount of travel from its young execs. But Travis enjoyed the thrill and sense of importance all of it gave him.

Yes, Travis was living the good life. He had his beautiful wife that he was in love with and his precious little daughter Allie. He lived in a beautiful house and drove a maxed out Hummer. He was brilliant, had a quick wit and had a solid body that didn't gain excess weight and needed little sleep. As soon as he had earned his degree, he was earning eighty thousand a year. In two years, he would be in six figures and all he had to do was work sixty hours a week. Yes, Travis was thrilled at being a fast-rising, lavishly compensated young marketing exec at Hicks-Bahr. He also was absolutely sure of ten things in his life (things he loved—some things more; some things less).

Job-Career at Hicks-Bahr.
Melody.
Allie.
The house and four acres.
The Hummer.
Mom and Dad.
Grandpa.

God. *He admitted that God should be number one. Although he had been raised going to church every week, he had backslid once he hit college.*

Being a Cherokee? *The question mark was because it wasn't all that important to him personally, but everyone else in the family thought it was important.*

Everything else.

He had written the list in the back of his Hicks-Bahr leather portfolio one day, and although he looked at it from time to time, he had never revised it. And in all honesty, the longer he had been at Hicks-Bahr, the less attention he had been paying to the arrangement of the items. Seems like most of the time he was maintaining a pace that even Superman would have a hard time keeping up with.

For the past three or four weeks, he had been pulled from the depths of sleep several times a night by an inexplicable, uneasy feeling that vexed him through each day. He looked through the window of the Boeing 757 that was flying him from Dallas back to Chattanooga. The stewardess brought him another cup of diet cola and he held it up against the window, examining the color. Translucent brown. His grandpa could probably tell a story about the color of the cola in the cup. Grandpa, always ready with a story, telling Travis to learn, saying, "The telling of stories is the essence of our culture. We must respect our ancestors and learn their stories to keep our ways alive for the sake of our children's children."

Yeah, right. Travis lived in a world where the standard was working sixty-hours a week, playing golf with the right partners, and climbing his way to the top at Hicks-Bahr. That was his standard of success, not a bunch of stories about fire and possums and water beetles.

He sipped the cola, which tasted good, and almost started into his work, but his eye was drawn to a little girl a couple of rows up that kept counting, "One two three four five six seven. One two three four five six seven." Over and over she counted until Travis thought he might go crazy. Didn't it bother her mother? Apparently not. He leaned back and closed his eyes, in his mind hearing Grandpa tell him about the Cherokee's fondness for the number seven. He knew that seven was-is-whatever ... a sacred number to the Cherokee; a seven sided council house, the sacred fire which was kindled with seven different kinds of wood, the seven directions and the seven Cherokee festivals.

One row up and across the aisle; an *annoying* little girl was *annoyingly* counting to seven, that *annoying* number which *annoyingly* reminded him that for years he had neglected the culture that his Grandpa had tried to instill in him. "*Duyuktv,* "the right way," the Cherokee way. Patiently, Grandpa had tried to teach a twelve-year-old Travis about a way of life that realized harmony with nature. A sustaining life embracing personal freedom, and balance between work, play, and praise.

Pressing the button that enabled his seat to recline, Travis couldn't suppress the something that stirred within him to again watch his grandpa using tobacco to smudge the air, asking and thanking the Creator for life and energy.

Not much energy today, Travis thought to himself. He placed the empty cup into the pouch in front of him and opened the thick file on the successful presentation he had finished in Dallas. Travis was good at his job and he knew it. He knew that the best presentation tool he had was not his product samples or slides or props, but *him*. He had a natural way of engaging the buyers. He knew how to make and maintain eye contact with them. He had enthusiasm, had mastered a professional volume and pitch of his voice, understood the savvy use of silence, and had developed good listening skills. A professor at college had pulled him aside one time and said, "Never forget Travis...*You* are the presentation."

As the plane sat down in Chattanooga, Travis was glad to be getting home. He had to leave again in four days for the biggest presentation of his life. He, Travis Joel Coker, would single-handedly be responsible for getting Discount America, the largest discount chain in the country, to sign an account with Hicks-Bahr.

As he drove north on I-24 towards his exit, Travis recalled the day Art Cuthbert had requested him to come to his office two weeks earlier. Upon entering, Travis was surprised to see that senior execs Egan Mohler and Juan Fuentes were seated with Mr. Cuthbert at the small table by the window.

After shaking hands with each of them, Travis sat down in the one empty seat and smiled, trying not to look nervous nor over confident. Mr. Cuthbert cleared his throat and began to speak.

"Travis, we called you to come and meet with us to discuss the fact that your fifth anniversary with Hicks-Bahr is less than a year away."

"Yes sir."

"You've been at or near the top of the monthly list for the majority of your time with Hicks-Bahr and the members of the marketing executive committee have taken notice."

Travis swiveled nervously in his seat and said again, "Yes sir?"

It was then Travis was given the impressive assignment of flying to Northwest Arkansas, to Bentonville to be exact, to meet with the buyers and work out the details of signing the deal with Discount America to handle Hicks-Bahr's line of household cleaning products.

At the end of the meeting, he shook hands with Mohler and Fuentes and remained in the lush corner office with his boss.

"Travis, we really want to get our products into those stores. When we do, we'll be the eight hundred pound gorilla."

Travis smiled at that. Cuthbert had a way of using a lot of southern expressions to get his point across.

Cuthbert continued, "Diane'll make your arrangements, get you into Bentonville on Thursday afternoon, uh, October 4. You'll be meeting with the household buyers on Friday morning, and golfing with 'em on Friday afternoon. you have to stay the weekend, but then you'll meet with 'em again on Monday and fly back here on the Tuesday red eye."

"Sounds good, sir."

Cuthbert stared at his young star. "I shouldn't tell you this, Travis, but you remind me of myself when I started out. Brilliant, aggressive, personable; you'll make senior someday Travis. Not too far in the future either. Marketing is a young man's game nowadays. Hicks-Bahr needs ya."

Travis glanced at the floor.

"I'm making you uncomfortable. I know that. But I got a good feeling about you during the first two minutes of our interview at UT. That's why I hired ya. Every one of your actions has purpose. There is a reason for everything you do. That's why we're sending you to Arkansas. You know signing a deal with Discount America means a potential economic windfall for the company and a big year-end bonus for you."

"Yes sir. Thank you sir."

Cuthbert patted Travis on the back as he left. "You'll get it done, son. You can charm a rattlesnake out of its fangs."

As he drove the Hummer out of the parking garage, Travis knew that he needed to give his wife that weekend. Likewise, Allie was growing so fast, it boggled his mind how she had gone from newborn to toddler so quickly. Therefore, he was going to try and put work aside that weekend so he could love his wife, play with his child, go to Sunday School (or at least church) with his family, and visit his grandpa. Granted, however, he had a lot to do to prepare for his trip to Northwest Arkansas; he had to make sure he was properly prepared for the trip business-wise and that he had everything with him that he needed when he traveled. He saw the trip as a test of his worth to Cuthbert and the others and was determined not to fail.

Chapter Two

Later, as he sat snarled in traffic, Travis was tired and was glad that if all went well tomorrow, he planned to work only a half day, taking a rare two and a half day weekend for one reason: Melody. Three seventy-hour workweeks had already placed him in the doghouse with his better half who chafed at even his usual sixty hour norm. He couldn't think of how to justify a full day tomorrow which would probably lead to at least a half day on Saturday, leaving her home alone again with Allie.

Travis agreed that it had to be hard looking after a nineteen month-old by oneself all day and all night. Melody's parents lived about forty-five miles northwest of Nashville, so they were not close enough to lend a hand. Travis's parents still lived at Cowan, where his dad was an attorney and his mom worked at the bank and in her spare time volunteered at the hospital over in Winchester. Suffice it to say, Melody was pretty much tied down at home.

One of the reasons Melody, a devout Christian, had originally agreed to date Travis was the fact that he had been raised in the same faith as she. He had used that fact to his advantage when he was wooing her. He was dressed and ready to pick her up on time for Sunday School every week, even carrying his Bible, but that was then. After settling in Cowan and starting to work, things were different. The difference being that Melody drove to church alone every week over in Cowan, taking Allie to her Sunday School class and then sitting in the pew with Travis's parents. Every week she would ask Travis to go to church with her. Usually he declined, saying that he had brought work home from the office, had the lawn to mow, or a myriad of other excuses. To appease her, however, he made an effort to sit with her each evening as she would read a chapter or two aloud from the Bible, even though his mind was usually in the office.

* * *

Travis and Melody met in Knoxville through one of Travis's roommates at a pizza restaurant near the university. Looking back, who would have thought that they would end up for better or for worse? Travis, popular and outgoing, was two years older and in his last year of graduate school. Melody, conservative and quiet, was an undergraduate and admitted that she agreed to date him simply because she wanted a cute boyfriend.

It definitely was not love at first sight for her, but Travis declared that he was stricken by Cupid's arrow that first fateful night. To Melody's annoyance, he kept staring at her all evening. Even though Travis tried to be utterly charming and was handsome, she just wasn't interested.

Travis, however, was very persistent. Riding on his black motorcycle, he'd zoom past her sorority house, as if by accident, and pretend to be surprised to see Melody. She liked the attention but felt that he was too dangerous since he rode a motorcycle. But Travis had good looks, charm, and a way with words which would have made any girl giggle and he was determined. Fear engulfed her when she began to fall for him. She was intent on getting her degree in social studies and then going on to grad school. But Travis was just too tempting.

A few weeks before the fateful evening at the pizza place, Melody had become frustrated with herself. All through school, she had poured over her books just to get excellent grades, but for what? College was supposed to be enjoyable and she decided that she wanted to have fun. Her motto that semester became "be adventurous and grab a cute boyfriend." After all, graduation, grad school and life loomed the following semester. So, with encouragement from her sorority sisters, she decided that she wanted to have a boyfriend, but not just any boyfriend; he had to be cute.

Refusing all of Travis's requests for a solo date, Melody did invite him and his buddies to go along with her and three or four of her friends to movies and burger joints and the like. Week after week she rebuffed his every invitation to go out.

Then one night at a pizza place with their friends, he announced to the world that she was his girlfriend. Melody was taken aback, thinking, "I am his girlfriend? How did that happen?"

Travis then leaned in close and whispered in her ear, "I am going to marry you one day. I'm going to be rich. You just see."

Red-faced, Melody laughed to herself and mused, "I would never marry this guy. He's a motorcycle bum. I don't have a future with him. He can be my boyfriend because I just want to have fun. I hate my boring student life."

But despite her initial trepidation, she fell in love with Travis. One evening, they sat by the fountain and watched the sunset and wove dreams of being together forever and having babies one day. Amidst the old Beegees song, "How Deep is Your Love," time stood still for the love-struck couple.

The day before graduation, holding pizza and a dozen red roses, Travis took Melody by surprise as he knelt down and proposed marriage. "How roooomaaaantic," she gushed, "Yes!"

Melody knew when she agreed to marry Travis that they would end up living in or near Cowan, Tennessee, where he had grown up, because that was what he wanted. Then when he committed to work for Hicks-Bahr of Chattanooga shortly before graduation, Travis insisted that he would not mind the fifty mile commute. So, they began their house hunting, and after searching for just the right place, they settled southeast of Cowan, Tennessee, purchasing a Victorian home that was built in 1882. The house had already been restored by some eastern investor that thought he might enjoy retiring in the South. He had to rethink it though because his Yankee wife decided that she would miss her Yankee friends and fancy social doings. Frustrated, the man sold Travis and Melody the house for barely a penny over what he had in it. With financial backing from Travis's parents, the bride and groom were able to move in and set up house. To make things even better, the unhappy retiree left the house partially furnished with nice antiques.

The newlywed Coker's loved their quiet country home. In Knoxville while attending the university, Melody had lived with forty-five other young women in a sorority house that provided constant racket. Travis lived with two other grad guys in an apartment surrounded by busy traffic, yelling neighbors and the constant sound of blasting radios. Further, life in the city does not cease when the sun goes down. The late shoppers, the entertainment goers, the honk of a horn, perhaps a distant radio, bits of some argument or laughter, sirens; all of these were the night sounds of Knoxville. As if in another world, the hoots of an owl, the calling of a bird, the snapping of a twig, the hum of insects were the sounds of their Franklin County country home.

Before graduation, Melody had been ecstatic when Travis had been offered the position at Hicks-Bahr, but after the wedding, honeymoon and getting settled into their new place, she soon learned that he would be working long hours. Travis told her more than once, "You can't have a job like mine and clock out at five." Most of the time she didn't say much, but other times they would quarrel about his "abandoning" her out in the country, especially after Allie was born. Then Travis would say something sarcastic like, "I can just imagine waving goodbye to Mr. Cuthbert on my way out, saying 'Sorry, sir, but Melody needs me home at five thirty.' " Travis repeatedly explained to her that being on the executive fast track at Hicks-Bahr meant long hours with lots of golf games thrown in for good measure. Anything less and he would never make it to the top of the ladder.

Travis's office was on the third floor of the Lawrence Hicks Building, a modern, glass-encased edifice that rose six stories above the corporate headquarters on the southwest side of Chattanooga. On a clear day, Travis could see Signal Mountain and from the dining room he could see the city and the Tennessee River.

When he had first joined Hicks-Bahr four years earlier, he brought Melody and his parents up to his tastefully decorated office to see its dark wood paneling and luxurious carpeting. The senior Coker's were proud to see what their son had made of himself and happy that he wanted to show them.

Travis kissed Melody goodbye in the lobby after the short visit and she had been so proud. Travis had to admit that he stuck his chest out a bit that day as he gave his parents and wife "the tour." After all, Hicks-Bahr was the number one maker of household cleaning products, and had been in business over a hundred years with profits the previous year exceeding $10.3 billion.

Chapter Three
September 28, 2001

Travis's half day on Friday turned out with him actually leaving only an hour and a half early. He had tried to get away at about two o'clock, but he had continued working like a machine with one of the senior managers who was putting together a million dollar deal with a Florida supermarket chain. Melody wasn't happy. He drove a little fast on the interstate, making a deliberate attempt to be home for dinner and try his best to patch things up with her. She was, after all, his wife, and he loved her, and as Grandpa had reminded him more than once, she deserved to have him to herself once in a while.

As he drove along in the fast lane, passing every car and semi, he gave himself a pep talk, determined to make things right with his wife. As he pulled into the drive, he was pleased to see Melody sitting on the front porch, watching Allie play on the sidewalk.

He didn't bother pulling the Hummer into the garage; he just hopped out and ran across the grass, yelling, "Daddy's home!"

He picked Allie up and gave her a big kiss to which she replied with giggles. Sitting her back down, he pulled Melody up from the step and gave her a kiss on the lips. "I wanted to make sure to be home in time for dinner."

Melody's eyes narrowed and she pulled away from him and crossed her arms. "Is that so?" She made a deliberate show of looking at her watch. "What about working half the day?"

Travis backed away a bit and his immediate response was to be defensive. However, he calmed himself and figured he deserved that for promising to be home and then not showing up until after five.

"Honey, I'm sorry. I tried to get away. I really did."

Melody turned and went into the house. Picking up Allie, Travis followed and after setting Allie down in her playpen, went into the kitchen. There he found Melody staring into the open fridge.

Travis stepped in front of the refrigerator, blocking her view of its contents. "Honey, I'm sorry."

Melody looked up at him and at that moment they physically were very close. Travis could feel her breath, and it was familiar and good. He noticed again how petite she was. Melody didn't move, just stood there; one hand at her side and the other on the fridge handle. Just then the motor on the fridge kicked in and cold air from the open door began to blow on both of them, causing her to laugh.

In one swift movement, Travis kissed her and caused her to walk backwards over to the counter, where he kissed her again. "Hey, let's go to Heavenly Red's for barbecue. Allie loves it. I love it. You know you love it. Come on …"

"I'm not dressed."

Travis stared at her long, tanned legs. She was wearing navy blue walking shorts, with a white cotton t-shirt.

"With legs like that, you could eat in a five star restaurant."

"You're still not off the hook."

"I know, but I love you."

Ignoring the open refrigerator door, Travis teased, charmed and sweet-talked Melody and was able to get her into a good mood before they drove to the barbecue place.

Chapter Four

Heavenly Red's was Travis's favorite place to eat. It was located in Cowan in an old brick building that should have been torn down years earlier and would have been had it not been for the popularity of the barbecue. Behind the building, smoke poured from a large brick barbecue pit and the smell filled the air and tempted one's nose, mouth and eyes. There was always a crowd at lunch and on Friday nights there was usually a waiting list. After waiting about thirty minutes, they were led to a table covered with red-checked oil-cloth. Along the way, Travis stopped a few times to shake hands with old high school buddies and friends of his parents.

The menus were hand painted on the wall, but were completely unnecessary for most of the customers. "Two large diet colas, a kid's drink, an order of fried mushrooms, two Heavenly Red's specials and a corn dog."

The sweaty waitress took their order without writing it down. After she had brought their drinks and mushrooms, Travis grabbed Melody's leg under the table. She slapped his hand.

"Stop. I'm still mad at you."

"You're beautiful," he said. "When was the last time I told you that you are beautiful?"

"About two weeks ago."

"Two weeks. Hmmm."

"Don't let it happen again."

He grabbed her leg again and rubbed her knee. She allowed it and smiled at him, teeth shining in the fluorescent light, her soft brown eyes glowing. Her dark brown hair was wavy and fell a few inches below her shoulders.

The waitress brought their dinner. Travis ate his and half of Melody's. Still hungry, he looked at Allie's corn dog, but saw that Melody had torn it up into small pieces that made it unappetizing.

"Let's get pecan cobbler."

"Aren't you full?" asked Melody.

"Let's get one and share it." Not waiting for her answer or the waitress, Travis went to the counter and returned with a bowl of hot cobbler, two spoons, and a kid's ice cream cone for Allie.

As they ate, they tried to find all fifty states from among the license plates that decorated the black and white checkered walls. Melody wondered why the fish that had swum in a 1920's Roman gas pump were gone. All that remained was a couple of fake plants and a bit of gravel. Allie had always enjoyed seeing the fish on prior visits.

Travis finished off the cobbler and the cone part of Allie's ice cream. Finally full, he paid the check and the family climbed into Melody's SUV. As they drove home, Melody's thoughts were of babies.

"I want a little brother for Allie."

"I think we ought to wait a couple of years."

"What are we waiting for? You love Allie."

"Yes, I love Allie."

Melody turned to face the window and said nothing.

Travis did love Allie, but felt uninspired when it came to having another baby. He had decided that he needed to devote all of his energy to becoming the youngest marketing executive in Hicks-Bahr history.

Travis sighed, exasperated at Melody's sudden change in mood. He began recalling the events of his work day as he drove his family home. Once there, he carried the sleeping Allie into the house where Melody put her to bed while he headed to the shower. Twenty minutes later, he found his wife under the covers. He leaned over and kissed her. She did not respond.

In an effort to make amends, Travis spent Saturday morning digging in Melody's flower beds. She had mentioned that she wanted to set out fall mums. Behind him, the lawn sprinkler rattled and hissed and spit out water in a perfect semicircle. As he dug up the summer annuals, he was thinking about Melody. He knew what he should do: he should tell her how much he loved her and then sit down and talk with her about having a baby. He stood and wiped the dirt off of his knees and went into the house and found his wife in the laundry room. She was at the dryer, throwing wet clothes inside. He leaned against the doorjamb and watched her. She didn't glance up although he knew that she had heard him come in.

He watched her for a moment before he pounced, grabbing her and pinning her up against the washer. He bear hugged her for a good minute. He kissed her neck and tasted the sweet smell of her body wash. She just stood there, her arms hanging at her side. He noticed that her eyes were wet. *Those beautiful eyes*, he thought.

"I'd like a date tonight," he said.

Melody just looked away; the tears suddenly overflowing. Travis looked into her eyes, held her closer and kissed her like always. She said nothing.

"I want to go out with my wife. Mom can keep Allie overnight and I'll make reservations at the Highpoint at Monteagle. You know it's your favorite. Huh, what do you say? A castle, romantic, hmmm?"

Melody continued to look out the window, body tense, arms hanging.

"What cha say, hon? We'll go out for a nice dinner. Maybe see Al Capone sitting at the next table?"

Melody started to smile a little.

"We'll eat and stay out late and then come home and stay awake all night." Travis kissed her neck again, causing her to laugh and try to twist away.

"I want my husband back. Hicks-Bahr is taking you away. If you would just work ten hours less a week, it would be okay. I want you home more. I want a yard full of children. I want to fill up this huge house with brown haired babies."

Kissing her again, he held her close. "We will, I promise. For now, how 'bout we practice? Where's Allie? She asleep?"

"No, she's in her playpen and I need to start another load." She tried to pull out of his grasp. "Besides, you don't need practice."

Kissing her once more, Travis laughed and pushed the laundry room door shut with his foot. "Thank you, ma'am, but how about we practice anyway? I promise that we'll sit down and talk about a baby when I get back from Arkansas."

Appeased, Melody gave in.

Chapter Five

It's going to be a good day, Travis thought to himself Sunday morning. He had slept good and woken up early. He grabbed his favorite pair of button fly jeans, an old college t-shirt and tennis shoes and slipped out of the bedroom without waking Melody. He dressed in the downstairs bathroom while coffee brewed in the kitchen. He poured some of the coffee into a thermos and left half a pot on the burner, along with a note saying he'd be back in time for breakfast and church. He didn't brush his teeth, shave, or comb his hair. Grandpa wouldn't notice.

Outside, the birds were starting their busy morning. It was still copperhead season and Travis watched the ground as he walked, stopping for a moment to look across the hills. The faint glow of sunrise licked the treetops and mist kissed the ground in some places as the first light calls of warblers, towhees, and cardinals trickled through the woods and the calls of katydids faded away. The feeling rose in him again, whispering that he ought to thank the Creator for all of the beauty. He didn't, of course, and the moment passed. He climbed onto his motorcycle and started down the drive, turning left on the county road that would take him the back way to Grandpa's house.

He knew Grandpa would already be up, would have said his prayers and had his usual breakfast of shredded wheat. He had lived alone ever since Grandma had died a few years back. Two weeks after Grandma's death, Grandpa had come down with a terrible cold and everyone supposed that he would take pneumonia and die. But he fought it, saying that it wasn't his time yet.

Grandpa's name was Horace Coker and he still lived on the farm that had belonged to his parents out by Decherd, a few miles from Cowan. Franklin County, Tennessee, and the area around Cowan had been home to Cokers for almost two hundred years. In the early 1800's, a half-Cherokee man named John Coker had settled in the area and married a Cherokee girl named Annie Ratliff. John had bought a grist mill and he and Annie had eleven children. Those eleven children had procreated what seemed like thousands of Cokers and Coker kin. Every cemetery in Franklin County was home to Cokers awaiting the return of the Lord. Many still lived in the neighboring communities around Cowan. Many more lived all around the country. Suffice it to say that Travis had a lot of family.

When Travis would think back to his childhood summers, he clearly remembered traveling to Grandpa's log cabin. Not much had changed over the years; the same narrow, winding road, snaking through a grove of trees. The true magic of the trip still began behind those ancient oaks and hickories. At the end of the bumpy driveway was the cabin, and beyond that, a sparkling lake.

As the motorcycle slowly bumped up the drive and through that thick curtain of trees, Travis felt the same way he did when he was a kid; sort of like a soldier returning home from war.

Growing up, Travis was always free to do what he wished at Grandpa's. Those days had passed in a blur of pure bliss. Travis had spent his time there swimming, fishing, and talking with Grandpa.

Grandpa taught (or had tried to teach) Travis the importance of prayer and faith in the Creator. He said that life would be a winding road and at times Travis would lose his way, but he would never be afraid if he took the time to pray. For through prayer he could keep faith and hope alive, and that as long as he held on to those there would be nothing he wouldn't survive.

Also, Grandpa had tried everything to get Travis interested in Cherokee traditional practices. Grandpa was a respected gourd dancer and Travis was always proud to see his Grandpa in the circle, carrying his rattle and fan, wearing his cowboy hat and boots, with his red and blue blanket drawn across his shoulders.

But Travis's fondest memories were of fishing. Grandpa fished at every opportunity in the summer. When Travis was little, around six or seven, he would call Travis's mom up the night before to ask if Travis wanted to go fishing. The answer, from Travis, was always yes. Travis smiled as he thought about spending restless nights waiting for the morning.

Grandpa would show up early, usually while it was still a little dark outside. That early morning twilight time was still a precious, almost sacred time for Travis. The whole world was sleeping as they drove to a nearby lake. On the floor of the truck would be a small tackle box, a Styrofoam box with worms in it, an insulated jug filled with cold lemonade, and a small bag of grandma's homemade sugar cookies.

The drive was usually quiet. They would sit in the silence and let the scenery roll by. Travis loved the quiet transition into the morning, interrupted by a pat on his leg, or by Grandpa's large tanned and calloused hand carefully producing a sandwich bag filled with lemon drops and offering them to him with a twinkle in his eyes.

One particular day was different from their other fishing days. Normally they set up on a small, mowed clearing and fished for bluegill most of the morning. Travis later came to understand that he was fishing for bait for Grandpa's other fishing trips but he didn't care. He grew to be an accomplished bluegill fisherman and was very proud of that fact.

On that morning as Travis unwound the line on his pole, he walked over to Grandpa, who looked him square in the face and said very seriously, "Travis, you like fishing, and if you're gonna fish, you need to bait your own hook."

And that was it. Grandpa had always carefully skewered the worm on Travis's hook, and Travis never thought that that might change. But you didn't argue with Grandpa. There was no question what would happen. Either Travis would suck it up and bait that hook, or he could put his pole down and sit until Grandpa was done. So he skewered the worm with Grandpa laughing the whole time. But it was a good kind of laugh, a proud laugh. It made Travis feel warm, taller, and older somehow. He had been let into the secret fraternity of the hook baiters. He was a real fisherman. He took a long swig of Grandma's lemonade and set to fishing.

He remembered once when he caught a big fish that had struggled until it broke the line. Just when Travis felt like giving up, Grandpa said, "You can't win every time." Or the time when he was messing around and dropped his fishing pole in the lake, Travis knew he was in trouble for sure. But all Grandpa had said was, "We make mistakes, Travis."

While they fished, sometimes they just sat really quiet, but most of the time they talked. Other times Grandpa would put his hand on Travis's shoulder and for a long time leave it there. He wouldn't say one single word but Travis knew how much he cared.

* * *

At last, there was the cabin. Travis slowed his bike to a stop. Sitting there, on the rocky driveway, more memories flooded his mind. He thought of the time when he and Grandpa had caught that twenty inch bass. Against Travis's childish wishes, Grandpa had made him release the fish. With a huge kiss on its gaping mouth, he reluctantly let him go. Grandpa then explained to him again about taking animal life and that sort of thing. That day had ended by watching the sunset over the shimmering lake. What times Travis had had with his grandpa.

After sifting through a million memories, Travis finally motored on up to the cabin. Sure enough, down at his little dock, Grandpa was fishing. Parking the bike, Travis walked down towards the dock, hands in his pockets and although he knew that Grandpa was fully aware of his arrival, the older man seemed oblivious, even when Travis squatted down beside Grandpa's old woven lawn chair.

At last, Grandpa reeled in his line which indicated that his bait had been stolen. "Siyo," he said.

"Hi, Grandpa, catching anything?"

Grandpa was 72 years old, stood five feet eleven inches tall, with a lean build and distinguished gray hair. And in spite of his humble, down-home appearance, Travis's grandpa was brilliant. He had retired from his career as a civilian engineer at Arnold Air Force Base near Tullahoma at the Arnold Engineering Development Center. Grandpa had worked in the wind tunnel area where rocket engines were tested.

Travis and Grandpa sat on the dock for a bit, reminiscing and telling fish stories. At last, Grandpa said that he was hungry and stood up, "Let's scrounge something to eat."

As they walked to the kitchen door, Grandpa stopped and picked a couple of handfuls of late strawberries for them to share. Over a fried egg sandwich, Travis told his grandpa that Melody wanted to have another baby. "I feel that our family is already complete for now. We've got a nice house, I make a good income, and I want to focus on making it to the next level at work. I'm not ready right now."

Grandpa nodded, saying nothing as Travis continued. "Grandpa, already me and Melody don't have a lot of time to spend with each other. I want to try again later; a year or so maybe. Do you think I'm being unreasonable in not wanting us to have another baby right now?"

Grandpa poured himself some more coffee before answering. "Travis, the Creator has programmed women to want children, so it's hardly surprising that Melody wants another baby. Many women have one child less than they want. Try to focus less on what you want and focus a little on what she wants. Take your emotion out of the equation and come to a decision based on other factors. Ask yourself how would you feel if you learned that you couldn't have another child? Sad? Relieved? Listen to your first reaction to this question. Most importantly, talk to Melody and make her feel loved. Try to spend as much time with her as you can."

Grandpa paused. "She supports you even with you at work all the time. You must support her too, my son."

Grandpa then leaned back in his chair and Travis knew that a story was next.

Once a little boy heard that the circus was coming to town. He wanted to go and see the circus parade. He went and told his grandpa that he wanted to go to town to see the parade. His grandpa said they could go as soon as he was finished weeding the garden. The little boy was stressed because grandpa took a long time. At last they went into town. When they got there, the parade was starting already. The crowd was large and the little boy could not see because they were in the back of the crowd. When the parade began to pass by, the grandpa reached down, picked up the little boy and put him on his shoulders so that he could see. The little boy said, "Grandpa, you can't see the parade!" The grandpa replied, "That's okay, when I was a little boy, someone once placed me on their shoulders so I could see the circus parade.

Grandpa paused for a moment to allow the story to sink in. Placing his hand on Travis's, he said, "We all need to sit on someone's shoulders sometime. We also need to let someone sit on ours."

Aware of the time, and that Melody would have already left for church, Travis told Grandpa that he had to get home. As Grandpa walked him out to the bike, Travis told him about his upcoming trip to Bentonville, Arkansas. In turn, Grandpa told him that the Trail of Tears had gone through near Bentonville and that he should try and visit Tahlequah and perhaps the Pea Ridge battlefield while in the area. He also told Travis about their ancestors that had fought in the battle at Pea Ridge, especially Daniel Ratliff who had been a Mounted Rifle for Colonel Stand

Watie. He urged Travis to drive out to the battleground and look around. "Kill two birds with one stone," he said, visit the Trail of Tears, and see a battlefield that was involved in Cherokee history."

Out of a sense of obligation, Travis promised that he would.

Travis went home to find Melody and Allie in the kitchen eating peanut butter and banana sandwiches. Melody wasn't talking to him so he grabbed the Sunday paper and went in and flopped down on the couch.

In a few minutes she came into the living room. "I need to talk to you. And I need you to talk to me, too."

In other words, we need to talk, Travis thought. He could hear her stare: How dare you just lie there? But he ignored it.

Finally, he said, "I'm sorry I didn't get home. I was with Grandpa."

"Whatever." Melody got up and he heard the bedroom door close. He then heard the antique lock slide shut.

Travis got up and tip-toed into the kitchen and slipped a butter knife from the drawer. He knew that it was not a time to knock. The blade slid smoothly, silently into the archaic lock, a subtle turn to the left and click, he was in.

She was expecting him. She turned to face him, mock surprise on her face. Dropping the butter knife, Travis dove onto the bed so hard it was a wonder that it didn't fall. Trying not to laugh, Melody rolled over and turned her back.

"I said that I was sorry."

"You're always sorry."

"You love me?"

"No."

"I love you," he said in baby talk.

More silly giggles and all was well again in the Coker household.

Travis felt pretty sure of himself by the way he always seemed able to bring Melody around by either acting corny or tickling her or seducing her.

Deep inside, however, he feared that one day his luck would run out and she would tire of him.

The rest of Sunday passed quickly. Travis rode the riding mower and cut the grass before he drove into town to rent a movie and fill the Hummer up with gas. Later, Melody baked a cobbler and made potato salad while he cooked steaks out on the grill. They ate dinner in the den in front of the television. She had fed Allie in the kitchen and put her to bed early. While they ate the cobbler with ice cream, Travis put his sock feet up on the coffee table. Melody smiled at him and was cheerful. Travis was content. They were a family.

They were at home.

Chapter Six
October 1-4, 2001

At five a.m., the alarm clock signaled next to Travis's head. He staggered across the bedroom, heading for the shower. He dressed quickly and kissed a sleepy Melody goodbye. Twenty minutes later, he was headed south on I-24 towards Chattanooga where a busy Monday and an eleven hour day waited. The work week passed quickly and on Wednesday, the day before his flight, Travis managed to get away from the office at 5:15, pretty good considering. He called Melody and asked her to start the grill and thaw out some chicken breasts. They watched television in the bedroom while Travis packed for the trip and turned out the light by 9:30. With so much riding on his trip, Travis wanted to be well-rested, "at the top of his game," as Cuthbert always said. He had to be at the airport in Chattanooga by 8:45 or so the next morning to catch the 10:20 to Dallas where he would connect to Northwest Arkansas.

Unable to relax, Travis lay restless and unsleeping late into the night. His legs burned. He could feel each of his muscles aching as if something were pulling them away from the bone. Every inch of him hurt in one way or another, and he kept up a slow, constant movement, trying vainly to find the one position of comfort which eluded him. Next to him, Melody slept on, occasionally mumbling some bit of dream conversation. He lay there for a long time, his eyes probing his closed eyelids until at last he opened them. The ceiling above him became a canvas for the unknown imagery that pressed in on him. He tried to think about work. So much was riding on his presentation Friday morning; not just his future with the company, but also the company's future with Discount America. Before he had headed out that afternoon, Cuthbert had reminded him again that it was unusual for a junior team member to be given such an assignment. Then, as he patted him on the shoulder, he also told Travis again that he was ready and that

Hicks-Bahr was confident in his ability to "get the John Henrys on the dotted line."

Travis rubbed his eyes, dwelling on the fact that his presentation to Discount America could make or break his career. What if he failed? What if they just didn't want to commit? *What if? What if....*

Desperate for sleep and although he knew he was prepared, he clinched his fists and tried to go through the whole proposal again in his mind. But as he stared at the ceiling, he was distracted by glimpses of his grandpa and scenes from his childhood. Bits of an earlier conversation with his mother also crept in and nagged at him. He rolled over and turned his back to Melody, hoping that forcing himself to think about the meeting would somehow steady his mind and bring slumber. It did not. Melody was sleeping soundly beside him. He looked at the clock on the nightstand beside the bed. It was eleven minutes past four. He could rest another hour or so before he needed to get up. He tried to relax so he could fall asleep for at least a few minutes, but his mind had started to run again with thoughts about his presentation. It didn't help that Melody had started tossing and turning beside him.

"Are you feeling OK?" he asked in a whisper.

"What?" Melody responded, sleepily.

"Are you feeling OK?" he asked quietly again, "Because you've started tossing and turning, and moving around the bed."

"Hm-mm" she said. "I'm fine, don't worry."

She then turned towards him and put her arms around him.

"I'm pregnant."

Chapter Seven
October 4, 2001

Travis arrived at Northwest Arkansas Regional Airport at two o'clock on the afternoon of the fourth of October, a Thursday. He picked up his rental car, and was delighted at what Cuthbert's assistant had reserved for him: a silver 2001 BMW M3, a dream ride.

It was a small car but it was comfortable. He placed his suitcase and laptop in the trunk. The spare tire took up too much room to fit much else. The airport was out in the country a few miles outside of Bentonville. It was early, by then only about three o'clock, so he decided to drive around for a bit and enjoy the Beemer before finding his hotel. Therefore, when he left the airport, he turned in the direction heading away from Bentonville. While he drove he took in the sights and sounds of the road, the small hills that surrounded him, and the creeks he crossed. There was plenty of farmland and livestock to see, cows and sheep, horses, large commercial chicken houses and fields of what looked like some kind of beans. There were small towns to pass through, names he had never heard, and places he had never seen before, with church steeples and mechanic shops. Every so often a large Discount America truck would trundle past him in the lane to his left, its driver letting it run like an unbridled horse along a path.

He kept at or below the speed limit, knowing that every few miles an Arkansas state trooper or some local sheriff probably lurked in the bushes along the side of the road, like a crocodile lying in wait of its prey. Sure enough, as he drove along the Benton County highways, he noticed several cars getting pulled over. Mindful that Hicks-Bahr frowned on an employee getting a traffic ticket while on a business trip, he didn't mind having to hold back on his speed.

He circled through Benton County with the windows open, the convertible top down and the sun beating down on him. The fall heat was like syrup. The sun drove shadows deep into corners, leaving them flattened on the road. He looked into the rearview mirror and darn it, his hair was starting to curl. Although he had the air conditioner on, it did little good with the top down, and his shirt was sticking to his back on the leather seat.

When he got into the town of Bentonville, he decided to check out the downtown area. The Bentonville town square was pretty with an old courthouse, a Civil War statue, benches, a fountain, and beautiful gardens, and quaint little shops. He could tell that the area was famous, historically speaking, for a battle or two during the Civil war. He saw the Massey Hotel building and learned that since around 1840, there had always been a hotel on that spot and that during the Civil War, several Union officers had stayed there when it was the Eagle Hotel. As Travis slowly drove around the square, he didn't really stop to read any of the historical markers, except the one about the Eagle Hotel. He could read it while stopped at the intersection. As he slowly circled the square for the second time, he looked at the statue of a Confederate officer of some sort. Feeling dramatic, Travis thought to himself about the man, *He patiently stands there, never questioning the sacred cause for which he sacrificed. Now his musket will always be quiet, he will always be young; his eyes always empty as he looks back. Because you know, this is 2001 and he's really not a soldier at all, but an image created by men.* Realizing how phony he sounded, Travis slightly rolled his eyes and raised his eyebrows as he caught one last glance of the officer's marble eyes and then drove away. He knew that somewhere around there was the battlefield-Trail of Tears site that he had promised Grandpa he would visit. *Oh yeah, Pea Ridge,* he thought to himself. He figured he would take a drive out there sometime over the weekend and read a historical marker or two about the Trail of Tears and see some remnants of a battle, preserved for tourism purposes. At least he figured that he could learn enough to tell Grandpa about it.

All that stuff was so long ago, Travis thought. There, even in the presence of such history, he felt little or no connection between the past and the present. The faces he saw around him as he drove, and the sounds he heard were squarely in the then and there to him. In the one hundred or more years since the great Civil War battle, many folks had moved to Bentonville to work for the great Discount America. He doubted if the business-type people of the present really cared much more about the Civil War or the Trail of Tears than he did. More than that even, he hadn't been all that interested in the Trail of Tears or Civil War stuff back home in Tennessee, so he certainly didn't care about it in Arkansas.

    He spent another hour or so cruising around in the BMW, ever mindful that he was scheduled to meet with the buyers the next morning. The heat of the day was beginning to catch up to him, so he decided that he should find his hotel and review his notes. Using the map Diane had printed out for him; he found the Suites Hotel, parked and went inside. The person at the reception desk was very helpful, even sending someone out to his car to get his suitcase. The fellow's southern accent was very different to Travis's, and the fellow made him think of a younger version of Cuthbert. It was a nice room, with a Jacuzzi bathtub that he figured he wouldn't have time to use. He ordered room service and called Melody to let her know he had arrived safely. While he waited for his dinner, he checked his e-mail with his laptop, and listened to his voicemail before settling down to go over his presentation again.

    But try as he might, he couldn't concentrate. He felt distracted about a hundred things, the least of which being the changing fall leaves that were framed perfectly by the large hotel window. For what seemed like an hour, he sat with his feet propped up on the window sill, gazing at the leaves as they helplessly floated one by one to the ground. With each falling leaf came a different thought about his life. He knew that he needed to try and be home a little more. He entertained thoughts about Hicks-Bahr and then again battled guilt about never being at home. He thought about Allie and how much she had grown. He thought about the new baby that would be coming. He thought about his Grandpa. But perhaps overshadowing all of his thoughts was Grandpa and the Cherokee heritage he had deliberately turned his back on.

    He loved his Grandpa but hated the power he seemed to have over him-power to make him feel guilty simply because he chose to not embrace his legacy. He was frustrated that his legacy seemed to call his name. But he was not going to let it control his life. He was a businessman. He didn't have time (or the desire) to spend weekends going to pow wows or any of the other things Grandpa wanted him to do. If he ever decided to do so, it would be on his own time, his own terms.

    The next few hours he spent going over the presentation until his growling stomach reminded him that room service had never delivered his dinner. Looking at his watch, he realized that it was 8:30. He called for room service again and then called Melody while he waited. They talked until the knock at the door announced his dinner. Sitting cross-legged on the bed, he watched a crime show, ate his dinner and crawled into bed, turned out the light, and called Melody again to say goodnight.

Chapter Eight
October 5, 2001

Travis had given himself plenty of time for his appointment so, when he arrived at Discount America he had some to kill. He had overcompensated because, not knowing how heavy the Bentonville morning traffic might be, he wanted to play it safe because so much was riding on the outcome of the meetings. He regularly amazed his friends and family by arriving at family gatherings and such at almost the exact time that he had promised. He had an uncanny understanding of the behavior of time, somehow knowing exactly how long it would take him to get somewhere, somehow factoring in traffic, weather and other possible delays. But on that day, as the bright morning sun welcomed him when he came out of his hotel, he factored in additional time for unknown traffic in an unknown city and was early by almost a half-hour.

The Bentonville streets were busy, but nothing at all like Chattanooga at rush hour. He knew the address where he was headed by heart and went to seek it out. He had been told to park in front of the building in the spaces designated for suppliers.

Since he had never met the people he would be meeting with, he wasn't too worried about being seen by any of them while he scoped out the building. Although later, during his presentation, someone might remember seeing him outside if they happened to be on the street at the same moment. But with so many faces around, the chance of that embarrassing event happening was unlikely. And if it did, he would worry about it then. Being late was one thing, it would certainly cast him and Hicks-Bahr in a bad light, but whether Discount America might think he was snooping around outside the building was harder to predict. It could make him look silly on the one hand, or dishonest, but on the other it might endear him to them. Neither outcome troubled him much for no one seemed to pay him the least bit of mind. All he wanted was to get in there, locate his samples (which had been shipped ahead), meet the buyers and give a dynamite proposal. In truth, he felt confident and enthusiastic about the whole meeting, and that was good. The whole trip fitted quite nicely with his image of himself as a better than average member of the "young and upwardly mobile" generation.

To him there was nothing special about the Discount America building, with its plain non-descript architecture. He had expected it to be a much fancier and modern structure. Instead, it reminded him more of a government office of some sort. It seemed like hundreds of people were headed into the building. Some appeared to be suppliers or salesmen, others appeared to be administrative assistants and others probably were executives. From where Travis sat in the BMW, he could spot at least five security guards, declaring to all that this building was of an authoritative nature. Meanwhile, the sunshine was brightening, giving the building a more attractive look.

Still a tad bit early, Travis continued to sit in his car and look at the Discount America building. He felt it held some promise for him as he looked at it from the outside. Perhaps it was the lure of going inside and meeting with the buyers, pulling off the big coup that would make him a star with Hicks-Bahr. He wasn't sure if that was it exactly, but it was merely the most rational reason his mind could attach itself to.

He still had over twenty minutes until his appointment time, but he was getting too restless to stay sitting in the car. He just wanted to get on with it, the butterflies were beginning to flutter and his mind was starting to create a drama. He imagined the room and the faces of the buyers, and the questions they would ask, and what his answers would be. His daydream went into full swing, though his awareness of a security guard that kept looking his way prevented him from talking out loud to himself as he often did when alone in his car. And anyway, he decided to just go on in and see about locating his samples. So, feeling self-confident and ready for action, he got out of the car and walked through the doors of Discount America. By that time, he was only fifteen minutes early but such was the advice he had always been given about important meetings, so maybe it would make him look good.

He held the door open for two ladies that were coming up the steps and then he stepped into a reception area, beyond which he could see what appeared to be hundreds of cubicles across the whole first floor of the company. The place was clean and efficient, with more security officers posted near the door and near the reception desk. Television monitors in various corners showed national news and weather stations. People were sitting singly or in small groups, appearing to be waiting for admission inside; Travis figured they were suppliers like him.

The receptionist greeted him. He told her the reason for his visit. She asked him to sign in, presented him with a badge and asked him to wait in the seating area. Shortly, a young woman appeared and looked around the room.

"Mr. Coker," she said.

"Yes," he replied and got to his feet.

"Hello, I'm Lisa, Mr. Kougl's assistant," she said with a pleasant smile. She held out her hand and Travis shook it, one of those quick business handshakes, short lived with a slight squeeze that needed to be administered with expert timing.

"I'm pleased to meet you," Travis replied.

"If you'll follow me, I'll take you to the room where your samples are. Mr. Kougl and the others will join you there in about a half hour. Will that give you enough time to get set up?"

"Yes, thank you."

As he followed her through the doors into the sanctum of Discount America, Travis was again somewhat disappointed in its austere appearance. All that he saw was what appeared to be acres of cubicles. He followed Lisa until she stopped and indicated a small conference room with a window which gave a view of the hallway. As he went inside, Lisa smiled before turning and walking away.

Travis saw a white board, a cork board, and his boxes of samples. Working quickly, he assembled his display of household cleaning products and sat down to wait.

Shortly, a 30-ish looking man wearing khaki's and an IZOD shirt walked in and introduced himself as John Kougl. Travis rose and shook hands. Kougl was personable enough, but Travis could tell from the way he asked about his flight and went right into telling him "a little about Discount America," that it was a canned speech. He stared Travis straight in the eye, while shifting his head from side to side like a bobble-head doll, and placed great emphasis on names and titles of Discount America's cleaning product buyer muckidy-mucks that might drop by and say hello. Travis got the impression he was being lectured, that this was information that Kougl didn't want to have to be repeating, but at the same time wanting it to be known that he wanted Travis to think that he was the one official spokesperson for Discount America hierarchy.

Kougl continued, "While we're waiting, let's have a look at your handout."

Travis reached down into his briefcase and took out one of the Hicks-Bahr brochures and handed it to him. As Kougl leafed through it, nodding, Travis began to relax, feeling that his knowledge of his products and his own self-confidence, would speak for themselves.

Another man strode into the room. Like Kougl, he was dressed in business casual.

"Hi, I'm Brian Mulabay, and you must be Travis," he said, too loudly.

"Yes, pleased to meet you, Brian."

Another brief handshake, "I can't stay long, John, but I wanted to meet Travis before I left. I have to go out for an appointment, but I'll catch up with you guys this afternoon at the golf course. The weather is supposed to be nice."

"Sounds great," said Travis, feeling the need to engage in this banter to show how personable he was. And there was something about Mulabay that compelled him to respond that way.

"Paper said it is going to be sunny and not too hot," he said.

But he wasn't sure either man was listening to him at that moment, as Mulabay took his seat alongside Kougl across the table. He noticed them exchanging a fleeting glance.

"Would you happen to have another copy of your handout, Travis?" asked Mulabay.

Of course he did, and handed him a copy of it. Mulabay put on his glasses and arched over the document in front of him, studying it closely. Kougl started talking.

"We're looking for a supplier who can provide us with a variety of household cleaning products to fill gaps in our current products. Discount America is continuing to build more and more stores and is getting busier and busier. There seems to be no shortage of customers and we are trying to meet their needs and wants in a bigger and better way than our closest competitors. The way things are going for us is really great, knock on wood."

Kougl made a fist of his left hand and gently rapped the top of the table with his knuckles. Travis noticed his fingers were thick and short and that he wore no rings.

"And we are very interested in finding a supplier that can be creative," he continued, "a company that has a long, impressive track record, such as Hicks-Bahr, and a company that is environmentally friendly and that can inject fresh ideas and convenience into the average customer's busy schedule."

By then Mulabay had finished reading and his gaze had alighted on Travis. His face had a nice relaxed demeanor but his eyes betrayed nothing, the upward curve of his lips not causing them to change shape nor to crease wrinkles in their corners. Travis knew the time had arrived for him to stand and present his products.

"Could you tell us a little more about your company," Mulabay said, "we want to know more about Hicks-Bahr, if we end up signing a contract with your company."

This last remark made Travis feel more confident still. Even if he didn't end up getting the contract, he wanted to be the one in control of the meeting.

With much pride in his voice, Travis spoke of the history of Hicks-Bahr and the things it had accomplished over the years; the different types of products they had brought to market, the office and staff expansions, the growth in sales, and its emergence as an industry leader. All the while Mulabay and Kougl were nodding, as if Travis were telling some kind of soothing bedtime story they had heard many times.

Travis explained how Hicks-Bahr studied consumer activity cycles to identify need gaps, and then worked to design new products to address those need gaps and develop concepts for new product ideas, all the while continuing to provide the standbys of their product line—products that historically were bought by consumers. Hicks-Bahr considered itself to be a household name in its product line.

He then concluded by telling (in his own words) the official version of Hicks-Bahr's company history by saying, "We all pull together and we're really like family."

The meeting continued along the usual lines with each party to the negotiations asking and answering questions. Travis was having a ball, felt on top of his game and knew that he was gaining strong business experience from the meeting. He could tell that his presentation was becoming more and more attractive to the buyers. With his innate talent for knowing what people liked to hear and wanting to win over the buyers, Travis felt more and more confident that he would fly back to Chattanooga Tuesday morning, signed contract in hand.

Another short while passed before Mulabay stood up and announced, "I've got to be going now. It looks like Hicks-Bahr might have the product line and company experience we are looking for, Travis. Tim O'Neil will be coming in a few minutes to discuss our weekly shipment needs and see if we can make this thing happen. What do you say, are you interested?"

"Oh very much so, Brian," he replied, trying not to betray his professionalism by jumping up and down with glee.

"Very good then. I'll leave you with John until Tim gets here. He can answer any other questions you may have. You'll be able to get Travis to the golf course, John?"

Kougl nodded and swiveled back and forth in his chair. Travis began to feel that the possibility of his company and Discount America coming together was becoming more real, more rapidly, than he had expected. And the push seemed to be coming from them. There was an air of inevitability to it. It excited him, as it always did when things were going the way he wanted.

Chapter Nine

As Mulabay was getting to his feet, forcing Travis to his also, a tall young man appeared in the doorway. He looked close in age to Travis, and carried his height impressively.

"Oh here's Tim!" Mulabay said and Travis noticed both he and John had become almost joyful.

"We were just meeting with Travis here about Hicks-Bahr's line of household cleaning products," said Mulabay, "and I'm about to leave, so it's good you are here. I won't be able to make it for lunch, but I'll catch up with you three at about 1:00 and beat you all at golf."

The young man reached out his hand and introduced himself, "Hi, Tim O'Neil. Are these two guys treating you well?"

"Indeed they are," replied Travis.

"That's good." Tim paused a moment, observing Travis.

Tim closed the door to the hallway, sat down at the head of the conference table, cleared his throat and opened a Discount America folder. Travis noticed that Tim already had a copy of the Hicks-Bahr handout he had brought with him. He also knew that in spite of their friendly presentation, these men were tough and canny businessmen with wills of steel.

After a moment, Tim spoke, "Hmmm, ah Travis, how are all the folk at Hicks-Bahr?" Before Travis could answer, Tim spoke again, "How was your flight to Bentonville?"

Travis had "read the book," so to speak, about the importance of small talk and knew that people tended to view a good conversationalist as being more intelligent and confident. So, after replying that his flight was good, he threw in some affirmative comments about the Northwest Regional Airport.

Apparently, Tim O'Neill had read the same book, because from his body language, Travis was aware that the meeting had reached the point where, as Cuthbert would say, "the rubber meets the road." Without looking up, Tim plunged ahead, "Travis, in order for Discount America to be in a position where it can sign a contract with Hicks-Bahr, we need talk about numbers of cases per week per product. What kind of numbers did they send with you?"

"Six thousand cases a week was the figure they kicked around," Travis lied. He didn't want to be too cautious. He had been told by Cuthbert that the optimal figure was to be five thousand.

"Hmmm, for sure eight," said Tim, looking down at something he had written on a spreadsheet. "If you can go higher, then I think we can help each other."

All three men were silent for a moment as a palpable impasse filled the room. It was Tim who spoke again first.

"Discount America already has a pretty good idea of what we can sell Hicks-Bahr products at. And we think we can sell a lot more of it than six thousand cases every week. It was six you said, right Travis? At six we might be paying too much to move it and keep our prices low. So, Travis, you're a smart guy. It's all down to volume or the whole thing might fall through."

Travis could feel the pressure then. He knew that Hicks-Bahr would feel some strain at first to come up with an extra three thousand cases each week for Discount America. He also knew that Discount America was a big fish (as Cuthbert would say) and that doing what it took to reel them in would realize a huge return to Hicks-Bahr. He also knew how desperately he personally wanted to take a signed contract back to Chattanooga.

Tim leaned back in his chair and turned towards Travis. "Well Travis, what about eight thousand? Can you do that?"

"I will call Chattanooga and see what they say." Travis answered. "But if we can do eight, we will."

"OK, Travis." Tim had closed his folder, put away his pen and stood up. "Let's wrap this up for now and go on out to Big Sugar and have some lunch at the club. Brian will meet us and we'll play a round of golf. You let us know soon. We would like to have Legal start preparing a tentative contract and get it signed before you leave on Monday."

As Travis pulled out of the Discount America parking lot, he was cautiously elated. However, he knew that the issue of cases per week had to be tackled head on or there would be no deal. He called Cuthbert immediately on his cell phone as he followed Tim and John to the country club. After explaining how well the presentation had gone, he moved right in to telling him how they were moving along in the negotiation phase.

"That's wonderful, Travis, I knew you could get it done, son."

"Thank you, sir. I need authorization for eight thousand cases per week."

He was anxious to get a sense from his boss of how capable Hicks-Bahr was of increasing its production capacity, and how fast. Before he pulled up at the country club, Cuthbert got back to him.

"Travis, are they gonna pick up from our plant in their trucks, or do we ship the stuff? We gotta figure out the logistics end and make sure our costs are factored into the price. We prefer they haul it."

Travis agreed. Whether Discount America would pick up and haul in its own trucks or if Hicks-Bahr arranged for shipping, would make a huge influence on price. Before he had left Chattanooga, he had prepared himself well for the trip with charts, freight rates, and detailed figures for Hicks-Bahr's production and shipping costs.

All through lunch at the country club, he was on the phone with Chattanooga and negotiating with John and Tim. Later, as they approached the eighth hole, shipping had been decided, but it was beginning to look like he would not be able to get the number of weekly cases up sufficiently to make Discount America happy. Brian, John and Tim had determined the number of cases that they wanted per week and that was that.

Cuthbert managed to pass off another piece of wisdom to Travis during one phone call. "Tha other half of sellin'," he said, "is buyin'. Remind Discount America what kind of service we'll give it. Encourage 'em to invest in *us*, rather than the other way around."

Travis had a difficult time concentrating on his golf game. Cuthbert had said he would get back to him about the extra three thousand cases and Travis waited nervously for that return call. He wanted the deal to go through. He wanted to take home a scalp from Discount America so that the big wigs at Hicks-Bahr would be impressed.

Finally, as he waited his turn on the sixteenth hole, his cell phone rang. Travis walked a few feet away so that he could speak privately. It was Cuthbert with Egan Mohler and Juan Fuentes on speaker with the following proposal: three months at five thousand cases and after that it would be eight thousand per week and the price would drop twenty percent.

"That Discount America business is too important to let slip away. You know who'll get it if we don't? Our favorite competitor, that's who!" said Mohler.

"You get 'em to sign the contract and let us worry about fulfilling it. We gotta go whole hog, Travis," added Cuthbert.

"So you're saying for me to go ahead and commit to eight thousand cases after three months with a twenty percent discount, correct, sir?" Travis said, and a small smile returned to his lips.

"Travis, Juan here. Yes, production can do it. The southeast plant will be finished upgrading its equipment in about forty-five days. Tell your buyers that we can assure them eight thousand cases after three months. What you need to do is get us an estimate of an initial shipment date on the contract."

In his delight, Travis failed to say anything in reply. Instead, he made one of those silent screams and shook his fist, punching the air before giving an "OK" sign to the three buyers with his right hand.

"Travis, are you there?" It was Cuthbert.

Travis cleared his throat. "Yes sir."

"Okay, son, get it in writing and we'll see you back here next week. Good job."

"Thank you, sir. I'll see you all first thing Tuesday morning."

Travis snapped his cell phone shut and walked over to the waiting buyers and told them what his superiors at Hicks-Bahr had told him.

"Travis, that's great news," said Brian as the three buyers shook hands with Travis. "What do you say we get together tomorrow morning for nine holes and an early lunch? That way when we meet on Monday morning, we'll move this along quickly with Legal."

The men played the remaining two holes of their game and went into the bar where they all ordered soft drinks and basket snacks. Mohler made arrangements for them to tee off the next morning at 9:00.

Later, as Travis drove down the handsome, tree-lined streets of Bentonville, he smiled as boys on bicycles stopped and stared at his rented BMW M3. He waved at an overweight woman jogging down the sidewalk sweating profusely. There he was, Travis Joel Coker, twenty-seven years old, and he had arrived. He was getting what he had prayed for. It was coming to pass. The feeling of power lingered and he loved it.

Chapter Ten
October 6, 2001

Saturday morning, still feeling on cloud nine, Travis jumped out of bed early, showered, dressed in his favorite jeans and polo shirt and put the top down on the Beemer. After the way things had gone yesterday, he was feeling on top of the world. Travis eased the car out of the motel parking lot and headed out of town. As soon as he reached the highway, he fiddled with the radio, tuned it to a classic country station and turned up the volume. As the car sped down the winding road, the pale morning light became brighter, polishing the dazzling view of the countryside. Travis loved the adventure of driving up and down the hills of Northwest Arkansas and got a kick out of the slight vertigo the downward plunge always brought to his stomach. The road had some sharp twists as it winded and curved, while the hardwood trees overhanging the road provided a riot of color.

This is one hot car, he thought as he zoomed around the curves of Highway 62 towards the Pea Ridge Military Park. It was six-thirty in the morning, Hank Williams was yodeling "Rambling Man," and Travis felt happy. He had enough time to drive through the battlefield (at least he could tell Grandpa he had visited the place) before heading over to meet the guys from Discount America for another round of golf. He sang along with Hank, at one with the spirit of the song. That day, Travis felt like the epitome of a Rambling Man.

As the car sped by sleeping housing developments and quiet farms, Travis felt bullet-proof. He loved the way the BMW M3 handled. Perhaps the Hummer would have to go. *Perhaps I should get one of these*, he was thinking. He felt like the only person on the earth. Soon, all of the sleeping houses would empty their occupants who would head into town for breakfast or shopping or whatever. But right then, on that early weekend morning, the Beemer was sailing and the road was empty all the way. Travis felt exhilarated as the fresh morning air enlivened his senses.

Wow, what a car, three hundred and thirty three horses! he said out loud to himself. This dog has a bite that's as bad as its bark. Oh, to be in Germany right now, driving this toy on the speed-limitless Autobahn. I'd even settle for Montana right now. These Arkansas roads must not have a straight mile in them. Wow!

He shifted down to second as he approached the turn into the national military park. *Perfect cornering,* he thought.

To honor his word to Grandpa, Travis spent a modest amount of time looking around the park, reading the signs as he drove the seven mile long loop through the battlefield. He then got out of the car and walked around a bit, reading other signs about the battle itself, viewing the Elkhorn Tavern and checking out the cannon. He then took a moment to see where the Trail of Tears had gone through and remembered that his g-g-g-grandpa Richard Ratliff, his son Daniel and daughters Eliza and Lizzie had passed through the area.

Looking at his watch and feeling the complaints of his empty stomach, Travis jumped into the car without even opening the door, cursing as his knee came down hard on the gearshift. He still had time to grab a latte and some sort of pastry before hitting the links. Humming along with Faron Young's "Hello Walls," Travis decided to head to Bentonville, via Highway 72, so that he could check out a few more of the winding Arkansas roads.

The morning was warm. The trees were turning their respective fall shades; the shades of richness, the summer having passed. The road was quiet and traffic was light. Quiet homes set far off from the roadway didn't mar the beauty. Travis was in his element, at one with the Beemer. He shifted down into third as he came around a sharp curve. He noticed a yellow pickup truck coming in from a side road. Suddenly, time stopped, the yellow pickup slowed and then pulled onto the highway right in front of him.

Chapter Eleven

A sudden bang and all communication ceased between the steering wheel and the wheels. The car swerved sideways and skidded on the dewy asphalt. Travis's hands gripped the useless steering wheel. It offered no resistance, spinning in a limbo of its own. The car continued to skid; the seconds passed in infinitely slow motion. Travis felt his head spin, although in reality it was the scenery around him that was spinning at an astonishing speed. The BMW skidded like a top on the dew-slick asphalt-until the wheels slammed into a boulder. The front end then skidded into the air and was stopped only by a hickory tree. The hood lunged toward the sky. In one last effort, the car rotated on its axis and ejected its driver, by then much too heavy for the gravity-defying pirouette.

Travis's body was hurled into the air, falling back down to crash into the ditch. The BMW completed its long careen lying on its back, half on the highway. A plume of steam rose from its entrails, and then it breathed its last. Travis lay still, peaceful, at rest. His features were calm, his breathing slow and even, there might even have been a small smile on his slightly parted lips. His eyes were closed-he seemed to be sleeping. His dark brown hair framed his face, his right hand lay across his midriff.

The fifty-five year old driver of the yellow pickup blinked hard. He had witnessed everything. He had caused everything. "Just like in the movies, only this time it was real," he would later say. Shaking, he opened the door and started to step outside. Changing his mind, he clawed frantically for his cell phone and dialed 911.

Within ten minutes the Benton County EMS arrived. Two sheriffs were already on the scene. David Newman, the ambulance driver, ran over to Travis's body lying in the ditch and yelled to his colleague to come quickly. Using scissors, he cut through jeans and T-shirt.

"Let's get an EKG and start an IV. I've got a thready pulse and no pressure, respiration forty-eight, cut on head, bleeding from the mouth. Looks like possibly an internal hemorrhage. Get me two units."

Newman's partner Jackie, a rookie paramedic, pasted electrodes on the young man's chest, connecting each one with a different-colored wire to the portable electrocardiograph. She switched it on, and the screen instantly came to life.

"What's it show?" asked David.

"Nothing good; he's going. Pressure, eighty over sixty; pulse, a hundred and forty; lips are blue."

"Give me a number seven endotracheal tube. I need to intubate."

The paramedic finished placing the IV catheter in Travis's arm and handed the bag of saline to one of the sheriffs.

"Hold that good and high."

Travis's temperature began to fall rapidly, while the tracing on the EKG grew erratic. At the bottom of the green screen, a small red heart began to blink, followed at once by a short repeated beep, a warning that heart failure was imminent.

In under a minute, they had secured an airway. Newman asked for a report on his vital signs, and Jackie replied that respiration was still stable but pressure had fallen to fifty. She had no time to finish her sentence: the short beep was replaced by a shrill alarm from the machine.

"That's it; he's in V-fib. Give me three hundred Joules."

David picked up the two paddles of the apparatus and rubbed them together.

"Go ahead, you have the juice," yelled Jackie.

"Clear, I'm hitting him."

Under the jolt of the discharge, Travis's body arched brutally, before falling back.

"Nope, no good."

"Try three-sixty, let's go!"

"Three-sixty, go ahead!"

"Clear!"

Give me another five of epinephrine and reload to three-sixty. Clear!" Another jolt, another spasmodic leap. "Still fibrillating. We're losing him: inject one unit of lidocaine into the IV and reload. Clear!" The body heaved upward. "Give him an amp of bicarb and reload to three-eighty stat!"

With the new shock, Travis's heart seemed to be responding to the injected drugs and had returned to a normal rhythm, but not for long. The alarm signal, which had briefly ceased, shrilled out louder than ever, "Cardiac arrest!" exclaimed Jackie.

Immediately, David began a cardiac massage with extraordinary determination. As he worked to bring Travis back to life, he was begging, "Don't do this to us. It's gonna be a fine day today. Don't be stupid, now. Come back!" He told his partner to reload the machine.

Jackie tried to calm him down. "Let him go, David, it's no good."

But Newman would not give up; he again yelled at Jackie to reload the defibrillator, and his partner complied. Yet again David shouted, "Clear!" and once more the body arched. But the electrocardiogram remained stubbornly flat; David went back to cardiac massage, his forehead beaded with sweat. His young partner realized that David had lost his sense of reality. He should have stopped trying and pronounced the time of death. But nothing could stop him. He went on massaging Travis's heart.

"Give another shot of epinephrine and go up to four hundred joules."

"David, stop. He's dead. I don't know what you're doing."

"Shut up! Do it!"

The sheriff looked questioningly at the paramedic kneeling beside Travis, but David was focusing on his patient. Jackie shrugged, injected another dose into the IV tubing, reloaded the defibrillator and called out the threshold level of four hundred joules. David delivered it without even asking to clear. Jolted by the current, Travis's body jerked violently upward. The EKG remained hopelessly flat-line. The senior paramedic did not look at it. He pounded his fist into Travis's chest. "You stupid idiot! Don't die!"

Jackie just stood there, unsure of what to do. Spellbound, the sheriff watched the two. David slowly raised his head and said, "Time of death: seven-fifty."

Jackie turned to the sheriff who was still awkwardly holding the IV bag and said, "It's over. There's nothing more we can do." David rose, and walked toward the ambulance.

Jackie began picking up the equipment, stood and looked down at Travis's body. Her expression froze when she looked at the young man's chest.

"He's breathing!"

"What?"

"He's breathing, I tell you. Get behind the wheel. We've got to get to the hospital."

Twelve minutes later they pulled up at Saint Mary's Hospital. Travis was wheeled into the emergency room where it was determined that his lungs were moving and his heart was beating on its own. A radiologist came in and mounted a CT scan on the view box. The images showed a blood clot on the brain. The attending physician picked up the phone. "I need a neurosurgeon," and arranged for an operating room.

Upstairs, the surgical team surrounded Travis's body. Behind his head, a monitor displayed the rhythm of his breathing and heartbeat. Dr. Winters, the surgeon, entered the room.

"How are his vital signs?" he asked the anesthetist.

"Stable, unbelievably stable. Sixty-five and one-twenty over eighty. His blood gases are normal. He's asleep, you can begin."

To relieve the pressure on his brain, a hole was drilled in the back of Travis's skull and a fine needle passed through the meninges, controlled by a screen and directed by the neurosurgeon to the site of the hematoma. The brain itself appeared unharmed. Fluid began to drain through the tubing. Almost instantly the intracranial pressure dropped. The anesthetist adjusted the respirator to increase the flow of oxygen to the brain. Once decompressed, the brain cells reverted to a normal metabolism, gradually eliminating the accumulated fluid. Minute by minute passed; one skilled move following another. Two hours later, Dr. Winters snapped his gloves off. He asked the team to close the incisions and transfer the patient to the recovery room. He ordered the nurses to take Travis off the respirator once the anesthesia had worn off.

Travis was taken from the OR to the recovery room. The nurse connected the cardiac monitor, the electroencephalograph, and the respirator. A technician took a blood sample and left the room. The sleeping patient looked peaceful. Half an hour went by, and the nurse called Dr. Winters to say that Travis had come out from the anesthesia and that his vital signs were stable. Also, because she wanted to be sure about the next step, she asked Dr. Winters to confirm his previous order.

"Disconnect the respirator. I'll be down in a while."

The RN turned back to the bedside, detached Travis's breathing tube from the tubing leading to the machine, allowing her patient to try to breathe on his own. A minute later, she pulled the tube out altogether, freeing Travis's throat. Taking another look at the IV, she went back to the nurse's station, turning the light off behind her.

After bringing Travis's chart up-to-date, she returned to the room and checked his vitals and IV again. She then picked up the phone and called Dr. Winters.

"It's me. We have a deep coma with vital signs stable. What do I do?"

"Find a bed on the fifth floor, and thanks,"

The nurse feared the worst—that although Travis's vital signs were stable, only his brain stem was still functioning. His cortical function, the function that made him Travis Joel Coker, made him see, feel and act, made him a loving husband and father, made him a human being, seemed to be completely gone.

Chapter Twelve
October 6, 1861

Travis lay on the ground, a ray of light breaking through the thick fog of deep sleep. A frown marred his brow as he flung one arm over his face to shield his eyes. Something wasn't right. He should be back in Bentonville by now. In fact, in all probability he should have finished his presentation and be well on his way back home by now. Now not only would Melody be wondering where he was, but his boss would be wondering too.

Without opening his eyes, he reached in his pocket for his cell phone, intending to call home. Not finding it, the frown on his face deepened. From under the cover of his arm, he slowly opened his heavy lids and blinked a couple of times to clear them. Through the blur he saw a canopy of trees. He closed his eyes, waited for a minute, opened them again, and quickly snapped them shut. *Where in the world am I?* he said out loud, looking around.

He sat up only to fall back down, nauseous and dizzy. His head pounded like nothing he had ever felt before. To make matters worse, in addition to not knowing where he was and the nausea and dizziness, there was also an inexplicable cold that began to gnaw at him. October in Northwest Arkansas could be cool and even cold, but this was not like any cold he had ever felt before. It penetrated his clothing quickly and bored its way right to Travis's bones.

Lying on the ground thinking for a few more minutes, he decided to quit trying to find an explanation for his situation and instead turned to considering his options. There were really only two. He could wait there for someone to come along or else he could start walking and maybe find help.

He rested on the ground for a while longer before he was able to get up by holding onto a small oak tree. He stood looking around him. Where was the highway? There was no highway, no ditch, no fence, nothing; just trees and grass and the sounds of busy birds in the trees. Where was his car? Holding onto the tree,

Travis turned around. Remembering the yellow pickup truck, he wondered if he had been thrown out of the BMW and into the trees. Then panic began to set in. *Easy Travis*, he thought to himself, *let your eyes adjust, you may have a concussion.*

But even after a few minutes, there was still nothing but green woods all around him; no rocks, no empty beer cans, nothing. Leaning back against the tree, he tried to clear his head. Then he remembered the highway again and decided that he had to try and find the road. Taking baby steps, walking from tree to tree and holding on for support, he again tried to find the highway. Nothing. His heart was beating ninety miles a minute. The shock was then beginning to wear off and fear and panic were taking its place.

Turning around, he went the other way, same results. It was as though there was nothing except him, millions of busy birds, and trees.

Feeling he might pass out again, he sat down, back against a tree and buried his head in his arms. Then he noticed the sound of people talking in the distance. Getting on his hands and knees, he struggled to his feet and walked towards the sound.

In just a short distance he got a pleasant surprise. Directly ahead of him he saw a lighted cabin.

Oh, he thought. *Why didn't they hear the wreck and come check it out?*

But that wasn't important then.

The cabin was small, cozy looking and more importantly it had light coming from it and the door was open slightly.

Never was he so glad to see such a small cabin in his entire life. He walked toward the cabin as fast as he could - even though the pain in his head and his blurry vision made running difficult. By the time he reached the cabin, he was winded and had to stop to catch his breath.

"Hello," he called, "anyone in there?"

He walked up to the door and peeked inside. He could tell immediately that no one was inside because the cabin was small, just one room. He stepped inside and looked around. Not much to see—one room with a window, some rustic furniture and a very inviting fire going in the fireplace. He took the liberty of shutting the door and then went to stand near the fireplace to warm himself.

As he stood near the fire, he heard what he supposed to be the cabin's inhabitants stepping onto the porch. The door flung open.

"I ..." Suddenly his throat was dry and he only croaked something. He saw that the man entering the room was older, well-built, clean-shaven with his black hair cropped short, and for whatever reason, Travis thought he might be French. Most of all, the man had a rifle pointed at Travis's head.

"Is he a Yankee?" asked an unseen woman's voice.

"I dunno. His pants are blue, but I don't think so. His clothes are unstained. And he ain't been wandering long, for no stubble's on his chin. But I ain't heard a no strangers guesting hereabouts."

The woman then entered the room. Still holding his rifle, the man approached Travis, who had raised his arms above his head like on TV and stood gasping. Travis saw that the man's coat and the shirt underneath were fastened with bonelike buttons and laces, and were of a heavy weave. About his neck he had fastened a strip of cloth tucked into his coat. These garments were all in brownish hues. He also wore a broad belt, with a large knife in a sheath at the hip.

Travis stood with his chest heaving and wildness in his eyes. The man said, "He must a run a long way."

Feeling like he was going to faint, Travis moaned and sat down in the chair by the fire and covered his face.

"If he's sick, best we get him to the bed," said the woman.

"No .... No." Travis looked up. "Let me rest a moment."

"He must be a Yankee," said the man, still holding the rifle aimed at Travis.

Travis shook his head as if it had been struck and got shakily to his feet. "What happened?" he said "Where is this place?"

"Where da you think?"

"I was driving; I crashed and woke up near here."

"He's mad," said the woman, backing away. "Be careful Cletus. If he starts to foam at the mouth, it means he's going mad."

"Who are you?" babbled Travis. "What are you doing with the gun?"

"Somehow," said the woman, "he don't sound crazed, only scared and bewildered. Something evil has beset him." Seeing blood on his collar, she move around and saw the huge knot on his head.

"I'm not staying near a man under a curse!" yelped Cletus, and he started backing away.

"Pshaw," said the woman. "Put the gun down. the boy's got a goose egg on the back a his head. Tell me boy, has the fighting started near here? Are the Yankees coming? Tell me boy is it coming here?"

Travis sat back down in the chair and held his aching head. As for the fighting, he didn't have a clue what the woman was talking about, and told her so.

"But please, *where* is here?" he said, looking up at the woman and then at Cletus. His voice was more dulled than before, now that the first terror had lifted.

"This is Arkansas, 'bout three miles from Bentonville," said Cletus.

"But that's where I was," Travis said. "Bentonville. What happened?" Again he buried his face in his hands. After a while he stood up and said, "My name is Travis Coker. I came from Tennessee. Something has happened to me. I got hurt and suddenly I was here."

The woman walked to the other side of the room and motioned for her husband to follow. Travis closed his eyes and listened as they talked back and forth; ultimately determining that he was not a Yankee because he was from Tennessee. Then they begin to speak in another language that Travis didn't understand. Then, hearing the door open and close, Travis opened his eyes to see the woman holding the rifle and looking at him. Out the window, Travis saw the man ride away on a mule. The woman watched her husband until he was out of sight, then placed the gun on the table out of Travis's reach, got a rag and gently washed the blood off of his head and asked him if he was hungry.

Later, Travis awoke just as Cletus rode up on his mule and he could hear the voices of other men outside. Soon, Cletus walked into the cabin accompanied by two scroungy-looking soldiers. The soldiers walked over to where Travis was sitting, and one of them said, "You told Cletus that you're not a Yankee, so you'rn one a us?"

Travis said nothing. Head pounding and still cold, he just continued to sit in the chair by the fire.

"How old are you?"

"Twenty-seven."

"Old enough to be in the army. Why ain't you joined?"

"I've been busy."

Both of the soldiers laughed.

"That's a good one."

The men laughed again. The leader suddenly became very sober.

"Believe we'll just conscript you."

"I don't think so," Travis said.

The leader suddenly grabbed Travis's arm and jerked him to his feet. "We'll take him back to camp and let the colonel swear him into the army, or else we'll execute him right here as an enemy."

"You're all crazy," Travis said as he tried to wrest his arm from the soldier's grip.

The other soldier then grabbed Travis's free arm and twisted it behind his back. Both soldiers wrestled him to the ground and tried to pin him down. Travis continued to twist and turn in their grasp until frustrated one of them struck him on the head with a pistol butt. As Travis collapsed into semi-consciousness, they tied his wrists in front and fastened a long rope to them. They then put him on the back of one of their horses and rode away.

Chapter Thirteen

For the rest of the day Travis rode behind the soldier through the unchanging landscape. They reached no settlement and met no people and it all passed in painful horror for Travis. His head was throbbing with a thick wrap of pain that went from his eyeballs up onto his forehead, out over the temples and all the way around to the nape of his neck. He kept his head bowed to protect his eyes from the white light of day. Only once during the late afternoon did they see a human; a horseman a few miles off. If he saw them, he showed no sign. He simply traversed the horizon like a silhouette in a movie and moved on.

They camped that night on a flat slab of damp ground that allowed no sleep, saying that they should be meeting up with the supply wagons soon and head on back to the encampment. They undid Travis's hands long enough to escort him to the creek where he was allowed to wet his face and head with the cold water in an attempt to take the edge off the pain. When he peed, he did so facing away from the soldiers, the sound of his urine echoing in his ears. The hurting in his head was growing deeper, like an infection entering the bones of his skull. The blow from the soldier's gun sure hadn't helped any. He felt as though his body was shutting down, that his bowels were constricting and his muscles were growing weak.

The soldiers shared their dinner of beans, coffee and hard, dried bread before tying Travis's hands and covering him with a blanket. As he lay there on the damp ground, he listened as they talked about Watie. Travis finally realized that they were talking about Stand Watie—part of the Treaty of New Echota group that had split the Cherokee Nation before the Trail of Tears.

What the ...? Travis thought to himself.

The soldiers continued talking, "... now that the Rebels have signed a treaty with us and made Watie a colonel ..."

"He's raising a good army," interrupted the other one.

Travis twisted uncomfortably and tried to untie his hands. He was floored. Where was he and who were these crazy people? He had heard about Civil War reenactments and hillbillies and moonshiners and the Ozarks, but never expected that it was like this. Travis thought perhaps he was where they had filmed the movie *Deliverance*. He didn't know much, but he knew that he was somehow caught up in this screwball scenario. Another thing he knew for sure was that his head ached and he was dizzy and he knew that he wasn't thinking clearly.

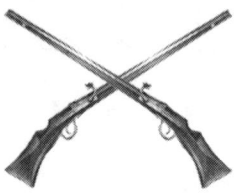

Chapter Fourteen

Travis realized there was something in his mouth, a rock of some sort; he rolled it round on his tongue, gradually awakening, before his eyes fluttered open and he tried to make sense of his surroundings. Trying to spit out the rock, he became conscious of laying on his back, with his neck twisted around at an awkward angle, his hands lying at his waist. It was then that he became aware of the rope and remembered where he was. Feeling sick to his stomach, he rolled over onto his hands and knees as best he could, and dry heaved for a few moments. He then realized that there was nothing in his mouth at all. The rock in his mouth was nothing more than his tongue, inflamed and dry and swollen. His head still ached, only the pain was much worse. With the slightest movement, it pounded out of his skull and clouded his eyes with pain.

Retracing a thin line of memory, the events of the previous day floated back to him, bit by bit. He remembered the BMW, the Memorial Park, the car accident, the cabin, the soldiers, and the forced horseback ride.

Once again the soldiers undid the rope and allowed Travis to relieve himself and wash in the creek. They then gave him some breakfast, which he attempted to eat but was unable to swallow more than a couple of mouthfuls.

The soldiers then tied only one of his hands and tied the other end of the rope to a tree, telling Travis he should rest and try to heal up, that they would be waiting there until afternoon sometime when they would rendezvous with the supply wagons.

Grateful, Travis lay down and covered his face and chest with the blanket and soon drifted into a troubled sleep. In his dream, he saw Grandpa's face close to his own, smiling and speaking to him in a flow of words that had no beginning, no ending and no meaning that he could understand.

In the afternoon the soldiers and Travis took off, Travis again riding behind the younger soldier until they caught up with four

Confederate soldiers who were returning from going for provisions. Travis then rode in the back of an army teamster's wagon, without being tied, for which he was grateful.

As he bounced along in the wagon, Travis again tried to figure out what was happening to him. He thought about the wreck, trying to visualize everything in slow motion. Perhaps he actually was dead, but didn't think so because of the pain in his head and eyes. Giving up, he began to look at the surrounding scenery. With a start, he realized that it wasn't what he was seeing that bothered him; it was what he wasn't. He realized that there were no housing developments, no farm houses other than cabins and wood plank houses. There were no highline wires, no radio towers reaching skyward. Nothing. What, where and why was this happening?

It's like I stepped into a black hole, he thought.

Chapter Fifteen

Just before daybreak, they splashed across a small creek. As they came out on the other side, they ran head-on into several dark figures.

"Halt or we'll fire." a nasal twanged voice snarled.

Horrified, Travis fought to keep control.

The soldier driving Travis's wagon grinned and said boldly, "Oh, now, hold your fire. We're jest on our way back right here to Fort Davis."

From where he sat in the wagon, Travis could see five or six Confederate sentries eyeing them suspiciously. Apparently unconcerned, Travis's driver began to climb down, saying, "We're just on our way back from Missouri. We've been to get supplies. We're with Watie's outfit."

One husky sentinel stepped closer and eyed Travis, his gun held diagonally across his chest.

"That a Yankee prisoner?" Travis's heart leaped so violently it almost jumped out of his shirt. Cold sweat beaded on his forehead. Not wishing to appear cowardly, he tried to nonchalantly look around at his surroundings. Besides the sentries, he could see the outlines of fifty or so horses hobbled and night-grazing close by. He could also see the shapes of men sleeping on the ground around small sputtering campfires.

There seemed to be little movement in the camp, and the entire scene had a presentment of impermanence about it. Travis could see piles of partly packed boxes of goods and equipment, several wagons, and stacks of cut wood.

What sort of hell had he blundered into? Surely this was one of those reenactments that his Grandpa and dad sometimes went to. Travis never knew that the participants took it so seriously.

The soldiers that had kidnapped him explained that Travis wasn't a Yankee and had been conscripted to join the Cherokee Mounted Rifles.

"Good. Ya'll get on down and come on in. Colonel Watie's camped right here, but I guess ya'll know that." Motioning with his rifle to the other sentries, he continued, "We're part of the Texas brigade that's joined up with Watie."

Ignoring Travis, "his" soldiers dismounted and led their horses a short distance away, where they began to unsaddle. Unsure of what to do next, Travis stood and began to climb down out of the wagon.

"You go ahead and fine a place to sleep till morning" the sentry twanged at him. "I guess then the colonel or sergeant or whoever'll, swear you in. Or maybe they won't. I dunno, cuz you sure look like a Yankee to me." Then with a gesture of indifference, he turned and walked away.

Moving to a grassy spot, Travis sat down and put his head in his hands. At last he lay down. The grass was wet with dew but Travis was too worried to notice or care. It felt good to lie still and relax. He was dog-tired.

But he couldn't sleep. Travis didn't know what to do. Even if he tried to walk out of here, where was here? They had to be miles away from Bentonville by then. Where would he go? These people that had him kidnapped were all fanatical civil war buffs. To them, this was actually 1860-whatever year it was supposed to be. They might actually kill him. Then remembering that most civil war reenactments only lasted a weekend or so, Travis turned on his side, and went to sleep comforted by that fact and decided to play along until he could figure out what else to do.

Chapter Sixteen

Travis was awakened just after daybreak by somebody stomping around on the ground near his head. A man's voice sang out, "Wake up, wake up, it's time to play."

Startled out of sleep and horror-struck, Travis opened his eyes to see muddy boots and large rusty spurs. Rising up on one elbow, he saw ugly dirty pants topped off by a wide belt holding a knife and pistol. Sitting up, Travis found himself looking at a stocky, weather-beaten man with deep-set eyes.

When the man saw Travis looking at him, his face broke into an enormous grin. "Well, I see we wake up to a one man Yankee attack!"

"I'm not a …"

"Wake up, boy," the man interrupted. "Hit the ground with Rebel pride and shoot a bullet through a Yankee's eye." The man then turned and stomped off, yelling "Day's a breaking, beans in the pot, sourdoughs a baking."

The sun was just above the eastern horizon. Feeling disoriented, and not amused by the man's rhymes, Travis sat back down and held his aching head. The birds were already at work with their fussy songs. He could smell smoke and heard something bubbling in a pot.

"Hey, you can eat with our mess," growled the spur man, coming up suddenly behind Travis. Startled, he spun around, causing his sore head to hurt and spin.

"Yes, sir." Squinting into the sun, Travis looked at the spur man and estimated him to be about thirty-five years old. He wore a medium-brimmed slouch hat. On the sleeve of his faded gray shirt were the stripes of a sergeant. He looked down at Travis and gestured towards the fire.

At the fire, a skinny-looking old man, who apparently was the cook, was roasting an entire beef shoulder on a hickory spit and baking sweet potatoes in the coals. The bubbling noise came from a large fire-blackened pot of coffee.

After watching some of the other men helping themselves to pieces of the meat, Travis realized that he was starving. He stood up, and after allowing his head to stop spinning, imitated the others and walked to the fire and tore off a large piece of the hot beef. As he ate, he looked around at the other men. Contrary to photographs Travis had seen of men in civil war reenactments that by and large wore nice blue or gray uniforms, these men were the roughest, raggedest bunch of men he had ever seen. Most of them looked like the very worst of homeless people or something on the back of a brochure for some charity. Most were dressed in tattered homespun gray, or dirty looking yellowish brown clothes. The men were all tough-looking, with shrewd faces and a proud demeanor.

Laughing to himself, Travis thought, *If these men are reenacting Stand Watie's men, then they are supposed to be Cherokee, but a lot of them look more white than Indian.* Still eating, he stared with interest at the men's weapons that never left their side.

Each man wore a pistol and many carried a rifle as well. In addition, they all wore some form of broad, straight, double-edged Bowie-type knife on their belts that seemed to have been made by local blacksmiths from saws, butcher knives, and files. Spur Man, whom the others called "Sam," had serrated the edges of his knife so it appeared particularly deadly.

As the men devoured the beef, beans and the sweet potatoes, they called the cook "Boney" and openly insulted him about everything from his food to his long thin face. The old man took the genial teasing good-naturedly. Travis saw that the nickname "Boney" was appropriate: the man was not much bigger than a skeleton.

Boney's food was well-prepared and tasty, and Travis bit hungrily into a second chunk of hot beef and continued to study the other men, who were all laughing and having a good time. Travis took comfort in the fact that everyone was so carefree. They were some of the most light-hearted men Travis had ever seen. But he figured it seemed right. After all, these men were just men taking a weekend away from their jobs and their wives, doing what they loved, reenacting a civil war battle. Probably by the end of the day, everyone would be heading home and he could hitch a ride with someone to the nearest phone. After eating, they all sat around on their heels, drinking hot coffee and smoking shuck cigarettes. Travis could tell from their conversation that they were getting ready to go into battle.

Travis wondered which one might be playing the role of Stand Watie. Needing to relieve himself, Travis stood up to go and try to locate an outhouse. He looked around for the two soldiers from yesterday but didn't see them. He noticed that no one seemed to be paying him the least bit of mind.

He watched for a moment and noticed men coming and going behind some bushes, so he headed off in that direction. As he walked, he was shocked at the size of the reenactment. He had assumed that the only men there were the fifty or so that were camped where he had eaten breakfast. But now, he could see literally hundreds of men. Some were sitting up, yawning and stretching, throwing off brown and gray blankets and patchwork quilts. Others were eating their breakfasts around campfires or saddling their horses. Scattered here and there he saw cannon and what appeared to be artillery caissons. He also noted dozens of wagons parked with their tongues up. Some had CSA stenciled on their sides; and a few were marked with US. Around the edges of the camp grazed a large herd of horses, mules and a few cows. Gasping with shock, Travis was astonished at the size and realism of this reenactment.

He located the latrine and then decided that he wanted another bite of the delicious beef. When he approached the fire, the cook noticed his lack of eating utensils. Grinning, he handed him a wooden plate and spoon and half of a crock jug that looked as if it had been blown in two. Taking them with a "Thanks," Travis looked around, and noticed that most of the other men had either a wooden or tin plate. For drinking, some of them had canteens. Others were using clay jugs, amber-colored bottles or tin cups.

Boney bent and poured Travis's half-crock full of coffee from the big pot on the fire. He took a sip and nearly gagged on his first swallow of the foul tasting stuff. It was all he could do to keep from spitting it out on the ground in front of everybody.

Seeing his face, Boney laughed and said, "Cherokee coffee."

"What's it made out of?" choked Travis.

"You pour cornmeal in a skillet, and stir it till its parched, then pour it in the pot and pour boiling water over it. You like it?"

Swallowing hard, Travis nodded yes.

Sam the spur man suddenly appeared next to Travis and said, "Let's go and see Colonel Watie."

Silently, Travis followed him. As they walked, the early morning sun peeked suddenly over the oak-covered eastern ridge, stabbing the scene with long streamers of light. Sam led the way down a wagon-rutted path cutting through the camp towards a crude building that reminded Travis of a motel. The long wooden structure had ten or twelve doors that opened onto a wooden walkway.

As they walked past an open door, Sam suddenly stopped and then backed up to look inside one of the rooms. Following Sam's lead, Travis looked inside and saw a handsome man wearing an unbuttoned shirt and yellow pants, busily stuffing some papers into a haversack. Travis assumed that the man was playing the role of Stand Watie for the reenactment. From the color of his skin, Travis thought that he looked like he was at least part Cherokee.

The man seemed to be in a hurry and unaware of them standing outside his door. Clearing his throat, Sam said, "Morning, Daniel. Where's the colonel?"

Looking up and then continuing to stuff the haversack, the man asked, "Morning. Who you got there, Sam?"

"Volunteer. Wants to join up with Colonel Watie."

The man stuffed the last of the papers and began to fasten the straps on the haversack.

Travis then noticed a Confederate uniform coat draped over a chair, and from the insignia on the collar, realized that the man was a major.

The rebel major scrutinized Travis from the top of his tousled dark brown hair to the soles of his dusty, expensive Dr. Marten oxfords. He saw nothing but a nice looking, clean cut man that looked a little scared.

The major then began to button his shirt and tuck it into his pants. Travis began to feel more at ease.

The man then turned, grabbed his coat off the chair and put it on.

"What's your name?" the major asked.

"Travis Joel Coker, sir," answered Travis.

A surprised expression came into the major's eyes. "Coker?"

"Yes, sir."

"Sir?"

Unsure of what to say, Travis replied, "Yes, sir."

Although he liked Travis's politeness, Sam laughed and nudged him in the ribs with his elbow, "The major ain't used to being addressed as 'sir,' Travis."

The major laughed then and began to button his coat. He then picked up his slouch hat and put it on; his long, black hair hanging down and sticking out underneath. "You swear him in, Sam. I was supposed to be meeting with Colonel Watie at headquarters right now."

Snatching the haversack off the floor, the major then strode out the door and over to a horse that was tied nearby.

Later, Travis learned that the major was Daniel Ratliff Jr., who lived in the Cookson area near Tahlequah and was one of Stand Watie's most highly trusted officers and personal friends.

And although neither of them realized it at that moment, Major Ratliff and Travis Coker were related by blood.

Chapter Seventeen

It was late morning, October 8, 1861, in Indian Territory, and just a hint of autumn nipped the air.

Travis was sitting in the area where he had slept earlier, wishing for if nothing else, a pair of sunglasses. There was a racking pain in his lower back and a great pressure was trying to burst out of his head.

He was scared yet curious at the same time, and kept reassuring himself that the reenactment would end probably at dark and he could get to a phone and a hospital. At least the wind was refreshing as it blew past his body.

So he sat, with his elbows on his knees, his hands covering his eyes and cradling his aching head, wondering what would happen next. He didn't have to wonder long, and held his breath as he heard footsteps and voices approaching.

"Yep, and if he's got hit in the head, ya'll take him over and see the doctor. Then Tommy can get him lined out."

Sam had the two soldiers that had conscripted him to escort Travis to the hospital. As they walked, he got a better look of the camp, which consisted of a rough barn and other buildings that looked like farm sheds, and some pitched tents, one of which turned out to be the hospital.

Travis was told to strip to the waist by a young blond army doctor with tired eyes that examined him.

"Quite a knot you got on yer head," the Texas doctor said, "Hurt much?"

"Yes, sir," Travis said. His mind was screaming to tell the doctor that he believed himself to be crazy ... or dead. Still remembering the threat of being shot, he didn't dare tell this quack doctor that his head ached, and he was dizzy, and he knew that he wasn't thinking clearly.

One of the soldiers spoke up, "Doc, we fear that he is touched in his remembering. When we got ready to bring 'em, he didn't know where he was, the first thing about the war or horses or who Watie was or nothing."

"Well, I think he's just got addled. Give him a week to rest."

"Can he fight and ride?"

"He's fine."

"Do tell," said one of the soldiers. "Guess as longs he's not crazy as a loon, he can shoot a Yankee."

The doctor and the soldiers laughed.

The other soldier said, "Tommy can teach him to ride and make sure he can shoot."

"Yep, lessen Tommy don't shoot him first."

They all laughed again.

"Come on," the doctor said, finally beckoning to Travis. "You rest up a week and then you'll be fine for battle…"

"Battle, what battle?"

The doctor just laughed as he handed Travis his shirt. "Most of you Cherokee young men can't seem to wait to go out and shoot at perfect strangers. Isn't that why you signed up?"

"Yes, sir," said Travis promptly. "I just want to do my part for the Confederacy." Recalling the soldier's remarks the day before about executing him had made him feel that he had to play along as long as the nightmare lasted—surely he was dreaming.

The doctor tapped Travis's arm with his dirty hand and laughed again. "I'll give you a mustard plaster to put on that bump. It's a pretty good one."

Travis looked down at his arm.

"You put the plaster on and try to sleep and get well just in time for the Yankees to shoot their minie balls at you," the doctor added. The doctor and the two soldiers laughed. Travis stared at them all, feeling extraordinarily depressed.

After that, Travis had no choice but to be sworn into the Cherokee Mounted Rifles. He was surprised and unsure how to answer when Sam pulled out a little book and asked him, "Where do you want your pay sent if'n you're taken prisoner?"

"Do we get paid?"

Sam just looked at him and raised one eyebrow. "Where to?"

Considering the question, Travis felt overwhelmed and troubled. Unsure of what else to say, he gave the man his address in Tennessee, omitting the zip code. Sam's next question was the name of his next of kin, to which Travis replied, "Melody Coker. Same address."

Travis was then sent to find the quartermaster. From what most of the other men were wearing, he wondered what sort of uniform he would be issued. What he got was one tan shirt, one pair of cotton socks and two pairs of what the quartermaster called "drawers." He turned down a pair of the ugly yellow pants, insisting on wearing his own Levi's. He was also issued a pistol and a blanket rolled in a waterproof gum blanket.

Aware that he was supposed to rest for a week, he went and sat down again where he had slept, but was soon joined by a young man that introduced himself as "Tommy." Tommy definitely looked Indian and had cut off his yellow britches below the knee and went barefoot. A raccoon skin bag hung from a thong at his waist. He was carrying a long-barreled rifle. The deer antler hilt of a hunting knife showed at his belt.

"I was sent to help you get a hoss. They said you were touched in the head and couldn't ride. Why'd you join up?"

"Seemed like the right thing to do," Travis replied, "How about you?"

"My family's Union. Me, I always been a rebel at heart, so I sided with the Rebs. Mama didn't want me to fight, but I runned away in the middle a the night. My papa's mean, and always was whipping me or locking me in the shed. I wanted to run away long 'afore this. I jined up for a gambol."

Travis looked at Tommy, who had brown teeth, brown eyes, brown hair, and didn't appear to be over twelve or thirteen years old.

"Can you show me how to use this pistol?"

"Sure," grinned Tommy, "an we'll getcha a shotgun or a rifle too. Be right back."

A moment later, Tommy was back with an old, well-used, short-barreled musket. He showed Travis everything about it. He also gave him a brief run-down on the Mounted Rifles, then stood up. "Come on," Tommy said. "Les go tell Sam that we're gonna fire yore musket a few rounds."

"Coming." Travis picked up the gun and followed Tommy. He had always sort of liked the way it felt to carry a gun, in spite of the fact that he had always shunned hunting; didn't like the idea of killing animals more or less for the sport of it. They found Sam down by the tents, again writing in some sort of book.

"Sam, is it alright if we fire off Travis's musket so's he can have a lesson?"

Sam continued writing for a moment before he looked up at Tommy and then at Travis. He then looked down and began writing again and nodded, "Go ahead. Shoot away from the camp and don't kill each other."

"Thank you, sir." Travis turned and followed Tommy about three hundred yards into the woods, where he would teach Travis the basic knowledge he would need in order to load, fire, and clean a musket.

Travis learned how to load his musket, and arrange his cartridge pouch so it would be ready to use. The ammunition was rolled in cartridge-paper, which contained powder, a minie ball, and three pieces of buckshot. To load, he had to tear the paper with his teeth, empty a little powder into the pan, lock it, empty the rest of the powder into the barrel, press the paper and the ball into the muzzle, and ram it home.

Over and over Tommy had Travis load and fire into a sand bank with both the musket and the Colt revolver.

At last satisfied with Travis's handling of his firearms, Tommy said, "Lemme go getcha a hoss."

While he was gone, Travis leaned against a tree and looked at his new firearms which, in spite of their well-used appearance, still looked competent enough. Travis felt proud of his rifle and thought he might carve his initials into the stock like he had done on the rifle his dad gave him when he turned fourteen. Back home in Tennessee, he had a .22 pistol and a lever action .30-.30. He was far from being a sharpshooter, but enjoyed target shooting and had recently taken up skeet shooting with some of the boys from Hicks-Bahr. But as he looked at his weapons, he couldn't help but think about how he wouldn't want to shoot anything. Likewise, he didn't want to be killed by men that died over a hundred years ago. How silly that sounded.

In just a few minutes Tommy was back, leading a huge, ugly, Roman-nosed horse that looked mean as a snake.

"This hoss is for you, Travis. the forage master said we got 'em from the Union Army. Name's Bolliver, and he's done been in the Yankee cavalry."

In spite of the horse's homely appearance, Travis watched as he daintily munched the small grass. He noticed scars over much of the horse's dull brown hair. He also had what appeared to be a botched attempt at branding on his left shoulder. Enchanted,

Travis strangely felt the thrill of ownership. He liked this ugly horse. He looked strong and intelligent.

"Yeah, the forage master said that he had been considering killing this hoss for the meat. He called him a red devil."

Travis just looked at the horse chewing the grass with lazy sideways motions.

Tommy continued, "He said you can't tie him up and if you picket him with the other hosses, he kicks 'em with those big ugly hooves."

Travis looked down at Bolliver's feet and had to admit that they looked as big as footballs.

Tommy kept on talking, "He just runs loose around the camp. Forage master said he tried to shoot him more'n once, but he'd always escape his shots. He said to tell you that tomorrow, catch him and take him to the forage master and he'll brand him." Turning to leave, he added, "Oh, and we'll have a lesson after supper."

Alone with his horse, Travis looked proudly at Bolliver, who seemed to be as gentle as a lamb and allowed him to comb the tangles from his mane. He stood as Travis cleaned the cuts and other wounds upon his sides, including one that Travis thought would leave a scar and appeared to be the graze of a bullet. "So, you were a Yankee horse, huh?"

After supper, when it was time to go, Travis couldn't wait to ride Bolliver. Tommy brought an enlisted man's saddle with tarnished stirrups. a saddle pad and a bridle, and showed Travis how to put them on correctly. Putting his foot in the stirrup, he went up one side of him and came down on the other in a heap. Tommy bent double laughing. Travis realized that perhaps he still wasn't entirely over his dizziness. He felt silly, falling like that in sight of the camp. But, with Tommy holding the reins, he got back on. For an hour or so, Tommy and Travis rode and soon Travis began to feel more confident.

Suddenly, Tommy kicked his horse in the ribs and took off. Bolliver leaped forward, nearly dislodging Travis from the saddle. Bolliver's jarring gallop hurt Travis's head so much that he pulled him back to a walk. Tommy circled back, a big grin on his brown face.

"Now you ready."

Chapter Eighteen

For whatever reason, Bolliver the devil horse, seemed to take to Travis. As he would sit and eat his rations, Travis would hear the sound of hooves coming up beside him and find a wet nose pressing against his hand.

Nonetheless, Bolliver remained a cussed horse. For it was quite another matter when the forage master had tried to burn the CSA mark into his behind. He kicked the red-hot brand from the forage master's hand and took off into the woods. That evening, Travis saw Bolliver wandering around the fringes of the camp. Travis laughed when Tommy said, "That explains the fact that the US brand on his shoulder is messed up. It seems that Bolliver will serve the Cherokee Mounted Rifles and the Confederate States of America on his terms, free of any brands!"

In spite of Tommy's good training about camp life and basic riding lessons, Travis soon found out that he had a lot to learn about military etiquette. He wasn't totally alone in that, however, for the men that comprised the Cherokee Mounted Rifles for the most part had been farmers before they had joined up. Therefore, they too had no military or cavalry training. The time spent at Fort Davis was to be a time for a sort of basic training for Watie's cavalry.

Nevertheless, recalling what he had seen in John Wayne cavalry movies, Travis figured that Watie's cavalry commander must have been the worst in the entire Confederate Army. The men rode with no semblance of formation or order. Some had their shirttails hanging and others had their pants legs hung in at least one boot. At least one rode barefoot. For the most part though, Travis was impressed with their horsemanship.

For an entire week the Mounted Rifles rode and drilled and it seemed to Travis that Bolliver had every bad habit possible in a horse. He balked, he went straight when Travis tried to make him turn, he would dance around when Travis tried to mount. One noon, when the troops halted for a few minutes and ate such as they had, feeling frustrated, lost and confused, Travis sat by himself and put his head down in despair, but then marveled at the fact that Bolliver went over and nuzzled him on top of the head. Then, when Travis mounted again, Bolliver behaved twice as good as any horse could. However, as Travis unsaddled him that same evening, he stepped on his toes and it seemed that no amount of urging would persuade him to remove his giant foot.

While learning to be a cavalry soldier, Travis was enjoying riding and the time spent outdoors in the fresh air, but he never seemed to totally understand the commands. The officers scolded him constantly and some of the other soldiers hazed him. If it wasn't for Tommy, Travis would have been the loneliest soldier in the camp. Tommy tried to help him all he could, but Travis knew that he would never adjust to army life. He also knew that he belonged in a 2001 world, and his fear grew each day.

One afternoon, he confided to Tommy that he was thinking about leaving.

"Bullcorn, Travis," Tommy said in alarm, "You can't just walk off from the army once you joined it. That's desertion. you know the penalty for desertion. They'll stand you and shoot you."

Travis's head still ached, his face looked pale, and his eyes were red. He clenched his teeth in desperation. "I'm just about homesick enough to chance it," he said, defiantly. Then his mood softened. "I miss my wife and daughter. I miss my parents, I miss my job, I miss my whole life. I miss my Grandpa."

"Will they starve, come winter?" asked Tommy.

Surprised at the question, Travis raised his head, "No, they won't starve."

Chapter Nineteen

As the days passed, Travis continued to spend as much time as possible with Bolliver. Thinking about all of the Tennessee Walkers in the area around Cowan, he figured that maybe he should have at least once taken a riding lesson. Now there he was, trying to get Bolliver to cooperate. Being a horse, Bolliver often had other ideas. Travis spent as much time enticing him to move as he did trying to make him stop. Occasionally Travis would wonder to himself, *Why I am up so high and moving so fast on an animal with so little brain?* However, in spite of the stubborn cuss's attitude, he had a fondness for his new partner.

Travis was finding out that something was definitely up with horses; he was not a fancy rider, but he was liking it. He had never been interested in them growing up. In junior high and high school, sports, especially football, had taken up all of his time; perhaps that was one reason. But the reason didn't really matter. What mattered was that something extraordinary began to happen when Travis swung onto the back of his horse.

Communication definitely took place between that big ugly horse and Travis Coker. He had learned and learned fast how to groom, feed and at least occasionally make sense of his horse. And once he got that far, he felt that the sky was the limit. He continued to put fat on the sores and scars that dotted the horse's coat. Where Tommy had called him ugly, Travis saw only beauty. Bolliver was big and sturdy and his coat was scruffy, but there was an alertness about him that to Travis signified wisdom.

Mornings, he would slip the bit into Bolliver's mouth, and spend as much time as possible on rubbing and brushing him until, at last, he could brush no more. The horse began to shine like a new penny.

Travis was surprised at some of the names in his unit: Mouse, Peavine, Ihaveseen, Bullfrog, Blister, a whole family of Buzzards, Bent Twig, Luther Stem, James Horsefly, as well as his new friend, Sawblade, another family of Pigeon's, three Squirrel brothers, John Tobacco, and others.

Soldiering can be a very dull job. Granting that Sam and most of the other sergeants managed to find a good amount of chores for the men to do, so far, no time had been occupied in actual fighting. The long hours in camp were often hard to bear by the men at Fort Davis. The soldiers whittled, told stories, sang songs or talked incessantly—the kind of juvenile banter Travis would have expected from guys on a long camping or hunting trip away from their families.

For often the chatter was punctuated by moments of candor, mainly about being away from home for so long. Most nights the men sat around the fire and talked, often about home and family.

"It's like missing half of my life," said a man called Vitaly. "The more yore here, the more you know yore missing everything."

"I just got married," said another.

"We all know what we're here for," said a baby-faced corporal. "We all know our job, but still it's a rough thing. It's not a good thing to take another human life—but every time we pull the trigger, we will do it to protect our wives and little ones."

At night the soldiers had lots of time on their hands. Although the men never drew any pay, they gambled just to pass the time. There were all kinds of card-playing, foot-racing, long-jumping and wrestling, and lots of storytelling. The men suffered from colds, influenza, sore throats, coughs, pleurisy, measles, diarrhea, as well as complaints about fevers, toothaches, insect bites and wounds from accidents.

Ernie Bobb, a Texas corporal from Cunningham, Texas, would sing sometimes after supper. Once, during an old spiritual, Travis started to sing along. After the song ended, they asked him to sing something. Unsure of what to sing, he knew most of the words to "Happy Trails" by Roy Rogers, so he sang that. The men all loved it and asked him to sing another and then another. It was then that the fellows started to warm up to Travis, the man from Tennessee.

One night the air was hazy with wood smoke and the dust of a thousand men's footprints. There was the smell of fall oak leaves, a smell that reminded Travis of Tennessee. He lay in his blankets and rubbed his eyes, trying to remember what day it was. He figured a couple of weeks had passed at least. He counted backward toward the morning he had taken the drive out to the military park. He tried to picture every sunrise in his mind, but they all ran together. There were sixteen or eighteen, he thought, perhaps twenty. It didn't matter in any case he figured.

It was then he recalled being told by the Texas doctor that he was to rest for week. *That never happened.*

His head injury seemed to be almost healed but he was still trying to come to grips with the fact that for whatever reason, in the span of a few weeks (or a hundred and thirty-some-odd years), he had gone from husband, father, son, grandson, friend and young corporate climber to a soldier for the Confederate States of America. *Melody probably has the FBI out searching for me. Cuthbert has probably fired me. Discount America has probably signed with another supplier.*

He wore a brown felt hat that someone had given him, a hat misshapen by weather and who knew what else. He also wore a brown coat with four mismatched buttons that someone else had given him to fight the cold. He still wore his Levi Straus button fly jeans stained with mud in gradations from the hem, and his Dr. Marten oxfords. For those clothes, and perhaps for even being alive, he was grateful.

Travis realized that he was coming to know his horse as he'd never known another animal. He had grown accustomed to the feel of him, the swell and release of his breathing. Bolliver's earthy scent was around him always, in the fibers of his clothes, on his hands, in his very skin. He came to know his temperament, his gestures; the manner in which he raised his head at a certain angle to smell the air, the way he sidestepped on being brought to a halt, as if he agreed to stop but could never quite agree to do so on his rider's chosen spot. Through the daily chore of saddling and unsaddling him, he'd come to know the feel of his coat, to find a beauty in the play of the light over his dark bay hair. He would groom him and run his fingers over him, amazed at all of the horse parts that made Bolliver completely a horse, perfect in every way.

One cloudy morning Travis led Bolliver by the bridle, listening to the progress of his own feet and the horse's hooves across the dirt, inhaling the rich scent of the massive trees, and watching the leaping of squirrels from branch to branch. He confided in the horse, telling him the story that he could tell no one else. He spoke of his wife and daughter in Tennessee, of his mom and dad, whom he longed to see again, and of his grandpa, who had grown in stature and wisdom in his eyes, such a kind, strong man, so rare in the world. Of Hicks-Bahr Travis spoke haltingly, as if Bolliver might judge him for placing such a high value on his job. He told his horse that there was a whole other world someplace that he just couldn't explain to him. How could he tell a horse how badly he wanted to go home. For that was what he most wanted, just to go back home; to be a husband, a father, a son, and a grandson.

He felt the tears sting his eyes, and still holding Bolliver's reins, he fell to one knee. Then he let his gaze rise up to where the sky was a deepening gray. The clouds lay like the underside of a great cotton blanket, with all its softness and ripples and curves and weight. The horse breathed slow, labored breaths, patiently waiting for whatever Travis might command. The wind started to get up, rippling his mane and tail in the breeze. Travis was aware of his own labored breathing and he could hear the sound of Bolliver grinding the bit in his big teeth. But those were the only sounds.

In the entire world, those were the only sounds.

Chapter Twenty

The Mounted Rifles, joined by the two hundred or so men of Welch's Texas Brigade, spent much time drilling and actually preparing for war. Like the other men, Travis was soon tired of the drilling and agreed with Sawblade when he complained, "The first thing in the morning we drill. Then drill, then drill again. Then drill, drill, a little more drill. Then drill, and then we drill."

A fortyish man, called Jack, told Travis a bit about being in the cavalry. He said that Watie's cavalry commanders followed the basics of the Poinsetts Cavalry Manual, but not religiously. He said that there were squads of eight members, which broke down into two ranks of four and that every time they would form up, either at assembly, with horse or not, moving out or drilling, that Travis would always fall in with his own squad. He said each member of the squad would guide off of the man in the number one position of the squad being the leader.

Jack was a patient sort of fellow and was friendly and soft spoken. Travis thought that had Jack had access to the technology, he might have worn glasses or had laser surgery, as he often squinted at objects in the distance. He moved with slow, even motions and tended to engage his face in a display of whatever thought process was going on within him. He said that before the war, he had been a sort of traveling salesman, toting kazoos, cigars, and jewelry. Jack was also quite knowledgeable about army life and cavalry matters, saying that he had ridden with a militia in Texas. He told Travis that he was half Cherokee and that he was married to a Cherokee woman in Tahlequah and had three young children. He seemed to like Travis and gave him a pair of saddlebags that were quite worn but seemed to be strong enough, and they beat what Travis had, which was nothing.

Travis learned from Jack that his sergeant, Sam, would call Assembly whenever he wanted the troops together without horses. "To Horse" would be when the men assembled with their horses. Jack said that the men would form up the same way every time, with or without a horse. "That way you know where you need to be and everyone can line up without bewilderment. And Sam'll be there to make sure you're not confused."

Over the next couple of weeks, Travis learned all he ever wanted to know about the cavalry terms such as *Assembly* and *To Horse* and *Rank*, and struggled with complicated maneuvers. He was taught the proper way to mount when he heard the command "Prepare to Mount," followed by "Mount," and "Form Ranks." It had all sounded simple enough when Jack was telling him about it, but when it came to mounting correctly, especially on a horse as tall as Bolliver, it all seemed so intricate and complex and downright impossible.

At the command "Prepare to Mount," the men in the one and three position of the rank would move forward one horse length. Then Travis was to place his right foot three inches behind his left foot and turn a quarter turn to the right. Then take two steps and slide his hand down the lead strap and secure the strap to the saddle ring, pick up the reins in his left hand, place his left hand on Bolliver's neck just forward of the pommel, and place his left foot into the stirrup. He then placed his right hand on the cantle, praying that Bolliver would stand still. Thus was the proper position for "Prepare to Mount."

The men were to hold the Prepare to Mount position till the Mount Command was given. *Give me a break,* Travis thought to himself. Bolliver seemed to know just when to sidestep, dance or try and bite or kick at the next horse. More than once Travis landed in the red dirt. The other men enjoyed laughing at the greenhorn from Tennessee.

In spite of his difficulties, Travis quickly learned which squad and rank he was in and how to get into position with the rest of the men when the irritable sergeant barked. His rank was made up of John Tobacco in the number one position, Sawblade in the number two, Travis in the number three position and his young friend Tommy in the number four position.

It was along about then that Travis discovered that he could speak and understand Cherokee. This occurred one day when some of the Texas troops were eating their meal not far from where Travis sat with some of the Cherokee men. He realized that he was hearing the Texans talking English and he could hear his mess mates talking Cherokee and realized that he could understand both languages. He was in awe that the words were just there in his mind. He didn't know how or when, but figured as he thought back to the first day, that the men had been speaking Cherokee the whole time and he had understood.

Travis enjoyed learning about the cavalry, which was valued for its speed and mobility, and used for reconnaissance, delaying actions, raiding parties, and pursuit and harassment of enemy troops. The mounted soldiers were trained to fight on horseback, using their horses for rapid transportation between engagements. When mounted, the men were trained to use six shot, .44 caliber Colt Army revolvers that weighed about two pounds. Only one hand was needed in the firing of this type of weapon. This was very important since the soldier's other hand was used to manage the horse.

They drilled and learned to use their horses as battering rams and weapons to mow down the Union troops.

The Mounted Rifles were also drilled to fight dragoon style. When in rank the men were always numbered by fours. When the command was given, "On Foot," they would dismount except for the number four soldier, who remained mounted to hold the other three horses. Instead of having to hold three sets of reins in addition to his own, each soldier would secure their reins so that they would not be dropped or stepped on by the horses. Numbers one, two and three of each set of fours would dismount and fasten their horses together by means of a short strap buckled to the pommel of the saddle and by means of a snap on the other end of the strap fastened to the bit of the horse on the right. Number four remained mounted, and led the horses of one, two and three, on his right by means of the strap from the pommel of his saddle. Thus the three dismounted horses would be linked together, and the number four man would only have to hold onto one extra horse. The dismounted men would then turn to face the front with their rifles. The horse holder would hold and move the horses as required.

When the command was given, the dismounted men would move out as skirmishers in the same manner as when they were mounted, with the mounted file pairs working together, one firing while the other was reloading. He was taught that if they were skirmishing without gaining ground, they should always be moving. He learned how the front rank would fire, then move back a few steps while reloading, and when that man was loaded he was to move back to the line and the rear rank would then fire, and then step back. This procedure would be repeated until cease fire was called. The horse holders would stay mounted and remain in place, keeping the horses calm.

One evening after drilling, Travis felt a twinge of pain in his left hand and found it difficult to eat because of the pain in his fingers. Beneath his fingernails, blue with dirt, the bruised knuckles were swollen frightfully. Bolliver had bitten his hand as Travis gave him his corn that night. To make it worse, instead of opening his mouth and releasing his hand, the horse had kept his teeth clinched until he finally scraped them over Travis's poor fingers. As a result it was difficult for Travis to manage his plate and spoon with his fingers so stiff and sore. He was thankful though that it was his left hand and not his right, as he was right handed and used his right hand for everything, including firing his musket if need be.

One day, when Travis was filling his canteen, he saw the cook drive the horses out of the creek and scoop up the water with his camp buckets, he lost all his thirst and swore not to take another drink until he was out of the nightmare of army life. However, later he relented when he wanted a cup of the Cherokee coffee. He was surprised at how good it was starting to taste, so much so that he could hardly remember what a chocolate latte even tasted like. He was getting better at filling his canteen out of the stream after searching for the clearest water he could find while trying not to think about dysentery, amoebas, typhoid and all of the other dangers of drinking dirty water.

No day passed during which Travis wasn't stumped by some insurmountable problem. No task was ever completed without a new one presenting itself. Just when a day's working or riding seemed at an end, his bridle cheek would break, or he would slip and gash his knee open, or his knife blade would snap off, or mosquitoes would swarm over the camp, devouring all exposed skin. Sometimes when he lay down to sleep, he would discover that he had placed his pallet on top of a rock or before dawn, the trees above him would rain down dew drops loosened by the wind. Other times a passing critter would stare at him with what seemed to be blatant taunt.

He was proud though of what the army life was doing to his body. He had grown leaner, yet stronger, a bone-deep strength that would never leave him. The hard labor of the past weeks had carved changes into his body. His hands were callused across the palms and bruised over the knuckles, making them puffed, rugged versions of their former selves. Cords of muscle fanned out across his back like wings growing under his skin and the muscles in his forearms bulged like solid balls. His knees and legs had grown accustomed to riding and his butt no longer ached after hours in the saddle. He was becoming comfortable and felt that he was really beginning to develop a partnership with Bolliver. When Travis would be in camp, the big horse would often come up to him and want to be petted. Travis realized that time spent with his horse personally gave him a great emotional high because the powerful animal seemed to trust and rely on him. Travis recalled that Will Rogers had said that, "The outside of a horse is good for the inside of a man." He personally knew that was true because Bolliver filled the empty place that was in Travis's heart. He was comfortable with his mount's movements beneath him, and it showed then in the way he sat the horse.

    Late in the month, Travis was put to helping dig a latrine near to where the horses were kept. For three days, he hauled buckets of dirt and rocks from where they'd been dug and dumped them into a ravine. Bolliver watched him with his disdainful eyes, as if he respected his efforts but doubted his skills as a ditch digger. In a bad mood, Travis couldn't help speaking to him under his breath, telling Bolliver about glue factories, dog food plants and how horse meat was used to feed zoo animals. Travis told him about every potential use for a dead horse he could think of in an effort to convince the animal of the short span of his life. He also blamed Bolliver for the abundance of flies that swarmed around him. They plagued his eyes, buzzed in his ears, and crawled over any patch of exposed flesh they could find. Half his efforts each day were spent in slapping the insects to death. He barely noticed the hours passing into days, and yet they did.
    Travis was homesick. He missed some things more than others. He missed the company of twenty-first century people. He missed the pleasure of a diet cola. Most of all, he missed Melody. Being with her, and especially sharing, was always on his mind. The more settled he became in the pattern of 1861 army life, the more he wanted to share it with someone, and when he thought of that missing someone, he would drop his chin and stare morosely at nothing.

* * *

It was during those tiring, lonely, boring, stressful days at Fort Davis, when he began to appreciate his grandpa, who with gentle simplicity had attempted to teach him traditional Cherokee wisdom through age-old legends and modern stories. One afternoon he was feeling especially doomed and at a complete loss about his predicament, when he recalled one of Grandpa's stories.

Travis, there's an old story about a frog who fell into a butter churn and no matter how high he jumped, the top was too high for him to reach. But as he was jumping, his webbed feet created the same up-and-down motion as the paddle, until finally butter was formed and he could stand on it and jump out.

"Oh, Grandpa, that's silly," he had said when Grandpa had told him the story.

Patiently, Grandpa had continued, "In our struggles we may think we can't go any further, not realizing that it is merely a turning point in our life."

Travis lay down on the ground and laced his fingers behind his head. Grandpa had taught him to lie down and look up to the Creator. "Talk to Him, pour your heart out to him and the answer'll come."

The thing was, Travis was afraid to start praying out of fear, that if he only prayed because he was stuck in the Civil War that God would turn his back on him and say, "You chose to believe in me when you needed me, at your convenience." Truth was, he wasn't sure if he even knew who or what God was to him.

He had grown up going to church and Sunday School every week with his mom and dad. He had gone to church camp for two weeks every summer and had learned all of the basic Bible stories. After high school, he had pretty much stopped going to church. At the University he did go a couple of Sundays, but since he didn't see anyone he recognized, he didn't go again until he had started dating Melody and wanted to impress her.

But as he lay there on the ground in Indian Territory, Travis began to realize that perhaps going to church and even believing in God had not made him a Christian.

Chapter Twenty-One

One morning the troops were sitting around a campfire broiling freshly killed rabbits for breakfast. The coffee was hot, sitting on the rocks bordering the fire, and the hoecakes were baking in the ashes. The smell of cooking meat, corn, and coffee filled the air.

"Smelling this food sure makes me hungry," said Travis, rubbing his hands together in anticipation.

"Fresh game and corn. Good food," Sawblade said as he bit into a piece of roasted rabbit.

"Good Cherokee food, anyway," Adahte added.

As the men ate, Hunter said, "I think it might be time for a story about rabbit."

Once there was such a long spell of dry weather that there was no more water in the creeks and springs, and the animals held a council to see what to do about it. They decided to dig a well, and all agreed to help except the Rabbit, who was a lazy fellow, and said, "I don't need to dig for water. the dew on the grass is enough for me." the others did not like this, but they went to work together and dug their well.

They noticed that the Rabbit kept sleek and lively, although it was still dry weather and the water was getting low in the well. They said, "That tricky Rabbit steals our water at night," so they made a wolf out of pine gum and tar and set it up by the well to scare the thief. That night the Rabbit came, as he had been coming every night, to drink enough to last him all next day. He saw the queer black thing by the well and said, "Get out of my way or I'll strike you." Still the wolf never moved and the Rabbit came up and struck it with his paw, but the pine gum held his foot and it stuck fast. Now he was angry and said, "Let me go or I'll kick you." Still the wolf said nothing. Then the Rabbit struck with his hind foot, so hard that it was caught in the gum and he could not move, and there he stuck until the animals came for water in the morning. When they found who the thief was, they had great sport over him for a while and then got ready to kill him, but as soon as he was unfastened from the tar wolf he managed to get away.

"My grandpa told it like this," said Sawblade.

Once upon a time there was such a severe drought that all the streams of water and all lakes were dried up. In this tragedy the animals got together to figure out a way to get water. It was proposed by one to dig a well. All agreed to do so except the rabbit. She refused because it would soil her tiny paws. the rest, however, dug their well and were fortunate enough to find water. the rabbit was beginning to suffer and thirst, and having no right to the well, was thrown upon her wits to get water. She figured that the easiest way would be to steal from the public well. The rest of the animals, surprised to find that the rabbit was so well supplied with water, asked her where she got it. She replied that she went out early in the morning and gathered the dewdrops. However the wolf and the fox suspected her of stealing and hit on the following plan to detect her:

They made a wolf of tar and placed it near the well. On the following night the rabbit came as usual after her supply of water. On seeing the tar wolf she asked who was there. Receiving no answer she repeated the demand, threatening to kick the wolf if he did not reply. Receiving no reply, she kicked the wolf, and was stuck to the tar and was caught. When the fox and the wolf got hold of her they talked about what was best to do with her. One proposed cutting her head off. This the rabbit protested would be useless, as it had often been tried without hurting her. Other methods were proposed for killing her, all of which she said would be useless. At last it was proposed to let her loose to perish in a thicket. Upon this the rabbit pretended great uneasiness and pleaded hard for life. Her enemies, however, refused to listen and she was let loose. As soon, however, as she was out of reach of her enemies she gave a whoop, and bounding away she exclaimed: "This is where I live."

The month of October passed into November in a dreary haze of endless work. The troops were up before the sun. They ate their breakfast as the sky grew pale, and they stepped out into the morning air as the first beams of sunlight touched the landscape, highlighting the tips of the grasses, bringing the camp out of its dull relief. The myriad tasks to be completed each day dwarfed any chores that Travis had ever known before. There was, of course, the constant drilling and maneuvering and the hours spent with Bolliver. Travis was quite proud that working with Bolliver had grown easier with experience. To Travis's reckoning, his riding skills continued to grow stronger each day.

Although Watie's army was pretty informal, duty rosters were prepared weekly and Travis had learned which days he would be in the saddle. Like most of Watie's men, he preferred the mounted patrols to camp duty or to standing guard. Each mounted patrol consisted of ten to twelve men. The scouting operations seemed to carry Travis into every part of the Indian Territory and provided him with great satisfaction.

"Man, I'm hungry," said Travis one day, digging in his bag for something to eat. While the scouts had been moving, they had had nothing to eat but corn bread for more than two days.

Squirrel laughed and said, "Yup, I'm so hungry I could eat that horse a yours, 'cept he's so ugly."

Squirrel passed Travis a thick piece of jerky.

"Well," Travis said, looking at the jerky, "I guess they won't starve us." He grabbed the waistband of his old Levi's between his forefinger and thumb and pulled it about three inches away from his stomach, and was amazed at the gap caused by his lost weight

"Well," Squirrel said, "come nights, we'll soon be doing some foraging from the families that's got plenty."

Because of the hard daytime training, the soldiers never seemed to get enough to eat. They were served bacon, beans, hardtack, and coffee three times a day but everyone yearned for more variety.

And so it was, the order came to begin foraging. Travis, Squirrel, and Tommy rode away in the dark and raided a hen house and a smokehouse and came back with six live hens, four eggs, and seven nice hams. Some of the other men came back with corn from a corn crib and flour from a miller's storage. Others came back with more live chickens, milk, and a goose. The next night was even more productive. For breakfast they were having coffee, corn, light bread, and beef. For dinner there was cornbread, peas, and bacon. For supper they had beef or chicken, dried fruit, turnips or potatoes, and bread.

During those days in Indian Territory, Watie's army ate well. Local farms gave up many hogs, chickens, and even a fresh milk cow or two to Watie's hungry army. Every night after dark the men left camp in small groups to add to their food stores. They were often shot at but not a man was hit as the cavalry rustled their own provisions.

One evening Squirrel, Tommy, and Travis were out foraging again. Travis had filled a small bag with potatoes, turnips, and onions, and Tommy had wrung the neck of a large gray goose. On their way back to camp they passed a deserted log house in the midst of a patch of large oak trees. Travis stopped, curious about the old cabin. "Let's see what's inside."

"Naw, Travis," Squirrel said. "We done got enough. Nothing there, anyways."

"Might be," said Travis. "I'm gonna look in." He pushed the door open and went inside. What he saw was a broken table, a bed, and some broken pieces of cups and plates. He was suddenly overcome with sadness for the family that had lived there. He fought to keep his emotions in check as he backed out of the cabin and mounted Bolliver for the ride back to camp. That night he could not sleep. His head was filled with thoughts of Melody, of Allie, of home, and of the pleasures he once enjoyed. Sadly, he was aware that those pleasures were gone and many sleepless nights would be spent in dwelling on their memory. He thought about the folly of his days at Hicks-Bahr, the sixty hour weeks, the many times he had disappointed Melody, placing his job over his family. As the tears flowed, he thought to himself, *If I could only go back, I would do everything so differently. I would love my wife and daughter. Why was I such a fool? I would give anything to relive the life I was too busy to enjoy. If only ...*

If only. If only he hadn't driven out to the military park that day. If only he had loved his wife more. If only he had listened to Grandpa. If only he ... If only. If only there was an antidote for the poison of *if only*.

Stand Watie was also sending scores of his Mounted Rifles to raid behind the Union lines in the vicinity of the Grand River, destroying the fields and gardens the Union sympathizers had planted on their small farms. It was Watie's intention to drive every Union Indian family he could find to the protection of Fort Gibson, compelling the Union Army to feed them from the supplies hauled in by mule and ox trains from Kansas. Watie's ultimate goal was to for the Yankees to evacuate the fort and leave the Cherokee Nation to the Confederates.

Travis was aware that some of the men had also been ordered to ride farther and farther away from camp to raid an innocent family's kitchen, or garden, or hen house, or clothesline. Although he knew that his day would come, he dreaded being ordered to ride on one of those raiding excursions, but when he questioned Tommy about it, Tommy laughed, telling Travis that provisions were necessary for the troops and that cavalry horses had to be fed. He explained that Yankee soldiers had supply trains from the north, but that Watie's Mounted Rifles were like all Confederate troops in that they had to live off the country. The search for food for the men and their horses had turned honest men into bold, shameless thieves. The men emptied smokehouses, corncribs, and root cellars. They swept up chickens, hogs, cattle, sheep, and anything else that might prove useful. Some of the men even carried off priceless heirlooms and keepsakes.

A few days later; Sam went out with Travis, Tommy, Johnny Tobacco, and Sawblade on a long ride to scour for food and supplies. As they came through a patch of woods, they began to see the outline of a farm. It was a complex of three structures, a two-story house and two barns, sitting next to a creek. Behind the house and lining the creek, stood the after-harvest remains of a nice sized patch of corn. Next to the house an old slave man was chopping wood, oblivious to the riders in the trees. At the back of the house, a woman and two little girls washed clothes, occasionally laughing and throwing water at each other. A black and white dog lay in front of the door. There was a nice patch of fall collards or turnip greens and here and there chickens scratched. At the end of a long tether, a goat munched on the grass at the edge of the field. The whole place conveyed a sense of peace and tranquility. Travis couldn't help but think of his own family, and his grass, his white house, his people and the quietness of his own place in Tennessee.

The men watched from the trees for a bit before riding forward at a walk. At last, Sam took a long drink from his canteen and wiped his mouth on his arm before saying, "Let's go."

Travis felt he could scarcely move, but when Sam repeated the order, he flicked Bolliver on the rump to get him going. He and Sam followed Johnny Tobacco and the others inside, stepping gingerly around the dog to do so.

For the next twenty minutes they ransacked the place. Johnny Tobacco seemed to be enjoying himself. He yelled out instructions, demonstrating the proper way to throw drawers and overturn furniture. To Travis's surprise, Tommy proved more than proficient at this, punctuating each action with hoots and curses. Travis went through the motions of searching, but was uncomfortably mindful of the mother and little girls sitting quietly at the table, saying nothing. The Negro man continued to stack wood outside, and still seemed oblivious of the motives of their work. Travis found a rifle cabinet, opened it, and stared at its contents as if he'd never seen such weapons before. He had just turned away from it when Sam noted his discovery and told Travis to carry the weapons outside.

Travis found nothing else of value. Left alone for a moment in the upstairs bedroom, he sat on the bed and stared at the photographs lining the dresser, daguerreotypes of an array of people. He found himself remembering his parents' home in Tennessee, remembering a dresser much like this one on which photographs of his own family sat. He felt his eyes go watery. The world before him blurred, and for a moment he felt that he'd forgotten how to breathe; overwhelmed by memories until a new round of shouting from downstairs brought him back.

That night, every time he closed his eyes, Travis could see the woman and the little girls, sitting quietly as he and the others had raided their home. Travis had been raised to believe stealing was wrong. Having a hard time rationalizing what had happened that day, he was unable to sleep. At last, he slipped noiselessly out of his blanket and walked to the creek.

The night was dark. The evening star was alone in the sky. Travis listened and looked back at the camp. All was quiet; it seemed that he was the only man awake.

He heard footsteps and then Bolliver nudged him in the back. Travis reached his hand up and placed it on his neck and grinned.

"Hey buddy. You're always here for me." They stood that way for a long time, man and beast, best friends, allies. With Bolliver by his side, Travis was amazed at how strong he felt. His discomfort about the day's raid, though he recalled it vividly, seemed far away. Not dim, but far away, like history. Evidently a part of army life, the raid was perhaps some sort of necessary rite or baptism, he concluded, a baptism that had catapulted him even further from imagination to reality. Like it or not, everything he had experienced so far had been real, the car accident had been real, the cabin had been real, the two soldiers that had conscripted him had been real. Bolliver was real. The raid that day had been real.

Becoming bored, Bolliver walked over to get a drink. As he watched his horse drink deeply of the water, Travis continued to come to grips with his situation. He knew for a fact that he was from the twenty-first century and not just some crazy person from the 1860's. How else would he know about such things as movies, Hummers and microwave ovens? *What about bottled water, and VCR's, and porcelain toilets, and helicopters, and, and, and ...*

He shook his head, laughing inwardly to himself and skipped a stone on the water.

I better come to grips with this right now.

Before he could think any further, his eyes caught something. Color was reflecting off the water on the other side of the stream. Travis glanced behind him.

An enormous harvest moon was beginning to rise. On pure impulse, he sat down on a rock to take in the magnificent sight of an enormous moon, bright as an egg yolk, filling the night sky as if it were a whole new world come to call just on him.

Chapter Twenty-Two

After that, Travis did his best to push his feeling about thievery into his subconscious and do his part. A couple of weeks later, the men came upon a small farm with only a corncrib, a ragged corral, and a small house. The solitary resident of the farm was an elderly woman. She was dark skinned and overweight and stood smiling by the door of the house while the men dismounted. While the other men loaded corn outside, Travis went inside. Silently, she took two grubstake bags from a peg on the wall and began filling them with supplies. She then handed the bags to Travis, who found the bags heavier than he'd anticipated. The old woman then placed her rough heavy hand on his cheek, saying something in an Indian language that Travis didn't recognize. He assumed that it might be Choctaw or Delaware.

Travis apologized to her for the mistreatment, then turned and went back outside and hurried with the bags over to Bolliver. Seeing that the other men were still busy behind the house, Travis laid the bags on the ground and sorted through the supplies. He found Lucifer matches, a large sack of flour, a smaller bag of cornmeal, half a block of bacon, a lump of lard, a number of twists of tobacco, and a wide-mouth jar of peach preserves. Unable to resist the temptation, he opened the jar and ate the preserves straight from the jar, poking it into his mouth with his dirty fingers, and savoring its golden, sugary taste. He shared some with Bolliver and then let him lick his fingers clean before tossing the empty jar under the bushes.

One evening the plunderers stopped early and set the horses to graze. The men slipped naked into the creek near camp and washed the filth off their bodies. Travis was hesitant because of the cold water, but once in the chilly water, he felt some of the tension within him slipping away. He imagined the water could wash him clean, not just cool and soothe his skin, but enter into him and wash away the stains, the pain, and the guilt that wrapped around his heart. He closed his eyes and leaned back, feeling the cool water relaxing him and quieting his thoughts.

He must have dozed off for a bit, because when he opened his eyes, the sun was setting and the rest of the men had gone back to camp. The sunset reminded him of Florida and he wondered if he would ever see Florida, or for that matter Tennessee again, or ever again feel that his life was in his own hands.

As if to answer his questions, Sam approached the creek. He spotted Travis and turned and walked toward him. Bare-chested, the sergeant seemed to Travis larger than usual. The skin on his chest was hairless, and brown, and his muscles were well-defined. After exchanging nods, Sam began to take his boots and pants off; Travis turned to look down at the water in which he sat.

Sam stepped into the water. The wince that ran across his face and then eased into a sort of relaxed pleasure indicated to Travis that Sam found the water as chilling at first as he had.

"You think raiding's wrong, don't you?"

Travis didn't answer, but could tell that Sam didn't expect him to.

"We have to fight. the Yankees for the most part have supply trains and the like. No one sends us supplies, the land has to support us. We have to raid."

Sam paused and allowed Travis to think about it for a moment. He met Travis's eyes then and waited for an answer.

Travis answered him with an "I guess."

Sam leaned toward Travis then. "You guess? I know you better'n that, Travis. You, me, all of us, we're doing this for our families, our land, our way of life. I can tell that you're not one to sell his soul for Yankee thinking. You got surviving in you just like the rest of us."

Travis nodded. He surprised himself; he actually *did* understand the need for raiding a bit.

Sam continued, "I respect you, though, Travis. If you think raiding and stealing's wrong, then it's got to *always* be wrong. Stealing don't get right jus 'cause we hafta do it, does it? You following me?"

Travis wasn't sure what to say.

Sam tossed a rock into the water. "You ain't following me. I ain't even following myself. Truth is, Travis, I hate it too. I ain't told a soul here what I'm gonna tell you. But Travis, before the war, I was starting to become a preacher. I still want to."

All Travis could think of to say was, "Wow."

Sam continued, "Trouble is, right now, I'm an officer. This army don't have 'nuff food for the men nor corn for the horses to go around. So we have to take it; some corn from this one, some rifles from that one, a cow from another. That's why I go along on raids when I can. Its 'cause I don't want the men taking more than we hafta. That's all there is to it."

Sam rose, his feet stirring the water. "Travis, in war, you just gotta look at things the right way." With that, he turned, waded out of the water and walked off, leaving Travis with a mind full of new thoughts to crowd out the old.

The next evening Travis and the other men were on their way back to camp with seven stolen horses, ten hams, twenty-two live chickens, bags of flour and clothing. It had been a good two days of ingathering for the Mounted Rifles. They had been riding in darkness for half an hour when the fires of camp appeared, like faraway dots. The strangeness of it was like a dream.

Home, Travis thought. *That's home.*

How could it be? An army camp in Indian Territory, populated by a thousand or so men whose life experiences were different than his, men that had died a hundred years before he had even been born, men fighting a war that had already been lost. How Fort Davis could even feel like home to him was a mystery that he wished he could explain.

But on that night he was too tired. That night the camp promised all the comforts of home. It was home and he was glad to see it.

The other men, with whom he'd been riding the last two days, were glad to see it, too. The horses could smell it and some were beginning to break into a trot.

Home.

Along with raiding, guerrilla warfare by Watie's Mounted Rifles was increasing. Although Travis continued to go on foraging raids, after the night at the creek, Sam never sent Travis out on one of the excursions to steal from or sabotage the Yankees. Watie knew that raiding made use of the cavalry's strong suit, which was mobility and faster rates of weapons fire. Watie used his cavalry to run behind enemy lines and create havoc, destroy supplies, gather intelligence, and tie up valuable Union combat forces.

Watie's position at Fort Davis was critical. When the Union Army sent two hundred cavalry down from Kansas as an escort to a Federal supply train, Watie's men boldly rode out and captured more than one hundred Union horses and mules.

Travis was amazed at the frequency and range of Watie's cavalry raids. Sitting around the fire after supper, he would listen as the men described some of the forays behind Union lines. Some of the men had traveled into Missouri to clean out supply depots, burn wagon trains, loot smokehouses, and steal livestock right out of the fields. Watie was determined to destroy or cart off everything that might give support to the Yankees. Other groups had gone over the eastern border of Indian Territory into Arkansas.

Once a stealthy group of ten rode into a small town in Missouri where they seized an undefended armory, arsenal and rifle works and quickly vanished into the timber under cover of darkness before a large force could be sent to intercept them. Each night, listening to these stories, Travis became more and more impressed with the fierce loyalty of the Cherokee rebels, both to their leader and to their cause.

Two of Watie's men that were part of a foraging group of six, were shot one night. They had ridden up to a house in the late afternoon. The family, a man and his wife and grown daughter had seemed very friendly and offered the men an early supper, which they gladly accepted. During the meal, the man excused himself from the table. Almost immediately shots were fired in through the window. One of Watie's men was killed. The other was badly wounded in the left shoulder, but was able to escape into the darkness and into the woods until he thought he could get away. He had managed to walk back into camp a bit before daylight the next morning.

Infuriated, the Mounted Rifles immediately mounted and hurried out to the place at once. The dead Cherokee had been thrown out into the yard and the soldiers found the house deserted. Feeling that the family had colluded to the death of a Mounted Rifle, the house was burned.

Chapter Twenty-Three

Fall seemed to linger, hesitant somehow to give itself over to winter. The trees along the rivers and creeks of Indian Territory were valiantly hanging on to their leaves of red and gold. Watie had received word that the Federal troops were on the move and sent out sentries and scouts to seek them out. For two days and three nights the Cherokee sentries scouted for the Yankees and found nothing. At last they went back to Watie's camp for rest. At the same time, however, the Yankees were on the move and after a long night march, the tired and hungry Federal troops were able to hit hard at the Rebel camp before Watie's pickets could warn the encampment. Caught off-guard, the Mounted Rifles offered little resistance. A Yankee cavalry charge, coupled with artillery shelling, routed the Indian troops.

Travis was sickened as he realized how he had somehow lulled himself to sleep in the belief that he was still just in some atrocious dream—that perhaps it was a really, really long reenactment—that none of what he was living was real. He had tried to preserve his sanity by actually starting to enjoy parts of the whole scenario and refusing to give in to his subconscious. But then, with the bluecoats coming in from out of nowhere; when there was yelling and shooting, Travis realized that this was no dream. He was really in the 1860's. Blood is never a dream. A few feet away, Billy Beaver dropped his musket like it was red hot and Travis saw that part of the man's hand had been blown away. And there, another staggered and fell with a minie ball through his temple, fatally wounded. Two men tried to help him walk towards the rear, but one of them got a minie in the side and fell groaning to the ground. Then out of nowhere, Sawblade grabbed Travis by the arm and together they ran to join their advancing comrades.

They found the other men of their unit loading, firing, and fighting with great deliberation and discretion. Several men had already fallen, some killed outright, some injured slightly, some seriously, and some mortally wounded.

Oh, brother, thought Travis. He brought his rifle around and planted the butt between his feet. He fumbled in his cartridge box, extracted a cartridge, and tore off the paper tail with his fingers. Then, as he began to pour the powder into the muzzle, his hand began to shake so badly that all the powder spilled on the ground.

Travis dropped the torn cartridge and reached for another. He was trying to remember everything that Tommy had shown him; every step he had completed as he had practiced loading and firing into the soft earth. But that was then and this was now. This was battle. He cursed as he noticed that all the other men had already poured in their powder and were replacing the long steel ramrods back into their guides. Travis could not even tear the new cartridge. He held it up in frustration and tried to stop his hands from shaking. Then to make matters worse, his eyes suddenly filled with tears: he could not load his stupid musket.

Just then Sawblade again appeared by Travis's side and lifted the cartridge gently from his fingers. "Here," said Sawblade. He tore the paper, poured in the powder, and started the ball into the muzzle of Travis's rifle, pressing it down with his thumb. Then he turned away and busied himself with his own musket.

"Thank you," said Travis, his face burning. He dried his eyes on his sleeve then finished ramming the charge. *Now to prime,* he thought. He brought the piece up, cocked it, and with finger and thumb plumbed his cap box for a percussion cap.

Now I guess I will drop the stupid cap, he thought, but he didn't drop it. In fact, when he brought his hand up, it was steady. He slipped the cap onto the nipple and lowered the hammer, embarrassed that he was the last man to load.

Being caught off guard, Watie's cavalry were not mounted and had to fight on their feet, dragoon style. Men with empty guns turned those guns into clubs, fighting to hold the camp.

At last Watie's men were able to drive the Yankee skirmishers back. However, many of the Cherokee men had already fallen. At last a Rebel cannon was hurried into position, the cannoniers loaded their weapon, and the big gun blazed and away went the shell. Travis joined the others in cheering as it exploded over the Yankee line. Cannon blast after cannon blast, sounds of musket fire, shouts of joy, prayer songs and moans of death—what a chorus assailed Travis's virgin ears.

At last, they could hear the Yankees retreating through the trees. The sound of the Yankee officers' commands and the snapping of twigs inspired a cheer from Watie's men. The Yankees were gone.

Still horror-struck, Travis got sick to his stomach. *How could this be? What has happened to me?* Once more he realized that he had foolishly allowed himself to believe that this was some sort of dream or even more foolishly, a reenactment. *How stupid. What an idiot,* he said to himself over and over. Later, in a last resort to hold on to his sanity, he asked an officer, "What is the date today?"

"December 1, 1861"

"Thank you."

As Travis turned and walked away, the earth seemed to roll beneath his feet, like a slowly undulating ocean that did not yet drown him but might at any moment.

Chapter Twenty-Four

Time passed and Travis did his soldiering as he was taught and as he was told. After the skirmish, he had finally come to grips with the fact that he was stuck somehow in the War Between the States. He just didn't know how he got there and he didn't know why.

His concussion, or whatever, had finally healed, but his mind was numb and weary and his heart was hollow with missing his wife and family. To keep from going crazy from thinking about it all, he put his body, mind and soul into whatever he could find to do, over and beyond what he was ordered to do as a soldier. He decided to keep busy all the time by doing anything at all to keep from thinking. He had learned to drill with the musket. He had learned to care for his horse. He had learned to drink the foul coffee and to eat whatever the cook doled out. He had learned much about the Cherokees that shared his blood and heritage. He grew as accustomed to seeing death as any person can. He had learned to deal with the clangor of wagon wheels on rocky roads, the sound of cannon fire, the pattering of incoming musket minie balls, as well as the periods of quiet so heavy it was palpable. He had learned to bury his new friends. He had learned about fear. He had kept going, and thus he kept on going, day after day, and for all of it he paid in full.

Most of the men were lonely or homesick to a degree. They missed their wives, or sweethearts, or mothers, or at the very least, the life they lived before the war. Travis missed all of that and more. He also missed an entire culture and the twenty-first century world. In a lighter moment, he had compiled a short list of what he missed the most, things that he would never again take for granted: toilet paper, bug spray, elastic, heating and air conditioning and preservatives in food.

After supper most nights, the men talked and smoked together and told stories. But for Travis, the acid loneliness ate into him. The end of each day found him oppressed by homesickness and longing for home. From the first, the evening silence after supper hurt him most, for a man needs his wife, as well as talk and tobacco, and after a time he dreaded the evenings so bitterly that he purposely exhausted himself every day, so as to pass from supper into sleep as quickly as possible. For the most part, the long days in the fresh air, combined with the stress he was feeling, burned out his strength thoroughly and daybreak brought him groaning out of his blankets to tend to Bolliver and eat his breakfast of coffee, bacon and bread. In time his days as a Confederate soldier became his wife and child, and he stepped into a routine which took the place of thinking, and the changes in him were so gradual that he no longer noticed the physical changes. A mirror might have shown it to him as he stood that morning by the fire, for the wind fluttered the shirt around his labor-tightened body, and his facial expression had developed a habitual frown.

Such was Travis on the evening that he and Tommy were down at the creek; washing away some of the grime and waiting for the cook to announce that supper was ready. Travis had just splashed his face with the cold water when a raucous cry caused him to start and look around.

Tommy was pointing into the sky where Travis looked up and saw two eagles fighting in the light of the late afternoon.

"They come here ever winter and they're battling for territory," said Tommy.

Travis had never heard the scream of an eagle that sounded like the one he had just heard. It had caused the hairs on his head to stand up. He was spellbound as he stood and watched. The eagles darted away. They flashed together with reaching talons and gaping beaks, and dropped in a tumult of wings, then soared and clashed once more until one of them folded his wings and dropped like a rock until he was out of sight behind a row of trees.

The conqueror screamed his insult before flying away.

For some reason, the eagles had made him think about Melody and Allie. It knew that the aching in his heart would never lessen for his family, yet he was aware that as week passed into week, the Cherokee Mounted Rifles were becoming wife and child to him. For conversation, he had the men that had become his friends.

He also was aware that as hard as he tried not to, in ways, he was enjoying himself.

He shrugged his shoulders and turned resolutely towards the camp after putting on his shirt and picking up his musket. By instinct he caught it at exactly the right spot, and the stock, polished by his and the previous owner's grip, felt smooth against the calluses of his palm. From the many hours of drilling, he felt pretty much at one with the musket.

That's a bad sign, I guess, he decided, and was still frowning as he walked back to camp. There lay his blankets, rumpled, brown with dirt, and he shivered at the sight of them; the night was sure to be cold. Before he fell asleep, he flung his arm over his face and listened to the men tell the ancient, oft-repeated stories, drifts of tobacco smoke passing his nostrils. As he drifted off, the deep voices of the men lulled him to sleep.

Then, almost immediately it seemed, he sniffed the air again and odors of burned bacon and army coffee permeated the air. *What's wrong with me?* he muttered to himself. The sound of his own voice echoed ghostly loud in his mind, and he shivered again. *I must be going nutty.*

As if to escape from his thoughts, he stepped out into the sun, and it was so grateful to him after the chilly night in the blankets, that he looked up and smiled at the sky.

More and more it seemed that the living things were speaking to him. For one full day a mockingbird spoke to him. The gray and white bird leapt from tree to tree, watching Travis with cagy sidelong glances, calling out to him in a variety of songs and whistles.

Late one night Travis lay down and closed his eyes. Then, when he awoke, he opened his eyes, and a little mouse was sitting less than a foot from his face. With his front feet drawn up, he studied Travis, as he studied him. Travis had never seen such a beautiful creature, so beautiful, so perfect and small. Each whisker vibrated his inspection of Travis's smell. His eyes were black and bright and he stared at Travis. The mouse was fat and full from eating whatever it was that he ate. The pattern of his hair ran together making him perfect. Travis felt an odd swelling of pure love for that little mouse. He washed his face and groomed his tail and Travis stayed so still. He barely breathed out of fear of disturbing the little mouse and betraying the mouse's trust in him.

Another night Travis bedded down kitty-corner from Sawblade and rolled himself tightly into his blankets and lay with his head on the hard bundle that served as his pillow. The moon had just risen above the trees, hauling itself up with tired resilience and casting its pale light across the camp.

Travis watched the moon's progress for some time, wondering if the same moon might be shining on Melody, or on his mom and dad, or grandpa. If so, would they be thinking about him?

He awoke late in the night. The moon was gone, having traveled its full itinerary across the sky and retired. The landscape was much darker. The fire behind him simmered low and the camp was silent. The only sound he noticed was Sawblade's nasal breathing. Travis saw nothing new before him and closed his eyes. He held them that way for several seconds, and then opened them again.

His eyes picked out movement in the dim light. Black and white creatures emerged from the cover of the bushes and waddled across a clearing of bare ground into view, and Travis found himself alone with a family of skunks. The creatures plodded to where he was sleeping like formally invited overnight guests. They tumbled and played and even sniffed his hand and face. Travis watched them frolic for some time and then he froze as the largest one made its way up to his face and brushed against his ear. He didn't move and neither did the skunk retreat from his foreign smell. It nuzzled into his hair, rustled around for a few seconds, and then lay still. Before long it seemed to sleep. Travis watched its black and white back rise and fall, rise and fall. He could no longer see the two smaller skunks. He lay still, afraid to move a muscle, like a father who feared waking his sleeping child. Some time later, while still contemplating this steady rhythm, Travis too drifted off to sleep.

He awoke to the early rays of morning light. He didn't move. He could hear Sawblade yawning behind him. The skunks were gone, having left no trace, sign, or footprint. Travis stared at the spot in which the large skunk had slept, then closed his eyes once more and feigned sleep for as long as the illusion would hold.

Chapter Twenty-Five

    The weeks had passed and Travis was still wearing the button fly Levi jeans that he had been wearing on the day of the accident. They had become too big in the waist and were wearing out down at the bottom of the legs where they had been walked on. From the time of the car accident, they had served as his only pants and now they were fraying all the way around the pants leg. This was very disheartening to Travis because the jeans and his shoes were his only tie to what he thought of as the "real world," and he had refused to relinquish them when he had been offered new pants. Perhaps their life could have been extended if at that point he had rolled them up in his blankets and accepted the offered pants, but to Travis, the old jeans were not pants that could be retired. For sure, the old jeans were not pants that would go quietly into the night. So, he had turned down the yellowish brown army pants and stuck to his jeans.

    However, not even the best denim can stand up indefinitely. One morning after a wash in the creek, he lost his balance and his foot went right through the crotch of the jeans to the ground. There by the water, he finally had to accept the demise of his perfect pants. He knew they could never be replaced and that no Confederate Army pants could ever compare. Bent over and pantless in the morning light, he was overwhelmed. A bleak and lonesome tear slipped down his cheek.

    He had to endure some good natured teasing when he walked back to the men barelegged. After some minutes, he was handed a pair of the ugly yellow pants. He walked over and sat down on a crate to remove his shoes before pulling on the coarse homespun pants. Although a bit scratchy, surprisingly, they weren't too bad a fit. He sat down again and pulled on his shoes. Next, he carefully cut the faded Levi Straus logo tag and the metal buttons off of his old jeans and stuffed them into his pocket. As he did so, his hand bumped something hard. Pulling it out, he inspected his find. It was a small round pendant, the chain tangled and knotted from being swirled about in the pocket of the pants. Just then the cook called the men for breakfast, so he slipped it back into into his pocket to look at more closely later. He then forgot all about the pendant until that evening after supper. Most of the men were lying around, playing cards, sleeping, or repairing equipment. Remembering the locket, he went over by himself and sat down, and took his first proper look at it. He saw then that it was made of gold, probably not very expensive, but a pretty piece just the same. It was dirty and he roughly cleaned it with his handkerchief. Turning it over, he noticed the tiny catch at the top and realized what he held was a locket.

He tried gently pressing the catch, but dust and dirt had clogged it and it refused to react. He tried again, pressing more firmly, still without result. Overcome with a sudden overwhelming curiosity to discover what was inside, he opened his canteen and cleaned the locket more thoroughly. He soon removed all the dirt and, after carefully rubbing it dry with the hem of his shirt, had the locket sparkling in the twilight. The chain, which he had managed to untangle, was surprisingly strong. The clasp of the chain, however, was broken.

Travis pressed the catch. This time, the locket sprung immediately open. It was so well made that it sealed securely so that no water or dirt had penetrated inside it. Looking inside, his hands began to shake so violently that he almost dropped the locket. Inside each half of the locket, protected by a transparent cover, he saw two tiny photographs, one of a woman and one of a baby.

It came as something of a surprise then, that he found himself so taken with the photographs in the locket. He didn't know why he was so attracted. For sure, the woman was attractive and the baby was well, cute enough, but Travis especially felt strong emotions as he gazed at the image of the woman. He was surprised when he realized that the hand holding the locket was trembling. Why did the photograph of the woman affect him so? He looked around, feeling ridiculous. Why was his heart beating so hard?

He continued to sit by himself, his eyes fixed on the locket. The photograph of the woman, though small and showing only her face, was clear in every detail. Her eyes looked back at him. She had a half smile. Her hair appeared to be dark brown. Travis could not tear his eyes away from the photograph. Somehow it was as if he knew her. The photograph had awakened the loneliness and homesickness that he fought daily to squash back down deep inside him. He closed the locket with a sigh, trying to shake off the aching longing inside of him. Even though the picture of the woman was then hidden, he could still see her in his mind, almost as clearly as if she was there with him.

Stop! Standing up, he put the locket back inside his pocket, determined to think of something else. Although he knew that he would never forget Melody, he determined to forget about the locket, at least for that night. He went over and joined some of the men. Cedar was beginning to tell a story.

In the beginning of the Cherokee world, there were two worlds: the heavenly world called Galunlati, which was placed high in heavens, and the lower, dark world where the forces of evil lived. Galunlati was populated with beings in animal, human and plant forms. All creatures spoke the Cherokee language and lived together in harmony. the earth was but a ball of water on which gigantic fish and reptiles lived. the universe of the Cherokees depended on harmony and balance. Light was balanced by dark; things of goodness balanced by things that hid from the light of day in the shadows of the darkness.

In the beginning there was no sun, but a Great Tree of Life grew in the center of Galunlati. It lit the world so that all could see and cast its light down on the dark waters below. So it was that the Creator lived by the Tree of Life where he tended the plants and cared for the animals. Sometimes, the waterfowl, the hawks, and the eagles flew down in the darkness below; giant turtles and muskrats swam on the water's surface and bathed in the pale light of the heavenly tree. the Creator led a solitary existence. When his work was done, he sat by the Tree, admiring his world around him and below. Sometimes he became lonely and longed for a companion, perhaps a daughter who would sit beside him in the evening, watching his creation live and grow.

Then, the Creator made a young lady whose beauty and grace touched his soul. He knew that she, too, would long for someone to run and play with so he created a man in his likeness and taught his children the things that he knew.

The Creator found that his daughter laughed and sang too much; and she talked constantly. She asked too many questions. Why do the leaves of the Tree of Life shine? Who created the Upper World? Who named the plants? Creator still loved her, for this was his daughter, but this constant laughter and questions, what could he do? the Creator had told them many times to stay away from the Tree of Life and not to play around its trunk. But like all curious children, she had to see why her father said these things. First Man would insist that she not go to the tree but every day First Woman would climb the tree to its highest limbs. One day she found a hole in the bottom of the trunk and started to go in. First Man was again insistent that she stay away from the tree but to no avail. She went in and fell out of the bottom of Galunlati.

Creator returned home to find First Woman was missing. He asked First Man "where is my daughter?" to which the young man replied "I told her not to go into the hole in the bottom of the tree, but she would not listen." Creator did not know what to do as he peered over the side of Galunlati and saw his daughter falling toward the awesome ball of water.

Creator summoned the birds of the sky, to catch his daughter that she might not drown. They created a great blanket with their wings on which they caught her. But, where should they put her? As they flew above the deep waters, the grandfather of all turtles surfaced. "Here, place her on my back," he said. the birds descended with the young woman, henceforth known as "Sky-Woman," and placed her on the surface of her new home. But it was not large enough, the Muskrat volunteered to find land and dove to the bottom of the waters and brought up mud, which he placed on the turtle's back. When she touched the earth that Muskrat had brought, it grew in all directions, becoming the earth that we know today as Turtle Island. the Creator knew that she would need more and so he sent down the plants and animals to take care of his daughter. He sent down the deer, buffalo, bear, rabbits, and squirrels to provide food and clothes. He sent the medicines of the plant people; cedar, sage, bloodroot, oak, and most importantly, tobacco. These, along with many other things, were to provide for future generations of the Cherokee.

When the First Woman, or Sky Woman, was happy with that world, Creator sent First Man down to help take care of his creation. First Man and First Woman were now husband and wife. They were happy and all things were good, but as in all good things bad will come and First Woman and First Man began to fight and argue.

Harsh words were said on both sides, and finally the wife said that she was leaving. Grabbing a few belongings, she began walking away from First Man. "I am going to find another place to live," she told her husband, "You are lazy and pay no attention to me." In a short time, the husband regretted his harsh words and tried to find his wife so he could apologize. Eventually, he realized *that she was too far ahead, and he prayed to the Creator to help him. "Slow her down, Creator, so that I might tell her how much she means to me," he begged. "Is her soul one with yours?" Creator asked. First Man replied "We have been one since the beginning of our time. We have been one since you have breathed life into our souls and we shall remain one until the end of time itself."*

Touched by the man's anguish, the Creator intervened. Seeing the way First Woman was walking he began to make plants grow at her feet to slow her down. To one side grew the blackberries and to the other grew huckleberries, but still she walked on. Again he made the plants grow and to one side grew the gooseberries and to the other grew the serviceberries, but still she walked on. the Creator knew that he would have to slow her down and so he went to his garden and grabbed a handful of strawberry plants and threw them to the earth. When they landed at First Woman's feet they began to bloom and ripen, First Woman looked down to see the beautiful leaves and berries of the strawberry plant and stopped to taste just one small berry. As she plucked and ate the berries she forgot her anger. Finding a basket among her belongings, she quickly filled it, and longed for her husband once more. First Man, hurrying on his way, was surprised to see his wife returning, and oh, how his heart did soar. She was smiling. She dipped her hand into her basket, and got a berry and placed it in his mouth. He smiled foolishly, and gave thanks to the Creator. Taking his hand, his wife led him back down the path to their home, feeding him strawberries on the way.

Cedar's story only made Travis think more about Melody. Later, when he rolled up in his blanket, his thoughts were only of his wife; how he would like to see her, to hear her voice, her laugh. He imagined being close with her, touching her, feeling her warmth. *If only ...*

As he finally drifted off to sleep, his mind was full, his dreams haunted by thoughts of his wife; dreams prompted by the photograph in the locket ...

... for it bore a strong resemblance of Melody.

Chapter Twenty-Six

Early in the morning, Sam sent Travis and Sawblade to try and round up some molasses, but after spending most of the day looking, there was no molasses to be had. As Travis was unsaddling Bolliver, Sam told him that he was to report to Major Ratliff as soon as possible. Curious, Travis gave Bolliver his corn and brushed him down with some dried grass and hurried in the direction of the officer's quarters.

Travis knocked on the door and right away, the Major answered. "Come in and have a seat," he said, indicating a chair.

Travis removed his hat and walked over and sat in the chair, the only seat in the room, which was next to a small desk. He noticed that the room was small and had been divided into two halves, one to be used as a sleeping room and the other as a sitting room. A calico curtain was hung to divide them and a carpet made of barley sacks covered the floor. A small fireplace, designed to burn logs vertically, was on the back wall. The entire room was not much over eight feet square and windowless, and except for the entrance, the room seemed from the inside much like a prison cell.

The Major seated himself on the edge of his cot. Travis could hear muffled voices coming from elsewhere in the building and the sound of boots on the creaky floors. He could smell tobacco and sweat. *What could I have done to be called in to see the Major? Must not be in trouble, otherwise he surely wouldn't have sat down on his bed?*

The Major suddenly got up and crossed over to the door that looked out over the camp. Travis could see out around him and saw horses sleeping. The Major began to drum on the door jamb with his fingers, yawning, causing Travis to uncontrollably yawn also. He stared out at the sleeping horses and tried to concentrate on them.

Suddenly the Major turned around. "Travis Coker."

"Yes, sir."

"I was looking over the roster and noticed that you come from Cowan, Tennessee."

"Yes, sir."

"Are you related to a woman named Annie Coker?"

Travis's eyes grew large and he had to think fast. *Oh yeah,* he remembered, *John and Annie had the mill!*

"Yes, sir, John and Annie Coker. They have the grist mill."

The Major crossed the room again and sat down on the bed. "Annie Coker is my aunt."

Of course! Travis thought, *this man is Daniel Ratliff. Daniel was Annie's brother.*

"Sir, was, is she your sister?"

"No, my grandfather Richard and my family came during the removal. Annie and her family stayed in Tennessee. Annie is my father's sister."

"Wow," said Travis. It was almost too much to take in. He was actually in the room with an ancestor. This man, this Major Ratliff, sitting in the room with him just then, seemed as alien to him as a platypus. What could he say to the man? But it was too late to worry about such things because Daniel was speaking again.

"Is she well?"

"Sir?"

"Annie Coker. Is she well? And her family?" Daniel stood up again and turned to watch Travis closely, as if at any moment he might crumble into dust.

"Uh…" Travis had to think fast, trying to remember the details of his family history. "Uh, Annie is well. John died in an accident when a tree fell on him."

"When was that?"

"Uh, a while after the removal, William, the oldest boy …"

"Uh-mmm," Daniel said.

"Well, he was getting married and John and the other boys went with him to cut trees. A big one fell on John and he died."

"I see." Daniel seemed solemn.

"They, uh, she is well and all of her children also. Her sons run the mill."

The Major sat down again on the edge of the cot. "I've been planning a short furlough to go and visit my family. I would like for you to ride with me and meet your grandfather Richard and the rest of my family."

"Sir?" Travis was confused.

"We are cousins, then."

"Yes. Richard Ratliff was Annie's father, Travis said. "So you want me to do what?"

The Major's face was set hard and Travis saw color rise in his sharp cheeks. "I would like for you to accompany me on furlough to go visit family."

"Yes sir, that would be nice, sir."

The Major rose then so Travis rose also. "Good, expect to leave on Sunday morning at first light. I'll let Sam know."

The Major had told Travis that it should take two days to ride from Fort Davis to Cookson, so he packed three days provisions, rolled up his blankets and had Bolliver saddled and ready about the time the horizon was beginning to lighten.

Soon the Major approached on his big horse, wearing his neat gray uniform coat and his slouch hat. Travis greeted him with a shake of the hand, doing his best not to appear too excited, although he was eager to get started. He took one last look at the camp before he climbed up on Bolliver's back. The Major glanced at Travis's saddle bags, nodded and turned his horse around.

It was still dark, but the Major led off on his big horse and Travis followed his shadow. As they exited the Fort, the sun peeped over the horizon, making the road easier to see. The morning air was crisp and as the red light crept up the sky, Daniel pointed as three or four deer bounded into the woods just ahead of them.

As the sun climbed higher, the two cousins rode side by side. The day was unseasonably mild for December. There had been a couple of frosts already, and the land lay sleeping. A mile or so from the Fort, the Major reined in his horse and dismounted. Travis watched as he removed his bedroll to expose a brown coat, which he draped over his saddle. He then removed his uniform jacket and rolled it up inside the bedroll.

As the Major slipped on the brown coat and remounted his horse, he smiled at Travis, exposing even white teeth. "Less conspicuous this way."

"Yes, sir, Major."

"You don't have to say sir all the time."

"Okay."

"And I prefer my friends and cousins to not call me Major."

"So what should I call you?"

"Call me Daniel."

"All right, Daniel," said Travis with a smile.

As they clip-clopped down the road, Travis was happy. He knew that he was on an adventure of a lifetime. He was especially excited at the prospect of meeting Richard Ratliff.

"Major," Travis said.

"Daniel."

"Sorry."

"No problem."

"Yesterday in your quarters, you said Richard Ratliff and *your* family were in the removal?"

"Yes. My father lived at Turkeytown, Alabama near Grandpa Richard's place. When the removal came, we went to Fort Payne, Alabama where the army had set up a camp. We left from there."

"Do you remember it? How old were you?"

"I was just a knee baby - about three."

Travis thought about what he was hearing.

Daniel continued. "My father has told me about it. the leader was an officer named John Benge. On the route we were on, there were a lot of horses and wagons. Most folks didn't have to walk."

"That helped."

"Yes, and the journey only took about three months. Only about thirty or so died along the way."

Just then Daniel pulled his horse to an abrupt stop and then motioned for silence.

"What is it?" Travis whispered.

"Something's not right."

Daniel's eyes narrowed as he looked ahead toward a stand of oaks and walnut trees.

"No birds singing," he said in a hushed tone.

Travis nodded and pulled his reins in a little closer.

They sat quietly for a moment, then nudged their horses ahead and swung off the dusty trail into the dense oaks. There they stopped their horses and waited. Daniel slipped off the back of his horse, pulled his pistol out and used his hands to tell Travis to stay put.

Travis dismounted as Daniel handed him the reins to his horse. Bolliver stood quietly, not even his ears were moving. Travis stood and looked at the trees around him, his eyes looking for anything and everything. Nothing moved. A chilly wind swept across a low circle of rocks. He fastened the three remaining buttons on his brown coat as the wind searched its way through a long tear beneath his right arm. He held the arm against his body and shivered, wishing for, of all things, duct tape with which to fix his coat. *That's stupid*, he thought, and wondered if December was really that cold in Indian Territory or if the cold came from his fear.

Where is Daniel? What's taking him so long? What if he doesn't come back?

At last he heard a bird whistle and then heard his name being quietly called by Daniel. Pulling the two horses along behind him, he headed up the hill in the direction Daniel had gone. He pulled up beside Daniel, who was kneeling and looking through a small collapsible spyglass.

"Yankee sentries." Daniel said quietly. "Taking a dinner break right over yonder."

Travis couldn't see anything. "Let me see, Daniel."

Travis had difficulty bringing the glass into focus. Eventually he caught a flutter of movement. He blinked and looked again. Sure enough, there were eight or ten blue coats huddled in the cold on a pile of rocks.

"What do we do?" asked Travis.

"We better clear out and get some distance between us and them."

The two men led their horses back down to the road and took off in a brisk trot, putting the Yankees as far behind them as they could without overtaxing the horses. As they rode, Travis's eyes apprehensively searched the wooded sides of the road.

Chapter Twenty-Seven

If there had been any talk in either Travis or Daniel, the jarring bounce of the trot wore it out of them. They rode in stolid silence through the woods and hills.

They only stopped once in the middle of the afternoon to water the horses as they crossed a creek. Travis walked a little distance away to relieve himself, and he came upon the half-decayed corpse of a Yankee soldier. The smell hit him at once, entering his nose and pouring down into his guts like a foul liquid. At first it looked as though the man died where he stood, as if the tree had grown up around him and lifted him from the ground.

As he stood staring, it became clear from the wounds that the soldier had been shot and scalped and then left like a statue of rotting flesh. Some animal had eaten into the man's internals and his legs were shredded, whether by teeth or claws was unclear. But most horrible to Travis's mind were the man's eye sockets, empty depressions that had been eaten away by birds or insect life. Once more this journey into hell had given him an image he'd carry ever after.

Before sundown, they stopped again at a spring to water the horses.

"We've been riding hard for four hours. My butt is tired. We need to find a place to camp for the night and take it easy tomorrow. Give the horses a chance to rest and eat," Daniel said.

Travis nodded. He knew the horses were tired and he knew they were beginning to show signs of the hard, fast ride. He also knew that horses had to spend nearly half their time eating if they were to maintain their strength and health.

"I know a place," Daniel said. "There's a cave near here where we can camp. There's good grass for the horses, as well."

"Sounds good," Travis said. "I'll follow you."

That night they relaxed in the shelter of the cave. It was near the Illinois River. Daniel gathered wood to build a small fire near the mouth of the cave, while Travis hobbled the horses near the water where there was plenty of dry grass. He returned to the cave just as Daniel was beating a leather pouch against a rock.

"What are you doing?"

"Don't have a grinder, so I'm beating coffee beans for coffee."

"You have real coffee?"

"Shhh," smiled Daniel as he put one finger up to his lips. "I brought it from home and I have some now and then. This seems like a good time." He then dropped some of the crushed beans into a small kettle and looked over at Travis.

"That enough?"

"I guess so."

"Well, you never know. I always thought that if a horseshoe nail didn't float in it the coffee was too weak."

Travis grinned at his cousin and dug jerky from his saddlebags, offered a piece to Daniel and began to chew. After their brief supper they bedded down around the small fire; the memory of the Yankee sentries and the remembering of the dead one made it difficult for Travis to sleep. His dreams that night came to him in patches and fragments.

He awoke to the realization that someone was shaking his arm. Daniel was kneeling beside him. "Get up, we're burning daylight."

Throwing off his blankets, Travis moved quickly to his feet, looking around him in the semi-darkness.

They brewed more coffee in the cold light of dawn and chewed hardtack and jerky. By good daylight they were moving again. Riding along, Travis kept glancing at the rising sun, wishing it carried more warmth. The one cup of coffee had failed to take the chill out of his bones.

As Travis and Daniel rode, they saw burned out farmhouses and barns in every direction, stark reminders of the war that seemed to overpower the beauty of early winter in Indian Territory. Red, orange and yellow leaves had fallen, and the sumac was clinging to its bright red foliage. Vines had dropped their leaves and their wooden skeletons were left entwined in the ruins of former homes and outbuildings. They rode past desolate fire blackened stone chimneys and the hips and rib cages of slaughtered livestock. Even though Daniel and Travis were both aware of the destruction, they did not speak of it.

Travis was somewhat nervous riding out in the open as they were, for they didn't know exactly where any more Yankee scouts or skirmishers might be. Hopefully, they were all at Fort Gibson or up in Kansas or Missouri. He hoped that the peaceful afternoon through which he rode with Daniel would remain peaceful for a little while longer. Anyway, there was nothing he could do about it, so on he rode, with Bolliver at a comfortable trot, trying not to think too much but remaining watchful all the same.

"What will you do, Daniel, when this is all finished?" Travis asked.

"Farm," Daniel said and then paused before saying, "and be a Lighthorseman."

"In the Nation?"

"Yes. Our people need to rebuild. And there is much to learn. Our children must know the white way if they're to survive. I will teach my children that."

"You said Lighthorseman. What is that?"

"Lighthorse is the name of the Cherokee police force. There are companies for the different districts. Our people had them back in Georgia before the removal. They administer the law, catch criminals, remove squatters, things like that. Before the war I was a captain over twenty-four men."

"Didn't know there was such a thing."

"What?"

"I said I'm impressed."

Daniel looked at Travis's face, threw back his head and laughed aloud.

"You're somethin', Travis."

Travis grinned and said nothing as he looked ahead at the trail.

Daniel continued, "I'll go back to being a Lighthorseman and I will work to preserve our ways. I want to teach the Cherokee way so it is not forgotten. Cherokee children must not forget who they are."

"That's good," Travis said.

He thought about his own grandpa; how he had not forgotten the ways and had patiently tried so hard to instruct him. He felt regret and ashamed then about the way he had disregarded Grandpa's efforts. Grandpa had known the importance of teaching him about his ancestors back in Tennessee, Alabama, and Georgia, so at least Travis knew stories about them anyway. He knew about Chief Pathkiller. He knew about John and Annie Coker and the mill in Cowan. He knew about Annie's father, Richard Ratliff, who was his companion's grandfather. The very thought that there he was, riding a horse beside his own third or fourth generation cousin Daniel Ratliff Jr. (try as he might, Travis couldn't figure out generations of cousins, and the whole thing seemed so unbelievable and bizarre.) He knew that Richard, Annie's brother Daniel (Daniel Jr.'s father) and little sisters Lizzie and Eliza had traveled west on the Benge Route during the Removal. They had settled in the Cookson area near Tahlequah. Richard then had served as a council commissioner in the New Cherokee Nation West in Indian Territory. Yes, Travis had heard the stories of those people all his life, but it had never seemed to matter to him all that much.

Until now. As they rode on towards Cookson, Travis continued to reflect on the joke that life seemed to have played on him. He had spurned his heritage, and had ended up dab smack in the middle of part of that heritage. Grandpa Horace was a Coker out of the line of John and Annie. Grandpa had never known his own grandmother Eloisa, she had died at the birth of Horace's father, Ben Coker, but his grandfather Eli visited the Coker farm near Cowan often and passed down the stories of the Real People. *Oh Grandpa, if I only had it to do over again. I would spend so much time with you and listen.* In spite of his remorse, Travis had a reflective smile as he rode the twisting trail and remembered his grandpa.

He was still looking a little wistful when Daniel spoke again.

"Travis, you've gotta a long face."

"I was thinking of my grandfather back in Tennessee."

Daniel nodded, his long dark hair shining in the bright sunlight. "The old ones also live in my head. It's good."

Travis nodded.

Daniel kicked his horse into a trot as they rode on top of an open sunlit ridge. "My grandfather told us about the white path. the Cherokee people must travel that path."

Travis nodded again.

"I will teach the white path, as well," Daniel continued.

"That's good," Travis said. "The young need to know the white path. When I get home I will teach my daughter and the little one that is coming the Cherokee way as well as the white way."

"We all need to know both," Daniel said.

Travis nodded in agreement and nudged Bolliver to trot a little faster. They rode in silence for some time and then reined their horses in and sat watching the horizon. The sun was warm and they were enjoying it. Neither spoke for a few minutes. Daniel broke the silence.

"What do you think of Stand Watie?"

"I find him to be quite an impressive man. How long have you known him?"

"All my life."

"He's a great officer." Travis said before clicking to his horse.

"He is that, good man, good Cherokee." Daniel agreed before changing the subject, "Ever see a country so good-lookin'?"

"Nope."

"Just good looking everywhere you look. Especially in the Cherokee Nation."

"Yup," replied Travis.

"Pretty quick we'll get to my place and stay a few days with my family. You can spend a couple a days with Grandfather Richard, too. You can learn from him, Travis. Go home and tell Annie you saw her pa. He'll enjoy hearing from you 'bout her too."

"I'm looking forward to it."

Daniel nodded.

Chapter Twenty-Eight

Late in the afternoon, Daniel turned and rode into a field. Travis followed and they rode quietly toward a big patch of oaks. On the edge of the oaks, Daniel reined up and sat quietly, watching. Travis said nothing. Daniel leaned in and whispered, "A good place for Yankee sentries to hide."

Travis nodded, and studied the trees and underbrush before him. He figured that they were close to Daniel's house. He looked at Daniel, whose eyes were careful and steady as he sat looking ahead. At last, the Major shook his head, reached into his pocket and took out a thin cigar, and lit it carefully with a Lucifer match. Travis watched Daniel's hands, and saw that they were steady. Then Daniel dismounted and unrolled his uniform coat, put it on and remounted. "All right, Travis," he said then, "Let's walk."

They rode out through a gap in the oaks. Travis saw a large white house. He relaxed as he rode along, looking at the structure before him.

He had been raised in a similar looking house in Cowan, Tennessee, and so Daniel's house seemed familiar to him; the quiet yard, the smell of brown grass and wood smoke and the bitter, dusty smell of the oaks, the shutters needing paint (his own dad had recently put plastic siding and shutters on their home in Cowan). He noticed that the yard was neat except for a wad of dying morning glory vines and a big wood pile almost as high as the house. From the chimney a pale feather of smoke rose toward the sky.

The hominess and the sight of the quiet house moved Travis in a way that he had not anticipated. The fact that he was stuck in the 1860's, and in a war no less, seemed to let go of him, to fade away into some other place and time while he remained, touched by a longing he barely recognized.

Almost without thinking, his hand touched the lump in his pocket that he knew was the locket. *Oh, man,* he thought, *I am so homesick.*

He heard Daniel laugh out loud and the world came back again. But the feeling the house had produced did not go away; and Travis didn't know if he even wanted it to go. There was no pain in his nostalgia as there once was—only a calm place, like a closet, where the images and dear ones of his 2001 life gathered and where he could still believe in the possibility of going home. He might have to permanently close the door to that closet soon, but not then. For the moment, he would look at Daniel's house and let his mind travel where it would.

Daniel laughed again and said, "All right, Travis, let's go." Daniel drew once more on the cigar and flicked it away. "Come on," he said, and kicked his horse into a lope. Not to be left behind, Bolliver took off also, and together Travis and Daniel rode the little way remaining to the house.

After being in the saddle since daylight, it was not easy to dismount. Travis got off and stretched, and Bolliver nuzzled him in the ribs. Travis rubbed Bolliver's Roman nose and waited to see what Daniel would do next.

Daniel straightened out the bottom of his Army jacket and Travis noted that the Major was a little stove up also, for he walked stiffly up the steps and across the porch. He had just raised his hand to open the door when a little girl opened the curtain and peeked out.

Before he even had a good grip on the doorknob, the door was jerked open, a shriek sounded and the little girl ran straight into his arms. After much hugs and kisses, Daniel turned and walked over to Travis and laughed as he sat the little girl down on the ground. She stepped over to Travis and offered him her hand, so he stooped down.

"Why, hey there, little lady," he said. "What's your name?"

"Is Emma, mister. I'm four. You gonna stay wiff us?"

"I believe I am," he chuckled, glancing up at Daniel and then back to Emma.

Travis slowly stood and looked at Daniel again. "Your daughter?"

"Yes," Daniel answered, scooping Emma up under one arm like a sack of feed and walking back towards the open front door, his spurs clanging on the wooden porch.

"Siyo, family, where ya'll at?"

Just then, a woman and three girls came around from the back of the house. Upon seeing Daniel, they all practically ran to him. Daniel sat Emma down began hugging them all.

Travis's heart was touched watching the hugs and tears and everyone talking at once. Then the lady, that Travis took to be Daniel's wife, glanced over at him and smiled.

"Daniel?"

"Oh, this is our cousin, Travis Coker."

Mrs. Ratliff walked over and offered him her hand. Unsure of what to do, Travis took it in his, not knowing if he was to shake it, kiss it or what.

"Welcome to our home, Mr. Coker."

"Thank you, ma'am."

Daniel then introduced Travis to his other daughters, Katie, age six, and eight-year-old twins, Josepha and Belle.

"Travis is from Cowan, Tennessee. He knows Annie."

They were all standing there in sort of a circle. It became quiet as everyone focused their eyes on Travis. Unsure of what to say, he looked around at them all one at a time. He couldn't tell what any of them was thinking.

"What you looking at so funny, mister?" said Emma.

Travis couldn't help it, he started laughing. Then Josepha started to chuckle, and pretty soon everybody was laughing.

"I think Travis is wondering who all these crazy people are," laughed Daniel.

"I'm just happy to be here," said Travis.

"Well Travis, we're all family here, so why don't you come inside."

"Got anything to eat?" asked Daniel.

Travis followed Daniel inside the house, taking in the rich carpet on the floors, the paneled walls, and the glow of china. Watching Emma almost broke Travis's heart as he thought of Allie.

Daniel's house was the first house Travis had been in since the small cabin on the day of his accident and the ones he gone inside of when they were raiding. He was impressed at how comfortable it was. It was cozy with spindle-legged chairs, a spindle-legged piano, brass fireplace andirons, fine woodwork, and a candelabrum of brass and crystal, and tall wax candles. In the wide fireplace crackled a mighty fire of oak and hickory; and on the mantle wax candles burned in silver candlesticks. Two Negro maids stood ready to attend.

Mrs. Ratliff said, "I will get something ready for you two to eat, but first you both need a bath."

A few glances and smiles went around the room.

She told the maids to boil some water and to start preparing an early supper.

"Josepha, you and Belle fetch us some clothes of your daddy's for Mister Coker," she added.

Within the hour, Travis thought he had walked into a tornado of activity. There he was being waited on hand and foot by two black maids, Mrs. Ratliff, and Daniel's four daughters and everyone acted like they were solely in charge of him being comfortable. And being allowed to have a real bath with real hot water and soap, he thought he had died and gone to heaven.

By suppertime, every inch of his body was clean and he was wearing fresh new clothes, with Mrs. Ratliff still fussing over the comings and goings of everyone in the house. Everyone had been so busy over him that it wasn't till the supper was on the table that he realized that dusk was falling and he hadn't taken care of poor Bolliver.

Travis walked over to the window and looked out and noticed that both Bolliver and Daniel's horse were nowhere in sight.

Just then Daniel came down the stairs looking as clean and polished as Travis felt.

"Where's the horses?"

"Oh, I've gotta a groom that tends to 'em. They're in the barn getting brushed and fed oats and good hay."

"Oh." Was all Travis could think to say in reply.

Just then Mrs. Ratliff called them to supper. She indicated a chair for Travis next to Emma, who was beaming as he sat down next to her. Everyone held hands as Daniel prayed and then the food was passed. Oh what food it was. Daniel's wife and maids put on a delicious supper that Travis knew he would never forget, with real tea that smelled so good and real sugar that was picked up with silver tongs. There was late corn and black-eyed peas and hot rolls that were so light that Travis swore they melted in his mouth. The maids brought in crystal dishes filled with preserved fruits and best of all, fried chicken which was juicy with a perfect crispy brown crust.

Stand Watie's name was on everybody's lips. The whole rebel country seemed to lean on him. His courage and military prowess were known far beyond the limits of his activities, and how his loyal service and constructive influence would surely prove to be a potent force in the history of his people. They were just finishing some apple pie when the door opened and an older man walked in.

He seemed breathless like he'd been running halfway across the country.

Already the man had taken three great strides around the table as Daniel stood up. And then the two embraced in true affection. Tears flowed from both sets of eyes. At last, Daniel turned and pointed his arm at Travis.

"Papa, this is Travis Coker. He's our cousin from Cowan, Tennessee."

The man looked at Travis as if he were looking at a ghost. Travis stood and pushed his chair back from the table. The man then walked over and took Travis by the arm and then hugged him. Travis patted the man on the back as Daniel said, "Travis, this is my papa, Daniel Ratliff."

At last the man let go of Travis. "I can't believe it! you know my sister?"

"Yes."

The man stepped back, eyes glistening as he continued to behold Travis with shakes of his head and smiles of wonder.

Travis was overwhelmed with it all. How could it be true that he was there, in Daniel Ratliff Jr.'s dining room meeting *the* Daniel Ratliff that he had grown up hearing about? And the famed Richard Ratliff was surely somewhere close to boot.

"Sit down, Papa and eat," said Mrs. Ratliff. He sat down, his shock and excitement apparently not enough to disturb his appetite. A maid brought in a clean plate and silverware and another maid began bringing the serving dishes around the table so that Daniel's father could serve himself.

"How you come to be here, Travis?" asked Daniel Sr.

"It's a long story, sir. I guess it goes to show what the Good Book says, that sometimes the Lord is guiding your steps when you least know it. I ended up in the army over at Fort Davis and never had a notion that I would get to meet up with any of you folks. "

"Has he met Pa?" asked the older Daniel.

"Not yet," replied Daniel Jr., "I told him to go up there tomorrow or the next day and spend a few days with him."

The older Daniel nodded as he gnawed on a chicken leg. As Daniel Sr. ate, Travis studied him. Daniel Ratliff Sr. was tall and square-built, with a kindly and friendly brown face, sun puckered around the eyes, with a thick mop of brownish-gray hair. His brown eyes smiled up at Travis.

After supper, the whole lot of them went into the parlor, where Mrs. Ratliff and her oldest daughters did needlework and the little girls played with dolls in the corner until the maids took them upstairs to bed. The two Daniel's smoked cigars and talked furiously, both catching up on everything that had happened since they had seen each other, before settling down to talk about the war. Travis just sat and took it all in, amazed.

Travis listened as Daniel and his father spoke further about Stand Watie, taking time to explain many details to Travis. At the very outbreak of the war, Stand Watie had organized, and been made Captain of a troop of Cherokees for the purpose of protecting the Indian Territory, especially the Cherokee border, from the Federal forces stationed at Humboldt, Kansas.

Between that point and the Cherokee Nation were the Osage Indians, who were nearly all Unionists, and ancient enemies of the Cherokees.

Daniel Sr. said, "There is no doubt that the wisdom and timely action of Watie and his men saved our people during those early days from greater hardships then we have now."

Daniel Jr. continued to explain that in May, 1861, Watie offered his services to General McCulloch of Texas, who had been given the command over the military district of the Indian Territory. His offer was gladly accepted and Stand Watie was given a Colonel's commission and authorized to raise an Indian regiment.

Daniel leaned forward towards Travis, "That is us, Travis. the Cherokee Mounted Rifles."

Daniel Sr. leaned back with his eyes closed and his sock feet placed near the fire. He explained that at the beginning of the war, John Ross, as principal chief, had signed the Treaty of Alliance with the Confederacy, but afterwards he had renewed his policy of friendship with the Federals.

Later, noticing that Travis was practically asleep, Daniel stood up, banked the fire and concluded that Stand Watie had never ordered a charge that he did not lead, yet so far he had never been injured.

Daniel Sr. said that many believed that Stand Watie possessed a charmed life and no bullet had ever been molded that could kill him and that his name equaled bravery.

* * *

If Travis had thought that the bath was like going to heaven, he later learned what heaven was like when he was shown to a downy bed upstairs, where he went to sleep, and slept as if he never expected to wake up again.

Travis did remain in bed until mid-morning the next day. Embarrassed, he went downstairs where he found Daniel reading a newspaper.

"Morning," Daniel said without looking up. "I was worried. You feeling okay?"

"Yeah, just lazy, I suppose. It felt good to lie there. I've been sleeping on the ground so long that bed felt like a hotel to me."

Daniel laughed and told Travis to go on in the kitchen and the maids would give him some breakfast.

As he walked towards the kitchen, he was surprised to see lying on a table a large Bible bound in tan leather with the name "Ratliff" engraved on it in gold. He stopped and touched the cover, gently tracing the Ratliff name with his fingertip. Then, as he headed towards the kitchen, a disquieting thought entered his mind. *What will be the legacy that I leave behind?*

He quickly forgot about the Bible, however, when he got in the kitchen. Katie, Josepha and Belle tended him like ministering but fussy angels. By then little Emma, who had been fascinated with the strange newcomer from the moment she had seen him, was one of his most devoted attendants, dogging Josepha's steps and babbling constantly to Travis with all the energy of a four-year-old.

Travis sat at the large oak work table eating ham and biscuits. It was a nice kitchen. There was a wide cooking fireplace made of native stone. Tall cupboards with glass doors hung on two walls. Overhead were white rafters from which hung an assortment of tools and utensils.

The girls stood or sat around the table, babbling and watching him eat. The maids were busy on the other side of the room, but each time his glass of milk was empty, one of the maids was there with a crock pitcher to refill it. She also continued to serve him more biscuits until he thought he was going to pop.

Travis stepped outside later to walk around and look at Daniel's place. He noticed that the house had a separate cookhouse that was attached to the kitchen by a breezeway. He saw the barn and went inside and talked a bit to Bolliver. There were two outhouses, a smokehouse, a chicken house and some idle garden plots. He also saw a nice tree house that he figured provided a cool place for the girls to play in the summertime.

Travis learned that in the Ratliff home everything possible was done to teach Daniel's daughters good breeding. They had to learn to sing, dance, play the piano, ride horseback, and read the classics. They were taught how to be good hostesses and how to manage a home. But they rarely did any actual cooking, or sewing, or cleaning. Apparently that was reserved for the maids.

Over the noon meal, Daniel told Travis just to take it easy around the house that day and to plan on going down to Grandpa Richard's the next day. He said that Richard still lived in the first house he had built when he had settled there in 1839. He had built a couple of rooms on, but other than that not much had changed.

He said that Richard had never remarried after his wife had died probably back around 1812 or 13, that he was very old and lived alone except for two slave women that cooked and watched out for him. He said both of the women had come with the family during the removal and that the younger one was the spinster daughter of the older one.

That afternoon Travis dozed with a white Persian cat on his lap as he listened to the girls practice the piano. Daniel had disappeared upstairs somewhere and Mrs. Ratliff and the slave women were going about their tasks in other parts of the house.

Then Mrs. Ratliff took him upstairs to get fitted for some new clothes to replace the rags that she had burning out back that had been his army clothes. She said that they would round up a new pair of boots for him too.

"We'll have you all spruced up before you and Daniel leave," she said.

Travis liked Mrs. Ratliff. "Thank you, ma'am."

Travis fell in love with Daniel's family and his home. Home was definitely the correct word to describe the place. *Family, pets, children, love—that's what makes this place a home.* He planned on telling Daniel and his wife that the visit had come at a time when the whole world seemed to be falling apart and that by inviting him into their home they had provided him with the most wonderful opportunity to rest comfortably among family: people that had one thing in common—love.

Chapter Twenty-Nine

As they ate breakfast the next morning, Daniel said, "Travis, why don't you go on up after breakfast and meet Grandpa Richard?"

"Okay. Where's his house?"

Daniel pointed with his fork out the window, "Up that trail, can't miss it."

"He's bound to want some of this food," Mrs. Ratliff said. "There's plenty left from our breakfast, isn't there Dora?"

"Too much," the maid replied. "And I can't stand to see nothing go to waste."

"I'll fix up a tray for him and you can take it down," Mrs. Ratliff said.

"Be glad to," Travis replied.

Just then a rider rode into the yard, and Daniel had to go out and see what he wanted.

Mrs. Ratliff gave Travis a napkin covered tray and he walked down to Richard Ratliff's cabin carrying it filled with corncakes, eggs, bacon, and a small pot of coffee. From the house as he glanced back, he saw Emma in the window watching him. He smiled and nodded his head in her direction. She grinned and blew a kiss at him.

As he rounded the bend, he saw what must be Richard's cabin. It was whitewashed and simple but quite pretty, with tied bundles of sage hanging stems-up under the eaves of the porch to dry. The cabin was hemmed in by fenced garden plots that had been neatly tended for winter, one or two still somewhat green with winter turnips. Chickens were scratching in the yard and Travis noticed carefully pruned apple and peach trees along the sides. A little creek cut through the far side of the clearing, running clean and clear over mossy stones. In every direction, oaks and other trees framed the peaceful image.

He knocked on the door and heard a man's voice call out from inside. He opened the door and went in. There was Richard Ratliff, still lying in the bed that had been made for him on the couch across the room.

He looked at Travis with a serene look on his weathered face.

"I brought you breakfast," said Travis, unsure of what to say.

"Sit it down there on the table."

Quickly Travis crossed the room and put the tray on the table and turned around.

"I am Travis Coker, sir. I come from Cowan, Tennessee."

Richard nodded and Travis realized that he probably already knew that he was coming.

"So you're enjoying your visit with family here?"

"Yes sir, very much. Family or not, this is a pretty remarkable place."

Travis glanced around the room before looking back at Richard and saw the old man smile.

"Where's your family?" he asked.

"They are all back in Cowan, sir."

"The war been hard on you?"

"Yeah ... it has, but I'm not complaining. God has been good to me. And now suddenly here I am with all of you folks. Who could have it better than that?"

"Speaking of all that, that breakfast getting cold?"

"Yes sir, do you want me to bring it over to you?"

"No, I'm ready to get up. I just need that coffee first. But if you don't mind, could you help me up?"

Travis went over to the couch. Richard reached up his free hand, and Travis took it and pulled gently. With a wince or two, he got himself up to a sitting position and then slowly stood.

"Thanks," he said. "I took a fall off my horse a while back and I forget sometimes how bad this shoulder of mine can be. But it's on the mend now."

Richard walked over to the table and sat down.

"You'll join me, won't you?"

"I've already eaten," Travis said.

"Then just keep me company. Where are the others?"

"They are all down at Daniel's house."

While Richard ate, Travis took the time to study the man who sat before him. The long white hair for some reason made him think of an older, darker-skinned version of Willie Nelson. He thought about the fact that Richard had known Andrew Jackson, Chief Pathkiller, and Davey Crockett.

"You live here alone?"

"No. Daniel, you know, is right down the path. And I have two maids. Lucy is as old as dirt, probably sixty, came with me from Alabama. Goldy is her daughter, an old maid, and she's a worthless girl, worst on the place, and she jus don't make much progress."

Travis nodded. Richard continued.

"She certainly is lazy. She's a bright yella mulatto, just the color of a pumpkin, with straight hair, and black eyes like a crow. She's odd to look at and unreliable. you give her any kind a work and you have to watch her."

"Why do you keep her?"

Richard looked at Travis before looking back down at his plate. "She's my daughter. Me and Lucy's. I hafta keep her and I can't bear to punish her. So she dawdles along, doing as little as she can get by with."

"Oh."

"Man gets lonely, you know?"

"Yes sir."

"My wife, Annie's ma, died you know. I never got another'n."

"Hmmm," said Travis.

"Both of 'em, lay up in the bed ever morning 'till almost dinner. But ol' Lucy makes sure the house's taken care of proper like. She takes care of me. Me and you, we'll go walking this afternoon."

"Sounds good sir."

During the afternoon's walk, Travis was amazed as Richard shot several squirrels right out of the trees with darts from a cane blowgun taller than he was. Richard said that he could smell squirrels, especially on damp days. At a distance of probably twenty yards, he was able to shoot plumed darts through their skulls with a single breath.

Later, Travis and Richard sat at the table as his maids skinned and gutted the squirrels as handy as one might an ear of corn. Lucy then washed each little body in cold water and stuck in a skewer from one end to the other and put them to roast over the fire coals. Meanwhile, Goldy was making bean bread by mashing pinto beans mixed with cornmeal and wood-ash lye. She then rolled the mixture between her palms (Travis hoped she had washed her hands) to form little loaves and wrapped each loaf in corn shucks that had been soaked in water. She finished the whole thing off by tying a neat bow around each little package out of pieces of torn shucks. She then set them to simmer in a big black iron pot. Lucy then brought out some chunks of yellow squash and cooked them at the edge of the fire until they softened up.

When the cooking was done, Travis thought that the squirrels looked an awful lot like dried mice, all brown and shrunken, but they were sizzling and shining with grease. It turned his stomach though to see their mouths full of long yellow teeth grinning at him.

Lucy and Goldy sat and ate by the fire while Richard and Travis sat at the table eating the squirrel supper. Travis did pretty good eating the squirrel until he noticed Richard snap a squirrel's head off, break it in two like a person would pecans and dig out the goody inside. That did it for him, he had gotten pretty used to eating a whole lot of disgusting things while being a soldier, but the sight of Richard eating the insides of a squirrel's head was just too much.

After supper, everybody switched, Richard and Travis taking the chairs by the fire while Lucy and Goldy cleaned up. Sitting in an old rocker made of twisted grape vine, Richard warmed himself at the open stone fireplace hearth in his original home near the Illinois River. Oak and blackjack crackled as they fueled the fire. Like Richard, the stone of the fireplace was very old. Brought from the river near the farm the large smooth stones made an attractive hearth. Richard would rock gently and puff on his long stemmed corncob pipe as Travis sat on a chair nearby.

The old man looked as old as time, and Travis knew that he was nearing a hundred or so. His eyes were as dark and deep as the memory of his people and their existence in the annals of history. They sat by the fire, neither feeling the need to speak. Travis couldn't remember ever feeling more at peace. At last, Richard puffed his old pipe, smiled gently, cleared his throat, and began to talk about how the world came to be.

When all was water, the animals lived above in Galunlati, but it was very crowded and they wanted more room. Dayunisi, the little Water-beetle, offered to go see what was below the water. It repeatedly dived to the bottom and came up with soft mud eventually forming the island we call earth. The island was suspended by cords at each of the cardinal points to the sky vault, which is solid rock.

Birds were sent down to find a dry place to live but none could be found. The Great Buzzard, the father of all buzzards we see now, flew down close to the earth while it was still soft. He became tired and his wings began to strike the ground. Where they struck the earth became a valley, and where they rose up again, became a mountain and thus the Cherokee country was created.

The animals came down after the earth dried but all was dark so they set the sun in a track to go every day across the island from east to west. At first the sun was too close to the island and too hot. They raised the sun again and again, seven times, until it was the right height just under the sky arch. The highest place, Gulkwagine Digalunlatiyun, is "the seventh height".

The animals and plants were told to keep watch for seven nights but as the days passed many begin to fall asleep until on the seventh night only the owl, panther, and a couple of others were still awake. These were given the power to see in the dark and prey on the birds and animals that sleep at night. Of the plants, only the cedar, the pine, the spruce, the holly, and the laurel were awake to the end and were therefore given the power to be always green and to be the greatest medicine, but to the others it was said: "Because you have not endured to the end you shall lose your hair every winter."

Men came after animals and plants. At first there were only a brother and sister until he struck her with a fish and told her to multiply, and so it was. In seven days a child was born to her and thereafter every seven days another until there was danger that the world could not keep up with them. Then it was made that a woman should have only one child in a year, and it has been so ever since.

"Good story," said Travis.

"Yes," said Richard. "Old stories help us know who we are. They also comfort us."

"Thank you, sir."

"But Daniel's woman had two children in one year," Richard laughed and emptied out his pipe. "Now, let's sleep. There is much to do tomorrow."

After Richard was settled on the couch, Travis got ready for bed, and remembered hearing his Grandpa tell basically the same story as Richard. Again he felt amazed at how well he could understand the Cherokee language.

He lay down on the pallet the women had prepared for him near the fire, and stayed awake long after he heard Richard's soft snores.

Chapter Thirty

The next morning, under Richard's supervision, Travis cooked a breakfast of corn mush and fried up some bacon. Richard ate heartily and Travis didn't think it was half bad, especially if he didn't think about the squirrels from the day before.

"You have your horse?"

"Yes sir, down in Daniel's barn."

"Hmmm. After breakfast, you get him."

"Okay."

Richard said to leave the dishes for Lucy and Goldy and to go get Bolliver. So Travis stepped out into the very cool morning and walked down to Daniel's, where they were just finishing breakfast. At Mrs. Ratliff's urging, he took a biscuit and preserves. She also insisted on making a grub bag for Richard's and Travis's lunch. Daniel then walked him out to the barn to fetch Bolliver.

Grub bag in hand, he rode a feisty Bolliver back up the lane, the horse snorting and letting him know that he felt like he could throw a good buck or two at any moment.

There was Richard out front with a big white horse that was fuzzier than any Travis had ever seen and he was wearing a huge ancient saddle that looked as if had come over on the Mayflower.

Richard told Travis to come in to the house for a bit. Travis followed him inside, hoping that Bolliver wouldn't hightail it back down to Daniel's warm barn.

"I wrapped us up some cookies that Lucy made a couple of days ago. What did they send us to eat?"

"I don't know, I didn't look inside."

"Well, Daniel's woman always takes care of me. She's a good one. I'll get my rifle and you put the stuff on the horses. Got a pistol or something?"

Travis nodded and helped gather the gear and pack it in saddlebags. "I'll wait for you by the horses," he said.

He looked at Richard. It still was impossible to tell just how old he was, and he didn't want to ask. Travis figured that Richard had probably always looked old. But just then, wearing his battered hat, tattered soft-fringed buckskin hunting shirt, faded blue trousers, tall leather leggings, with moccasins on his feet, he was a fascinating sight.

They rode off at a good clip. Travis had no idea of where they were going, he was just feeling high on adventure. Richard led the way through heavily-wooded areas, and rolling hills, mountains, and foliage. At noon they stopped next to a waterfall. In spite of the cold, Travis was having the time of his life.

"How did you find this place?"

"Hmmm. Did you notice the trail trees?"

Travis didn't know what he was asking about. "The what?"

"Hmmm." Richard chewed a cookie. "We will circle back home a different way, but I'll show you. They have 'em in Tennessee and Georgia too. you never saw none?"

"I don't guess so, sir."

"Hmmm. You should know 'em. I'll teach you."

Travis nodded and picked up a stick and began making marks in the dirt at his feet. It was if he was tracing his history in the sand. Richard smiled and leaned back against a tree. He closed his eyes and rested. Travis looked at him and saw the old man was asleep. Richard was smiling as he began gently snoring. His white hair cascaded over his shoulders. His brown wrinkling face was calm. Travis thought Richard's face looked like parchment. He watched the old man sleep for awhile and then walked down to the waterfall.

When he walked back, Richard was awake. "You ready?"

"Yes sir."

They mounted up and headed back a different way. Richard urged his old white horse forward past Travis, turned in the saddle, looked back at him and smiled. Travis smiled in return and fell in behind the old man.

It was mid-afternoon when Richard finally pulled his horse to a stop and swiveled in his saddle to speak to Travis.

"What do you see?"

Travis looked around. All he saw was winter-kill vines and trees.

"What am I looking for?"

"There is a trail tree here."

Travis looked and finally noticed a tree that he thought was deformed or diseased. He pointed to it.

"Long ago the Cherokee and other tribes bent young trees to mark the trail so we won't get lost."

"Wow."

"When the early settlers came here, for the most part, the rivers, the woods, and the Creator provided just about anything you might need."

"But one day, you decide that you need to go a little further, or you might wanna go to the trading post."

"So you figure it's a good idea to mark a tree along the way so you can get back home again."

Travis nodded and looked at the tree.

"Some folks used to cut notches, but someone a long time ago decided to bend young oaks in the direction of travel."

"Wow," again was all Travis could think of to say.

"Some will point the way to a hidden spring. Some to a creek. Some mark the trail. Some point to caves and hiding places. Some are message trees and have a hollowed out place you can leave a message in. Others could show where you buried your treasure."

"I'm impressed. Thank you Richard."

Richard pointed his finger at Travis and said, "Learn, my boy."

"I am sir. More than you know."

Richard turned around then and clicked to his white fuzzy horse.

That night after a hot supper of fried rabbit, gravy and biscuits prepared by Lucy and Goldy, Travis followed Richard over to sit by the fire. Richard dropped some finely ground tobacco into the fire.

"Good to let the Creator know we made it back home. Maybe he'll listen to our prayers. Have I told you how important tobacco is to us?"

"No," Travis answered. "I don't think so, anyway."

"Ah," Richard said. "Then listen to this."

It is said that in the beginning of the world, when people and animals were all the same, there was only one tobacco plant to which they all came for their tobacco. One day the Dagul'ku geese stole it and carried it far away to the south.

The people were suffering without it and there was one old woman who grew so thin and weak every one said she would soon die unless she could get tobacco to keep her alive. Different animals offered to go for it, one after another, the larger ones first, then the smaller ones, but the Dagul'ku saw and killed every one before they could get to the plant. After the others, Mole tried to reach it by going under the ground, but the Dagul'ku saw his track and killed him as he came out. At last, Hummingbird offered.

The others said he was entirely too small and might as well stay at home. He begged them to let him try, so they showed him a plant in a field and told him to let them see how he would go about it. the next moment he was gone and they saw him sitting on the plant, and then in a moment, he was back again, but no one had seen him going or coming because he was so swift.

Hummingbird said, "This is the way I'll do it. "

He flew off to the east and when he came in sight of the tobacco the Dagul'ku were watching all about it, but they could not see him because he was so small and flew so swiftly.

He darted down on the plant—tsa—and snatched off the top with the leaves and seeds and was off again before the Dagul'ku knew what had happened. Before he got home with the tobacco the old woman had fainted and they thought she was dead, but he blew the smoke into her nostrils and with a cry of "Tsa'lu! Tobacco!" she opened her eyes and was alive again.

It was Travis's turn to say, "Hmmm."

Richard smiled as he tossed bits of sage and sweet grass into the fire.

The next morning had hardly begun and Travis and Richard had only been out of bed long enough to drink one cup of the strong coffee that Richard liked when they heard a commotion outside. Travis pulled on his shoes, then picked up his cup again and wandered outside.

There was Daniel, scraping the mud off his boots. He said that Travis and Richard were to come down to his house that afternoon as his Aunt Lizzie and her family was going to come out, that they wanted to meet Travis.

"You never know when someone else might show up around this place," laughed Daniel. "People seem to come all the time out of nowhere."

"People like me!" laughed Travis in return.

When it was time to go, the sky was getting black and the thunder would roll from one end of the sky to the other. Richard told Travis to go on down, but that he thought he would just stay home by the fire.

Travis went down and knocked on the door, which was answered, of course, by Emma. She threw her little arms around his legs and told him that she was glad he had come back to visit her.

Soon there was the sound of a carriage pulling up, bearing Lizzie Ratliff Stem, her husband Jack and their son and daughter. Travis noticed that Jack's right arm hung at his side.

Just as they stepped out of the carriage, the rain hit so hard and so suddenly, that everyone just stood there in the yard for a second or two staring up at it. Then they bolted for the front door. They crowded through the door, soaking wet, with everyone laughing and all talking at once.

Daniel went to the fireplace to stoke it up and add a few more chunks of wood. Within minutes everyone was standing in front of it, beginning to warm up. The rain was pounding on the roof so loud that they almost had to shout at each other to be heard.

They didn't know it but Richard had started walking up to the house and had gotten about half way there when the cloudburst broke. A few minutes later the door opened and he trudged in, bundled up from head to foot.

Everyone just looked at him, wondering why he'd gone outside in the middle of the downpour.

"What you doing here, Grandfather?" Daniel laughed.

"Land sakes, I ain't never heard it rain like this." Richard said. "I didn't want to be alone up there with all this party going on."

Lizzie and Daniel's daughters made Richard a seat close to the fire and wrapped him in dry blankets.

Travis and the rest then continued to stand near the warm fire. It seemed like the rain was all anyone could talk about.

"It flooded here, when was that Grandfather, four years ago?" Daniel asked. "You remember that?"

"I remember," nodded Richard. "That was mighty fearsome."

"It didn't pour down like this," Daniel went on, "but it just kept raining and raining and never stopped. the stream and the river finally met and destroyed our crops and surrounded the house. We were scared it was going to keep right on coming until the house itself floated away. You remember that, Jack, when you came rowing over the water to us?"

Jack chuckled to himself. "Yes I do," he said. "That was some flood, all right."

Travis watched as Jack flicked his cigar into the fireplace with an awkward crossover movement with his left arm. His right arm remained limp and useless in his lap.

Everyone quieted then, each lost in their own memories of the flood. Then came a moment when everyone looked around at one another and all seemed to realize it at the same time. It was a strange feeling to Travis. He had to remind himself that the people there by the fire were his family. Lizzie looked at him and put her arm around him and kissed him on the cheek.

She asked him to tell her about her sister Annie. Travis started with the story, beginning about the time of the Trail of Tears and did his best to do a good job. Richard sat by the fire, eyes closed, nodding his head as he listened.

As he finished, Travis realized that part of the familyness in that room just then was knowing that they were family. There seemed to be a peculiar bond that he suddenly felt toward his Cherokee ancestors that he never had felt before.

"Travis," said Lizzie, "tell us about your own family. Are you married?"

Fighting to keep his emotions in check, Travis talked about Melody, Allie and the coming baby. He told how his dad was a lawyer. He told about Grandpa and his little farm. He passed around the locket so they could each take a look.

Mrs. Ratliff had the maids bring in some cold slices of ham and hunks of bread. They then parched corn and roasted pecans over the fire and everyone laughed as they peeled and chewed on sticks of sugar cane.

And so the afternoon passed as they continued to share and laugh and tell each other about their lives, even laughing about things that had happened years before. The rain kept coming down in sheets and no one even thought about going back outside. Gradually an hour slipped by, then another.

At last the rain let up some but was still falling steadily on the roof. The fire in Daniel's fireplace was toasting them, and everyone was so engrossed that no one even thought of moving from where they sat listening.

Chapter Thirty-One

On Sunday, Travis's last night with Richard, Lucy and Goldy prepared a good supper of deer steaks, baked sweet potatoes and boiled dry corn. Lucy even made a cake with sugar icing. Daniel had come down early in the morning and said he and Travis would need to leave the next day.

It had rained again, so Travis and Richard just stayed around Richard's house that day and talked. Richard shared some Cherokee teachings with Travis—teaching him the sort of things that are seldom spoken of. They also shared more about Annie and John, William and Ellen Jane, and all of the others back in Tennessee. Travis had gotten pretty good about talking about those folks in the present tense instead of the past.

Over leftover coffee and another piece of Lucy's cake, Travis told Richard more about his parents and Grandpa. He showed Richard the locket again and talked some more about Melody, Allie and about the little one on the way. He also told Richard of how ashamed he was about putting his job over his family. In turn, Richard shared with him his own story about placing his decision of moving to Arkansas over the best interest of his own wife and family.

Travis commented that it had been nice to meet Lizzie and Jack. Richard told him that Jack had been kicked in the shoulder by a wild horse a few years back and his arm had shrunk up and become useless. He told him about Eliza, Lizzie and Annie's other sister. Saying that she lived in Tahlequah and that her husband was a Union supporter and it was probably just as well that she had not been able to come out. In fact, no one had even told her about Travis's visit.

During the late morning, Richard talked about Andrew Jackson and about being a White Plume. He said a lot of it involved the Cherokee people near the Tennessee River being pitted against the Creeks. Then, in about 1812 or 1813, a man named Captain John Strother was in the Cherokee Nation seeking information about the Creek lands. He had devised a method of telling the Cherokee men from the Creek men in battle.

"That plan was that the Cherokee would wear either white bird plumes in their hair or a white deer's tail," Richard said.

"Your grandfather, Pathkiller, was chief of Turkeytown and principal chief of the Cherokee Nation. During the Creek War, in October 1813, Turkeytown was in danger of being attacked by the Red Sticks, a hostile faction of the Creek Indians. Pathkiller sent runners to Andrew Jackson's army in the north with a plea for help. Jackson responded by ordering a detachment led by General James White, which included many Cherokee soldiers, to relieve the town."

Richard then told Travis how he and many other Cherokees had been Jackson supporters and they had counted Jackson as a friend.

"That friendship, Travis, and our loyalty to him held devastating consequences to the Cherokee."

He told Travis in detail how Jackson's army at one time had come to his place and taken three hundred head of cattle and one hundred and fifty hogs from him.

"When we filed a claim, Jackson declared it null and void."

He told him how on another occasion, "A Captain Morgan and his soldiers came and took all my property and my Negroes."

Richard paused and relit his pipe. "Then they arrested me."

"That time though, Jackson made 'em give it all back and let me go."

The men moved over by the fire while the women cleared away the dishes. Richard stuck a match and carefully lit his pipe. Travis knew it was probably time for a story.

Richard leaned back and began to talk.

"You say you're gonna have a second little one. You must teach them both, Travis. And let 'em spend time with your parents and your Grandpa. Cherokee children get most of their learning from their elders. the boys get their training from either an uncle or grandfather, and the girls get theirs from an aunt or grandmother to learn the women's ways.

"My uncle Bear told me that a long time ago humans were able to talk to the animals. We were that friendly with 'em. They could understand us and we understood them, but at some point humans got into such a tight spot we had to take the life of certain animals for food and then we started getting sick. It turned out that various animals, even fish, were angry at us because we were eating 'em, so we started getting illnesses such as deer sickness and fish sickness.

"A council of our people got together with all the four-leggeds, creatures of the waters, and those that fly in the air. We gave 'em offerings and told 'em, 'My relatives, we have great need for you in order to live. When we hunt, we'll try to kill you quickly so that you will not suffer. In time, our bodies will lie down inside this Mother Earth and something will grow there so that our animal relatives can sustain their own lives. A cycle will be formed, an exchange, for the continuation of all life. In this way, we ask how to make our people well from the sickness you cause.'

"So the animals told us how to cure the illnesses and allowed us to hunt 'em because they knew that we were not killing 'em for sport; our need was to feed hungry people, and we used ever part of the animal for our survival. As long as we kept our word, no sickness came.

"That was the beginning of how our people began to have knowledge of curing different illnesses. And that's why our children are taught when they go out to hunt to never kill out of anger, nor for sport to see how many animals you can kill. Take just enough for survival and always be respectful of the four-leggeds. If you must kill, present an offering and talk to the animal, explainin', 'I need you for my family.'

"As young men we were not allowed to hunt until we became skilled with our weapons. We were taught how ever animal's made and exactly where to hit so it would die quick-like and not suffer more than it had to. When we brought back the kill, even that was a ceremony. We gave an offering to the animal, honoring it and explaining why we took its life.

"Young boys are to be taught never to eat their first kill. They are taught to give it to an elder. If you just killed and ate it yourself, that's about all you'd be able to do. You would not become a great hunter because you weren't showing much respect for the animal that you killed. But if you killed and made a sacrifice, giving that meat to others, then the reason for taking that life was based on generosity and respect. Those are the traits of a good hunter."

"Thank you, Grandfather Richard."

Before they turned in for the night, Richard blessed Travis with tobacco.

* * *

All too soon it was morning and time to ride back to Fort Davis. The groom had brought the horses around and Travis had complemented the man on how good Bolliver looked. The few days rest and good food had done the horse as much good as it had Travis and Daniel, for although his hair was wooly with his winter coat, it was clean and curried and his mane and tail were combed and free of burrs. Likewise his feet were trimmed and shod and had been oiled until they shown.

Even before they stepped out onto the front porch, it began to get quiet amongst Daniel and his wife and Travis. The good-byes were getting close and they all knew it would be hard.

Travis stepped off the porch and took Bolliver's reins. Mrs. Ratliff followed him and put her arm around his middle. "Here you are now, Travis. You are now a part of our lives. It's really wonderful how good God has been to us. I am so thankful that we have you in our family."

"Being here is the most remarkable thing I've ever experienced," said Travis.

"I am very glad you came home with Daniel. Take care of him for me," she said.

"I'll do my best, ma'am. But I am more grateful than I can say, both to God for letting me cross paths with Daniel, and to you all for opening yourselves to me the way you have. I feel like I've known you all for years."

"Travis, are you a Christian?"

"I guess I'm something like it," he answered. "I try, though I'm not as good as I would like to be. I know I've let Him down in the past."

Mrs. Ratliff squeezed him around the middle a little tighter and said, "The girls and I ... I hope we're sending everything you will need. We fixed you and Daniel new heavy blankets lined with brown linen and we put pockets at the top for soap, combs, brushes, handkerchiefs, and the like. We tied the linen to the blankets with strong tapes so that it can be easily taken off and washed ..."

Travis could tell that she was fighting tears.

They all stood around there in the yard, making small talk and pretending to be happy when they weren't.

Mrs. Ratliff stepped around to her husband. Travis could see that Daniel was fighting tears as he smiled back at her. He took her in his arms and gave her a big hug.

"I'll miss you." he said in a husky voice.

There was a great lump in Travis's throat. He tried to busy himself with his saddle while Mrs. Ratliff continued to cling to her husband on the other side of Bolliver.

"Do you have to go, Daniel?"

Travis tried to imagine how good it must feel to Daniel to have his wife's body pressed against his. If only he could have spent the past eight days with Melody. If only ... there were those words again, if only ...

"All our children are good," Daniel was saying. Travis turned and looked over his shoulder at the front porch. Josepha and Belle stood on the porch, arms around each other as protection from the brisk, cold wind whipping around the corner of the house. Travis pulled up the collar of the new woolen coat that Mrs. Ratliff had given him. He had sure been happy to see the old, torn brown coat burning out back the second day of the visit. Mrs. Ratliff had provided him with new pants, two bandanas to keep the cold off of his neck, two warm shirts, woolen gloves, underwear, and socks. Daniel Sr. had found him a nice pair of boots that were only slightly too big.

He waved at Emma and Katie who were standing inside between the curtain and the window pane. Katie smiled and waved while Emma energetically blew him a kiss. He returned the kiss, fighting back the lump in his throat and the ache in his heart that was more like homesickness than anything he knew.

"I wish this war would end," Mrs. Ratliff said softly.

"I'll be fine. Don't forget, I'm a Major. I must be about my duty. Travis, ready?"

"Ready, sir," Travis swung up into the cold saddle, chewed on his lower lip and averted his eyes as Daniel kissed his wife one more time.

The horses snorted and frisked in the cold as Daniel saluted his family, then led off at a brisk trot back towards the war.

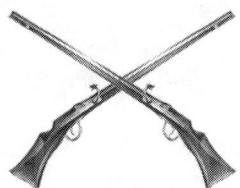

Chapter Thirty-Two

As they rode, Daniel told Travis to keep it on the hush-hush, but that the Mounted Rifles would soon be moving out.

"Where to?"

"Can't say right now, Travis. But we haven't seen a lot of Yankee action for a while, and I took this furlough because we should be moving soon."

"You think we'll get into heavy battle?"

"Probably."

Travis thought long and hard for a while before he got the courage to ask Daniel a question.

"Daniel?"

"Yeah."

"I noticed how your family always prayed over meals and I saw the Bible laying around."

"Yes."

"Do you feel, uh, how do know if you're ready to meet the Creator? If you get killed in battle, I mean? How do you know you're ready? I believe in God ..."

Daniel raised his hand before Travis could blurt out more questions.

"Travis, believing in God doesn't make one a Christian."

"Then what does?" He was plain lost then.

"Being a Christian means coming to the realization that you're a sinner. Travis, I know that even if it was only me that had sinned in the whole world, Christ would have still come just for me. But as we know, the Bible tells us that we all have sinned and come short of the glory of God. That means we've all strayed from the path God set for us. Each and ever one of us, Travis. We realize this and realize that our life just can't go anywhere without Him because we were created to worship Him. you see, we are made up of three parts, Travis, body, soul and spirit. Our body houses our soul, but our spirit is empty because our sin separated us from God. We try to find things to fill that emptiness, whether it is hunting, parties, whiskey, work, love, even being intimate with a woman. Everyone tries to find that perfect life."

"What do you do?"

"You gotta find peace with Jesus Christ. you gotta know what he did for you by dying on the cross. you have to submit to Him and accept that God sent His son to die for our sins so we can be reconciled to Him. Then ... then you can be ready to die in battle."

Daniel thought carefully before speaking again. "Travis, the Bible says that God sees ever sparrow that falls. And how much more important we are to Him than the sparrows?"

Travis shook his head. "What are you talking about?"

Daniel sighed. "It's in the Bible."

"The sparrow thing, too?"

"Yeah. And many other things. Have you ever read the Bible?"

Travis shook his head.

Daniel stopped his horse and looked at Travis.

"If you love Jesus, you ask Him into your heart to rule your life. you get to talk to Him every day and ask Him for help and He'll teach you right and wrong. One day you'll be with Jesus in Heaven. But if you don't ask Him into your heart then you can't have any peace going into battle, Travis."

Stunned, Travis stared at the Major. "You understand all of that?"

He nodded. "I have Jesus in my heart. I pray to Him every night."

For the first time Travis started feeling something break in his heart. This man, the Civil War Cherokee Mounted Rifle, the Major, his cousin, his friend, trusted God and loved Him and didn't see anything wrong with it at all. Travis knew that he must have spent thousands of hours in church. Why hadn't he ever paid attention to any of this before? Why hadn't he *heard* and really *listened* when he had been told that salvation was so simple? He had just thought that all there was to being a Christian was being good and going to church (sometimes), not a personal relationship with a living person, God.

"Do you have Jesus in your heart?" Daniel asked.

Travis gulped, feeling a knot form in his throat. "I ... No."

Travis simply sat there. He couldn't answer Daniel's question if his life depended on it. His eyes began to well up. He thought of all the information from the day, from the past week with Richard and with Daniel and his family, all the facts, including Daniel's words that salvation was free to everyone.

"Why?" asked Daniel.

He blinked at him. "Why what?" he asked, fighting to listen to him and deal with the truth that was ringing clearly in his brain.

"Why don't you have Jesus in your heart?"

"I don't know. And if we get into battle and I get killed, I want to go to heaven. My wife will be there. She is a good Christian. My little girl ..." He couldn't go on then for the lump in his throat.

He sat there on Bolliver in the middle of an Indian Territory road in 1861 and knew that he had to accept it. If he did, then something would change, that spirit part of him would wake up, and God would change him. He didn't understand how, but suddenly he felt like the worst of sinners, having spent his entire life living as he wanted, not even realizing that someone had died for him.

Embarrassingly the tears began to run down his cheeks.

"It's all right," Daniel said, leaning over and patting his gloved hand on Travis's arm.

"Just close your eyes and say," he continued, "Dear God, I want You to live my heart."

Travis opened his mouth to pray, but couldn't. Not a word came out.

"It's okay," Daniel whispered and patted him again on the arm.

Silently he said over and over and over, *I'm sorry. I'm sorry. I'm sorry. I didn't know. This is true. I've never had such a reaction to anything I've ever heard. In my heart, deep in my heart, I know it's true. It's in Daniel's eyes, in Melody's eyes. You're real, Lord God of Earth and Heaven. Forgive me. Show me how to be saved. Show me how to do it.*

He wasn't sure how long they sat there in the road until suddenly within him the pain and disillusionment of years faded away, and an unearthly peace filled him.

Then Daniel was pulling on his sleeve. "We gotta get Travis, or the Yankees be getting us."

The next night back at Fort Davis, after he was in his blankets and could hear Sawblade snoring, he felt at peace and knew that no matter what happened for the rest of his life. He would be okay.

Travis was a Christian.

Chapter Thirty-Three
January, 1862

About a week after Daniel and Travis returned to Fort Davis, about noon on Friday, January 10, Watie ordered his boys to prepare three days rations, pack up all their gear and prepare to move to an unknown destination.

The bugles blew at three o'clock the next morning. Travis didn't hear them but when Sawblade nudged him, he got right up, washed his eyes in cold water, and began to pack his stuff.

Tents were pulled down and rolled up and, with mess boxes and camp kettles, packed into the baggage wagons. Mules were fed and harnessed, horses saddled, cannon and ammunition dollies backed into line. Soldiers hurried to the creek, filling their canteens with water and saddling their mounts.

The night was black and still and bitter cold. A cloud bank was rising in the west and when fiery threads of lightning flashed suddenly across it, Travis saw them reflect dimly off the cannon, the guns showing black against the lighted night sky. Soldiers were hurrying with bundles of rifles or sacks of corn. Others were toting ammunition boxes. Behind him, the artillery gun drivers had their teams hitched and were standing patiently nearby. The cavalry men stood with their horses, ready to mount at the word. In spite of the fear that was always with him, Travis felt a flush of excitement. Unlike the rest of the time that they had spent at Fort Davis, this was the real thing.

Growing impatient, Travis patted Bolliver who twisted and squirmed in his tracks. What were they waiting for? He would explode if something didn't happen soon.

Daylight came finally, and the eastern sky was laced with turquoise and orange. The cloud bank in the west was receding. The wind blew up softly from the south, carrying upon it the musty odors of the creek bottoms. Travis could feel its cool flush on his face and see it move the tree limbs and rustle the brown grass close by. But still the Mounted Rifles didn't move.

Suddenly he heard a cavalry bugle blowing. Travis grasped his reins in his left hand and put one boot in the stirrup. He heard Sam's loud "Mount!" The men seemed to swing onto their horses as one, their rumps slapping the leather seats almost in unison. A dark-skinned lieutenant up front dropped his arm swiftly downward, and Stand Watie's Cherokee Mounted Rifles moved out.

Travis heard the creak of harness, the jingle of chains, the rolling of wagon and caisson wheels and the pounding of hundreds of hoofs as the horses and mules plunged obediently to obey. He thought it a remarkable sight to see the cavalry, followed by the wagons and artillery, twisting through the countryside in a column over a mile in length. The horses seemed to sense the seriousness of the journey and walked with a special quickness as if they shared their riders' pride and zeal.

Travis sat rigidly in his saddle, his head held high, giving Bolliver free rein to prance or walk as he chose. With furrowed brow, he assumed the demeanor of a courageous warrior with serious business on his mind. His heart beat high. Travis felt that they were leaving the last jumping-off place, taking him farther and farther away from the security of his old life. He knew that every mile they traveled took him nearer to a bona fide battle and farther away from the life he remembered from 2001.

The sun rose higher and higher in their faces, and the freezing morning grew a little warmer. Travis was glad that he had spent so many hours in the saddle; otherwise this trip would rapidly become hard work. Watie's army crossed rivers and streams. More than once the men had to dismount and lead their horses through boggy recesses that threatened to envelop them, They later sliced through dense woodlands that provided additional woes to cross-country horsemen.

Bolliver plodded forward, his hoof beats blending with thousands of others. Looking down at his hands, Travis was pleased at what he saw. Browned by the Indian Territory sunshine, his body was wiry and tough. He felt as if he could keep going all day.

"Here's water," somebody had called, and without waiting, the thirsty soldiers dismounted and ran through the woods. Carrying little canvas buckets, gourds and canteens, they crowded around a farmer's stone well.

Travis got one good drink and filled his canteen with the liquid which was not clear water but thick and brackish, evil-tasting, but it still moistened his dry mouth and swollen tongue. He then watched in amazement as his company scooped water so busily that soon all splashing ceased, and all he could hear was scraping on the well's rock bottom.

That night they bedded down near a small stream, but early the next morning they were back in their saddles, this time traveling almost due east. Day after day they moved; usually covering twenty to twenty-five miles from morning to dusk. The land began to turn into steeper hills and they encountered more streams, and there were more trees, mostly hickory, sycamore and oak. The cavalry plunged into the shadowy depths of the woodland, battling scratchy branches, dense undergrowth, thorny creepers and treacherous stretches of marshland. Each night they tried to camp beside a small river or stream, and as they made camp; they could smell the smoke from the campfires and hear the hiss of the bacon frying. After the meal the men usually sat around smoking and resting and trying to stay warm.

They spent the next night at a site called Casey Creek and the next evening they camped twelve miles south of Bentonville and Watie ordered sentries and guards posted and sent out scouts. "We're getting close," Sam told them. "Colonel says the Yankees are coming down fast from Missouri. Looks like we're gonna have a battle, all right."

The Mounted Rifles rode into the streets of Bentonville, Arkansas, just before noon the next day. Immediately the order was given for the men to rest. The town was in a near panic. It was January 14, 1862, two weeks after Christmas. Everybody believed that a battle would soon be fought. The whole town seemed frightened. Wagons and buggies and people jammed the square of streets around the courthouse. The normally beautiful walks and drives were cluttered with the foreboding equipage of war. All business appeared to be suspended. Storekeepers were boarding up windows and loading merchandise into wagons, ready for flight. Other folks were cooping their chickens, harnessing their teams, calling to their children and neighbors. Storekeepers and citizens seemed to be afraid of the Mounted Rifles, fearful that the troops would ravish their town. Many handed the men food or tobacco.

A storekeeper's wife gave Travis a small bag of hard candy and several hunks of beef jerky. Surprised, Travis muttered his "thanks." All afternoon he took in the sights and sounds of 1862 Bentonville. He remembered driving around the very square he was sitting in. He tried to compare it with how he remembered seeing it in 2001, but found it difficult. What struck him most was the dilapidated appearance of some of the buildings; apparently the old buildings had been refurbished by the time of his business trip.

He sat there all afternoon, leaning against a tree, watching the excitement and the confusion, while some of the other soldiers lay resting on the dead grass beneath several gigantic oak trees in the town square. Others of the Mounted Rifles were talking quietly, some playing cards, a few actually reading letters or writing them. Some sat up smoking. Others were killing lice. Many lay with their hats over their eyes, wandering through restless dreams of their own.

Travis, even tired as he was, did not feel like lying down. So, he sat on the ground with his musket on his lap. From where he sat, he could see the Eagle Hotel. Vividly, he recalled the day that he had driven around the square in the rented BMW. He remembered pulling over and reading the marker about the hotel from his convertible. But try as he might, he could not remember a word of what he had read.

In the west, the sun was sinking lower and lower. A quarter-moon was rising in the east. Moon and sun all at once, Travis felt it vaguely disturbing, perhaps a sign of bad things to come, although he had never heard of such an omen. He was sure of one thing though, something was bound to happen.

Late the next afternoon, the men were ordered to saddle up and file ranks. Colonel Watie rode up on a fine gray horse and, without dismounting, began to talk to his Mounted Rifles.

Watie said, "Men, we're going to have a battle. We're gonna go and try to hit 'em before they know we're coming. Don't shoot until you're ordered. Wait until they get close. Fire to hit 'em in the gut and don't get scared. It's no part of a soldier's job to get scared."

Travis was scared ... and excited. He was scared because he knew that he rode in the number three position and he would definitely have to fight. He looked over at Tommy and felt a guilty twinge of jealousy for young Tommy who rode in the number four position, that of horse holder.

They were waiting for the night to get very dark before moving out. The men were solemn, now that the hour of battle approached. Travis could sense it in their faces and hear it in their whispering. Some had painted their faces as their ancestors had done in times of war; several were wearing colorful turbans. Many were praying and others were singing quietly.

At last the command was given to move out. The troops moved out at a walk and rode in a northerly direction towards Missouri. Ihaveseen, big, broad, and straight, rode barefoot, bearing the Cherokee Braves flag. It was raining a dismal rain. Real wintery stuff that gradually wetted the men through until eventually they could feel it trickling down their sides and legs.

The night deepened. The pace slowed. The road wound up and down several small, rocky hills covered with timber. Once Travis saw the dark outline of a log house, although all the windows were dark and no dog barked. He felt thirsty and reached down for his canteen and took a drink. The water tasted cool and sweet. It was surprising how satisfying unboiled, unsterile, sometimes cloudy or muddy water could be. Travis was also surprised at how well you could see after you got used to the darkness.

Sometime after midnight they stopped. For what seemed like hours they stood by their horses. Then they were told to unsaddle and bed down in the roadside grass and rest for the night. The prospect was by no means a cheerful one, but the men lay down behind the horses to get what little sleep they could.

Travis checked the priming and the hammer on his musket, then lay down on the rough ground and slept.

Most of the men were just dozing off when "Saddles" was heard. The men grumbled and cursed, saying, "If we had kept awake, it wouldn't be so bad." As it was, they could barely rouse themselves. Travis was so tired, he didn't even hear the order and continued to doze until he felt a hand shaking his shoulder and heard Sawblade's voice whispering in his ear.

"Saddle up and keep silent. We're mighty close to the enemy."

It was cold and wet on the ground. As Travis got quickly to his feet, he could hear the other men stirring and getting ready.

Reaching into his pocket, he took out a cloth bag containing the last of his rations, a strip of cold bacon, some stale corn pone, and the last piece of jerky that the lady in Bentonville had given him. He had given the rest of the jerky away.

The officers seemed to be waiting for something. The men sat tense in their saddles, waiting for the order to go forward. Everybody was keyed up. Rumors were flying up and down the line that the men were to move up, dismounted. Would the order ever come?

At last, however, the cavalry was put in motion. It then started its slow crawl northeast with a company of skirmishers in front. Relieved that his squad wasn't selected for duty with the skirmishers, Travis felt a cool moisture on his face and looked up. A fine drizzle of rain that was little more than mist had started.

Travis's squad was in the second line of advance. He knew that the advance line, which had drawn the honor of meeting the Yankees first, was somewhere ahead.

As before, he felt relieved that he was not in that group, and immediately felt guilty for doing so.

"Ride at ease, but no smoking" was the order, and later on, "No talking." Even so, there were sounds enough in the middle of the night to tell the Yankees that a cavalry was on the move—creak of saddle leather, click of shod hoof, now and then the smothered exclamation of a man shaken out of a cavalryman's mounted doze. To Travis's ears all of it was loud enough to send any Union picket calling out the guard. Yet there was no indication that the enemy ahead was alert. Word came back from the skirmishers that apparently no Yankee sentinels were out. Ordered to dismount and leave the horses, they left the road on foot and climbed silently up a rocky slope stumbling and slithering in the mud, Travis could feel the cold, wet brush pulling at his pants and legs. When they finally crested the ridge, they halted panting silently, arriving in a sunken area, where they rested awhile. The rain increased, and the men were becoming clammy and cold. Despite the inky darkness, Travis knew through some sixth sense that they were near the Yankees.

Breathlessly he squinted over James Squirrel's shoulder and felt a cold chill run up and down his spine. In the valley below lay the sleeping Yankee camp. He could see the sputtering gleam of their campfires and hear their horses stamping faintly.

A half hour passed. The night wore on toward a gray dawn. Travis was on the north hill with his sergeant, Sam. Sergeant West was on the south hill. Between the two hills flowed Little Sugar Creek. The Yankee soldiers were camped along both banks. The slow rain stopped, and the stars began to shine brightly between broken patches of clouds.

Travis shifted, and for the first time in his life said silently, *Please God, please don't let me get killed,* wondering if God would really hear him.

"Be ready," came a whispered command. As Travis gripped his rifle, he heard clicks and sounds around him that told him that the Cherokee Mounted Rifles were set and ready.

It was almost daybreak. The country was open, and here and there Travis could begin to see dark objects. Keyed up, he felt no fatigue at all from the long hours in the saddle; although he knew he should have been dog-tired. He looked around at his comrades.

"I don't mind meeting the Creator," somebody whispered. "The thing I'd hate most is parting with my wife."

Travis put his hand in his pocket and squeezed the locket.

The stars paled. Birds began to twitter. Now Travis could see the live-oak trees taking shape all around him and smell the wintery odor of the woods. His hand accidentally brushed the stem of a sumac bush, and came away wet. Everything was dripping.

Suddenly away off to the south they heard a dull, heavy boom. It seemed to come from the direction of Sergeant West's ridge. Crouching in the sodden brush, Travis glanced at Sam, who was down on his knees next to him, peering intently through the leaves of a blackberry bush.

"What was that, Sam?"

"Our cannon," he whispered hoarsely.

The Mounted Rifles caught their breath, braced themselves, and looked at one another.

The noise of the cannon rudely called the enemy from their beds. Many were killed and many more were wounded. The booming of the Rebel cannon, with interludes of musketry fire, had announced to the sleeping foe that a battle was in progress where a battle had not been expected.

The distant booming began to come faster and faster. Soon it was answered by the much louder "Boom. Boom." of awakening Union guns firing from the creek below. Long ropes of orange flame streaked from the dark woods of the Yankee held creek.

"BOOM."

A deafening roar came from the Rebel battery located two hundred yards behind them. Travis ducked and heard the grapeshot rushing noisily through the quiet air over his head, as if projected by a giant slingshot. How the cannon bellowed, and their shells plunged and bounded, and flew with screeching hisses over the men. Their sharp rending explosions and hurtling fragments made Travis shrink and cower, despite his utmost efforts to be cool and collected. His eardrums throbbed and the ground beneath his feet shook.

Then the guns were all speaking deafeningly together. BOOM, BOOM, BOOM. Both ridges and the valley between were alive with long, slow lines of fire. The battle had begun.

A wild burst of cheering rang out one hundred yards below. West's line of attack lunged down the ridge and across a small field filled with small trees and onto the awakening Yankees who were still trying frantically to form a battle line in front of their tents.

Just then there came a different sound, an ill-omened rumble and growl, like thousands of beans being dropped into hundreds of pie pans. Travis knew what that was - musket fire. The firing continued at intervals, purposeful and scattered, as if at target-practice. "That's the enemy waking up," James Squirrel said.

Within a few minutes, there was another explosive burst of musketry, the air punctured by many missiles, which hummed and pinged sharply by spraying through the tree-tops, bringing twigs and leaves down on the men. *Those are real bullets*, Travis thought to himself.

Travis marveled, as he heard the constant patter, snip, thud, and hum of the bullets, *How can anyone live under this raining death?* He could hear the balls beating a merciless drumbeat on the trees, pinging vivaciously as they bounced off the bark, thudding at the rate of what seemed like a hundred a second. One, here and there, buried itself in a Mounted Rifle's body. Tall Tree, not five yards from Travis, flew backwards, and Travis saw that a bullet had gored his whole face, and penetrated into his chest. Another minie ball struck Luther Stem on the head, and he turned on his back, showing his ghastly white face to the sky.

Travis was scared, as he had never been scared before. But his head was clear. He was extremely alert, as though his brain was dictating that he would survive. He recalled reading somewhere that psychologists said that fear is a good thing; it stimulates the adrenalin glands and heavily loads the blood supply with oxygen.

He didn't know then, when it was that he realized that he wasn't frightened any longer. He suppose it was when he looked around and noticed that bullets were hitting six inches to his left or six inches to his right. He could have sworn that he could have reached out and touched a hundred bullets. He thought to himself, *Yankees certainly are lousy shots.*

Drawing in his breath, with solemn awe he watched the Rebel line strike the Union line, bending it to the rear and driving it in confusion toward Little Sugar Creek.

With his heart in his throat at the solid charge of the Rebel advance, Travis yelled at the top of his lungs. The Cherokee Rebel Yell drove all sanity and order from among the Mounted Rifles. It served the double purpose of relieving pent-up feelings, and transmitting encouragement along the attacking line. Travis rejoiced in the shouting like the rest.

It was time for the second line of advance - his line - to join the battle.

Chapter Thirty-Four

Hoof beats sounded behind him. It was Daniel, in his full gray major's uniform galloping up full tilt, jerking on his reins. As the big horse slid to a stop, it kicked up a shower of small rocks and gravel. There was an urgent expression on his dark face.

"Got your line formed, men?" he called loudly. "Be ready. We'll give the word in a minute," He kept looking back anxiously over his shoulder. Then his worried eyes swept up and down the line of men before him and stopped on Travis.

"Travis!" he barked, pointing with his gloved hand … "Get back down to the horse line. Bring the horses closer and bring up more ammunition, on the double."

Daniel looked at Travis for a long moment before heeling his horse around and galloping off along the ridge.

Travis stood and watched him ride away. Sam stepped quietly to his side.

"Better git."

Guiltily feeling relieved again, Travis stepped back out of line and ran, panting and still holding his musket, his new boots slipping and scraping as he ran, descending the same muddy hill they had marched up. Behind him the cannon were booming like thunder, and he could hear the clatter of musket fire and the wild, furious shouting of the second line of advance, his line, as it charged down the ridge without him.

After spending an hour or so looking for the horses, Travis finally found them and joined the men that were sitting there. "What's going on? Are we skunking them?"

"Ammunition!" Travis got the word out as a squawk, grabbing at the boxes the waiting men were sitting on. The men quickly opened the boxes and emptied the cartridges into their pouches and slung them over their shoulders. The men then quickly mounted the horses, each holding onto the remaining three horses in their rank. Except where was Tommy? Where was Bolliver? He yelled to the man nearest him, who replied that Tommy apparently had snuck away, wanting to be in the battle. The man then quickly loosed one of the horses he was holding and tossed the reins to Travis, who quickly mounted. As they headed towards the line, he saw Tommy's horse with dragging reins. And there was Bolliver, standing stolidly and still fastened to the other three horses. Wanting to ride his own horse, he jumped down, unfastened Bolliver and climbed into the saddle, leading the other three horses. The other men, each with a pouch or box of ammunition under one arm, solemnly followed Travis back the way he had come.

As they rode, Travis realized that the sounds of battle had faded and the woods were strangely still and silent. Birds had disappeared, rabbits had run away, and squirrels and chipmunks had vanished. He mentioned it to the other men, and they began to relax a bit, as they expected to find the Mounted Rifles with a victory under their belt. But as they trotted along the road leading the horses, they began to meet the Cherokee Mounted Rifles proceeding with difficulty along to the rear.

It was a ghastly sight. Many of the men had lost their hats and their guns. Travis recognized Nick Sparks in spite of the fact that he was covered in mud and blood from head to foot. His normally handsome face was distorted and frightful. Swelling had practically closed his throat and reduced his breathing to painful, gurgling gasps.

Dumbfounded, Travis jumped down from the saddle. In an effort to stop the bleeding, he ripped a strip of cloth from the right sleeve of his own shirt and wrapped it around Nick's neck. Little could be done, however, to stem the flow of blood gushing from the gaping hole where the minie ball had exited. In spite of his efforts, Nick fell and Travis realized that he was dead.

Travis stood up again and looked at his comrades. "How's the battle going?" he asked anxiously. He put the question to man after man, but they just looked at him with glazed eyes. Some crawled onto horses and others just kept walking.

He saw a lieutenant being carried by two of the Texans. Mounting Bolliver again, Travis looked back over his shoulder just as the flap of the officer's jacket fell away from his body, and he could see that the man's side looked as if it had been chewed by wolves.

Horrified, he nudged Bolliver on.

The wounded Mounted Rifles kept coming, many walking with wounds untended and still bleeding. Others wore crude bandages and used their rifles as crutches. All looked sick, defeated, and very tired.

"They skunked us," one man said, finally. "The Yankees rallied and drove us back. Hundreds of our boys got shot."

Shocked, Travis could scarcely believe his ears. "Why, we were winning it when I went to go get the horses and ammuni..." His voice just trailed off before he was able to say, "What happened?"

"They was too many of 'em. We drove 'em back at first, and I thought we had 'em licked. But they kept coming. They must've had twice as many men as us."

Feeling sick to his stomach, Travis turned Bolliver around, feeling floored at this calamity. The army - his army - had been clobbered. He felt like crying. In a somber frame of mind at hearing the bad news, he rode on, trying to find buddies from his own squad in each bunch of weary, disheartened men he passed. Finally he came across part of his company walking southward, through a potato field.

Dirty and exhausted, they wore a dazed, dispirited look on their smoke-blackened faces that suggested they had come straight from hell. David Davis was the first one Travis recognized. A bloody bandage was wrapped around his left arm, where a rebel minie ball had struck him. James Horsefly had torn off most of his own shirt to dress the wound.

"Are you all right, David?" Travis asked.

David just looked at him unhappily and, without answering, crawled onto a horse and trotted on toward the rear as though to put as much distance as possible between himself and the horror he had seen. James Squirrel rode double behind him, carrying David's gun. He had lost his hat. There was dirt on his face and a bloody stripe ran down his shirt.

"Grasshopper got killed," James said. "Shot in the face when our line charged. John Tobacco's dead too. He was cut down when we were retreating. More'n a few of our boys got hit. We were lucky to be in the second advance line. the first line lost almost half killed."

John Tobacco dead. The news saddened Travis. John had ridden in the number one position of Travis's rank, and he had counted him as a friend.

Quickly Travis nudged Bolliver to go on ahead. He felt like crying at the news of John Tobacco. He would miss Grasshopper too.

As Travis rode, he caught a glimpse of Sam, a stream of red running from a patch of blood-soaked hair over one ear. He swayed; his eyes wide open as those of the frightened horses, but he fastened them on Travis as if he was the one steady thing in an unsteady world. There was a dark circle around his mouth where the black powder had spilled as he had torn open cartridge after cartridge with his teeth. He spat out his tobacco, wiped off his chin with his free hand, and then wiped his hand on the leg of his pants.

"We just needed more men," the sergeant bellyached. "We chewed 'em up pretty good anyhow, I think. Your little friend Tommy showed up. He's a brave little cuss. At the first Yankee strike, Big Tree threw down his musket and run like a rabbit. But your little Tommy charged right in with our boys. I saw him later and he asked where you had gone off to."

"Why did he leave the horses?" Travis asked, but Sam had already moved on.

They went all the way back to Bentonville. Riding wearily into the town at sunset, they read their defeat in the frightened faces of the townsfolk staring at them on the streets. They didn't look much like an army and they knew it. Disorganized, they would have been easy prey for a Union pursuit. But the Northern army, as Stand Watie had planned, was itself too badly battered to follow up on its victory.

The fight that day, which had lasted less than three hours, was not much of a battle by most standards. Both sides had retreated and suffered about the same number of casualties. However, although the battle had basically ended in a stalemate, due to the ferocity the sleeping Yankees had exhibited, Watie knew that the Yankees were a force to be reckoned with.

Later Travis found Sawblade gulping cold water from a well behind a church He still had his musket with him, his face was crestfallen.

"Have you seen Tommy?" asked Travis.

"No."

Moonless, the night was growing very dark and cold. After they had eaten a little corn pone, they found a place to bed down there behind the church. Travis was exhausted and felt that he could sleep for a month. Lying down, he pulled his blanket over his chest.

Just before they dozed off, Sawblade said fervently, "Travis, I hope I never have to fight or shoot at anybody, long as I live."

Travis tucked a corner of his blanket around his shoulder and didn't answer. He too wished with all his heart that there would never be another battle, but he knew there would be. For he, and he alone, knew the outcome of the Civil War. He also knew that Major Daniel Ratliff Jr. had, in all likelihood, saved his life.

Thank you God.

Chapter Thirty-Five

At daybreak the next morning, Travis awakened to feel something hard toeing him in the ribs. Rolling over, he saw an ugly black shoe covered with red Arkansas mud.

Slowly his eyes traveled upward. Above the shoe and the dirty sock, was a yellowish-gray pants leg. Halfway tucked in the waist of the pants was a faded brown shirt. The man wearing the shoe, the pants, and the shirt was holding his musket in both hands. He was obviously a sentry. Travis recognized John Buzzard of his own unit. Behind him, Sawblade had thrown off his blankets and was stirring sleepily.

"Get up, botha you," the sentry said. "Yer mess is on the other side a' the square."

Travis wiped the sleep out of one eye with his dirty hand and then sat up, squinting. An orange glow had begun to illuminate the eastern horizon. He smelled bacon frying and felt a ferocious hunger. He hadn't had a square meal for about three days and he figured he wouldn't get another one for longer than that. Travis yawned and looked up questioningly at the guard.

"What's going on?"

Ignoring him for the moment, the sentry told Sawblade that the squads would reorganize due to losses and then drill right after breakfast. He then looked down at Travis pityingly. "You ain't drilling. First Lieutenant Su-A-Gee has got you down for duty with the hospital. you gotta report in twenty minutes. Dash, Travis, what did you do to deserve that stinking duty?"

Travis blinked uneasily and pulled his legs up under him and climbed to his feet. His legs still felt dead. Six hours' sleep wasn't nearly adequate after you'd walked and ridden and been (at least a little bit) in a battle.

Sawblade, sitting up blearily, his eyes half shut, was still stiffly trying to get up.

After breakfast, Travis told Sawblade good-bye and reported to the field hospital half a mile south of Bentonville. After the battle, most of the more dangerously wounded had been picked up and transported there.

Travis never forgot that day. Set up on the outskirts of Bentonville, the field hospital proved to be two large, gray tents thrown together in a clump of big oak trees. Cows were still grazing peacefully in the pasture. Travis's detail carried those who had bad leg wounds to and from the amputation tent, where the tired Texas surgeons that had already worked all night were destined to labor all day as well.

Finally only a dozen men were left. They lay on litters under the trees, awaiting the surgeon's saw. Their torn and bloody clothing, matted and hardened, was rasping the tender, inflamed, and still oozing wounds. Their groans and cries of agony wrenched Travis's heart. With teary eyes he walked among them, covering them as best he could to shield them from the cold, moving them into the shade, carrying water to them.

All day he had kept an eye out for Tommy, but never saw him. Then he heard, "Travis."

He spun around. Somebody had called his name. Carefully he looked over the litters on the ground. Then he saw a familiar figure stretched out on a pile of dirty straw. One long leg was crudely wrapped in bloodstained bandages. The face was gaunt and dirty. Coming closer, Travis finally recognized him. John Tobacco.

"John," Travis gasped joyfully. "They told me you were dead."

Travis tried to make him more comfortable by rearranging the blood-soaked rags which served as a pillow. John Tobacco grabbed onto Travis's hand and looked towards the hospital tent. One flap was turned back and John and Travis could see the surgeons working busily at their grisly tasks. John's hands trembled.

"Take a look at my leg, Travis," John begged. "Tell me if you think it'll be cut off." Travis raised the blanket and looked at John's leg. The leg was purple and swollen. Travis could see the bone. With tears in his eyes, he recovered the leg.

"Well," said John. Travis saw that in spite of the cold, John had big crystal drops of sweat on his grimy face.

"I don't know, John. It looks bad."

Just then the pain of his mangled leg struck John. "Oh." he moaned, "It hurts awful. I cain't stand it."

"Don't fret, Tobacco," counseled an older, heavy-set Texas man from the next litter. "This is gonna be lots better than dying with gangrene." Although his leg, too, was sheathed in bloody bandages, he was coolly smoking a loosely rolled cigarette.

Travis got them both a dipper of water from the bucket.

"Come on, John, I'm just glad you're alive. I felt bad when they told me you'd been killed."

John shut his eyes and swallowed painfully, then turned his head a little towards Travis.

"Naw," he said, with a touch of bravado. "I got it in the leg as we retreated."

John Tobacco's eyes kept darting uncontrollably from Travis to the amputation tent. "Some of our men was carrying me to the rear, but the Yankees was firing so quick-like, they had to drop me and run. The Yankee skirmishers found me, and one of 'em poked me with the toe of his boot. But the other'n thought I was dying and said just to leave me be. I laid out there on the battlefield 'til someone picked me up just a bit ago. Travis, it was awful out there alone, listening to the wounded and the dying a shrieking and cussing and praying and nobody there to help 'em."

A weary-looking surgeon in a bloodstained coat stuck his head out of the tent. He was trying to thread a needle. Unable to get the needle threaded, he dampened the end of the thread with his tongue and rolled it between dirty fingers. Threaded at last, he pointed with the needle to the heavy-set man at John Tobacco's side.

"Bring him in next," he mumbled wearily to Travis and the litter detail. Gently they picked up the litter. The heavy-set man took one last, deep draw on his cigarette, and pursed his lips, blowing out the smoke in a perfect smoke ring.

"See you later, Tobacco," he said.

Travis and the litter bearers carried him inside the tent and placed him onto a table. Travis looked around with awe. He had read stories about the horrors of civil war hospitals, but he was not prepared to see it for himself. The terrible sights and sounds that met him did little to relieve his mind. He saw what looked like a hundred of his comrades, lying on straw and on cornstalks, with wounds of all imaginable shapes and sizes. Then, as his eyes adjusted to the darkness, on the floor he noticed the animal manure, vomit, clotted pools of blood, and piles of amputated arms and legs. One man, his nose hanging only by a strip of skin, tried to grab Travis by the hand. The sights were terrible, but the sounds were more so. Men were moaning with pain, calling for water, begging that they might die. Travis was sickened by the lack of ventilation, bad lighting and the fact that many of the men lay almost on top of each other in their filthy blood-caked clothing. A disgusting stench assailed his nostrils. The place reeked with the sweet odor of blood and rotting flesh. Travis saw one of the medical orderlies washing a catling knife in a pail of dirty, dark-colored water. Another was cleaning human bone fragments from a small saw. When one of the surgeons motioned him outside, Travis was glad to leave.

"So long, Coker," the heavy-set man called after him. Then noticing Travis's stricken face, he added apologetically, "Try not to think about it son." Just then the orderly plucked the cigarette out of the man's mouth.

All too soon the surgeon appeared at the tent flap and gestured toward the unhappy John Tobacco.

"Your turn next," he said. John Tobacco's face turned chalk white. "Don't let 'em cut off my leg, Travis," he pleaded.

"I'm sorry, John," Travis tried to comfort him as they lifted his litter. "You won't even feel it. They have to do it to save your life."

"Soon you'll be all through with war, Tobacco," somebody else said as they carried John inside and laid him on the table.

"Travis, I don't wanta live if I hafta be a cripple for life. Please, don't let 'em do it." John grabbed Travis's hand and held on tightly. Impatiently the surgeon motioned him outside again.

Travis turned to go. He didn't want to stay a minute longer in the horrific surgical tent than he had to. His stomach felt like it would empty what little contents it held at any minute. His knees felt weak and his throat dry.

Travis ducked beneath the tent flap and went outside to find that more wounded had been brought in. One man had been shot through the bowels and Travis didn't think that he would ever see anything more horrible than that. The man suffered with a burning thirst and no sooner would Travis give him a drink of water than he would throw it up. Travis carried dipper after dipper of water to him until the man's litter was drenched. The man's suffering was so great that he died before he could be moved into the surgical tent.

Travis then was ordered to join a detail that had been assigned to burying dead Rebel soldiers. As he and his comrades guided their horses among the human wreckage, they sickened at the stench of burned flesh, clotted blood, splintered limbs, and disemboweled corpses. Mutilation, apparently by buzzards and wild animals, only added to the horror.

The dead had fallen in long swaths, reminding Travis of windrows in a hay field. They lay in curious convulsive positions with all sorts of expressions on their faces. The ground was scattered with soiled and torn clothes, muskets, blankets, and dead horses. Trees not more than one foot in diameter contained from twenty to thirty musket balls and buck-shot, put into them during the battle. Other trees were blood stained. Travis counted a hundred and ten dead men on a small spot of ground. His heart grew sick at the sight, and so he stopped counting and set to digging. Using pick and shovel, the men dug shallow trenches in the ice cold sunshine.

With a start Travis recognized the first victim they buried as Peter Hammer, who had been seen riding merrily into battle in his moccasins and a bright calico shirt. Hit in the side by artillery fire, he apparently had died during the night, his face twisted hideously by whatever he had suffered before dying.

When it came time to put Hammer into the rocky Arkansas soil that was to be his final resting place, Travis wondered again at the fact that he was there instead of sitting in his office in Tennessee. He thought about Melody and wondered if she would ever know what had really happened to him the day of the wreck. He wondered why any of this had happened at all.

After he helped ease the body into the shallow trench, he stood back, a lump in his throat, and thought how awful it was to be buried without any identification or without even a song or a prayer. He stood back as the men shoveled dirt over the dead man's face.

Later Travis's detail was ordered again to the Little Sugar Creek battlefield to claim the body of Sergeant Jordan. There they saw several Yankee burial parties busily interring their dead. The half-dressed dead and wounded Yankees showed what a surprise the Mounted Rifle's attack had been.

When he rejoined his outfit, Travis lost no time telling his comrades that John Tobacco was still alive and had had his leg amputated.

Sam's brown eyes swept the group authoritatively. "Well, Travis, it seems like Tobacco also had been shot in the back. I went to check on our men and saw him. They didn't take his leg off, 'cause they had seen that he was bleeding from his back. So they just moved him off to the side. the doc said he wouldn't last 'till morning."

The mood was somber then and Travis felt really sad about poor John Tobacco and decided to check on him first thing in the morning.

Finally Travis stretched and lay down wrapped in the blankets and the cotton quilt that made his bed and tried to think. All around him he could hear the snores of the men and smell the stench of their unwashed bodies. Slowly his mind began to go back over the last few weeks. Other than for the visit to Daniel's home, they had been difficult weeks for him. He tried to picture his office in his mind and was unable to do so. Instead, he tried to focus on Melody and Allie and soon fell asleep. He began to dream. He dreamed that he saw his Grandpa speaking to him, and it had seemed obvious that Grandpa seemed proud.

The next morning before breakfast, Travis hurried over to the hospital to check on John Tobacco. He found out that mercifully, he had died very peacefully in his sleep the evening before. Travis was sad but very thankful that the end came for John Tobacco a little earlier than was expected, putting an end to his suffering and fear.

Back at camp, Travis was still unable to find Tommy. After breakfast, he and some of the others rode back out to continue burying their dead. It was then that they saw Tommy's crumpled little body lying in a shallow gulley.

Fearing the worst, Travis and Sawblade slipped from their horses and moved to where Tommy lay motionless.

Tommy lay on the ground on his back. His hands began moving feebly to tear at the already torn shirt across his belly. There was a congealed mass of blood across the entire front of Tommy's shirt and pants.

Travis knelt and lifted Tommy's head and looked into his face.

"Tommy, we're here." Tommy opened his eyes, but they offered no recognition.

"Sawblade, hand me some water."

Sawblade hurried back to his horse and retrieved his canteen hanging from the saddle. He gave it to Travis and stood half-watching Travis give Tommy a drink of water while at the same time, scanning the woods for movement. Tommy took a slow gulp of water.

Travis then pulled Tommy's hands away from his belly and saw a small wound in the side. He couldn't see any other injury. He knew though that Tommy's delirium, his flushed face, and his fast breathing suggested worse trouble.

"We'll get you to the doctor," Travis said.

Travis and Sawblade gently lifted Tommy onto Bolliver. Mounting behind him, he grasped the reins with one hand and wrapped the other arm around Tommy and eased Bolliver back toward their camp, where they were met by Sam.

"Get him off that horse and to the surgeon," the sergeant barked.

Tommy was taken to the hospital where other soldiers ran to gently lift Tommy from Travis's horse and carry him to the hospital tent.

"Would someone take care of my horse?" said Travis. "I want to go with Tommy."

Chapter Thirty-Six

During that day more Confederate wounded were brought in. Every corner was crammed; and the ground outside was covered with the bleeding, mangled bodies. The surgeons, with sleeves rolled up and bloody to the elbows, stayed busy amputating limbs. The red, human blood ran in streams from under the makeshift operating table, and a pile of arms and legs, withered and horrible to behold, were voiceless evidences of the fierceness of the fighting. Travis had to fight the rising bile in his throat as he witnessed the blood and brains, mangled limbs, protruding entrails, groans, shrieks, and death. The deep and agonizing groans, the shrill death-shriek, the cries for water, whiskey, anything, even death, assailed Travis with the most horrific scene imaginable.

He wandered his way through the tent to where the Texas army surgeon was bending over Tommy. Flickering yellow light gave the room an eerie cast. Travis liked the surgeon, the same blond-headed Texan that had examined him that first day. As Travis approached, the doctor looked up and nodded a greeting. Travis stood and watched as the doctor probed the wound in Tommy's side. Dark blood oozed from the injury.

"It's deep inside," the surgeon said. "Bullet is really deep. Probably in his liver. Hard to tell for sure."

Travis tried to search the surgeon's face for a clue of Tommy's fate.

"Don't know how he made it. This should've killed him outright. Shoulda dropped him right on the spot."

"Tommy may be young, but he's brave. He was supposed to be a horse-holder, but he left the horses and went into the battle," Travis said.

The surgeon smiled and nodded.

Tommy turned his face towards the surgeon and asked, "Will I live?"

Travis's heart broke as he looked as his poor young friend as the surgeon replied, "No, son. I'm afraid the wound is fatal."

Tommy mumbled, "Doctor, I don't wanna die." There was a look of terror on his childish face. Travis stepped closer and took hold of both of Tommy's hands. "Tommy, it's me. Travis. Don't you recognize me?" The boy stared hard at Travis, his breath coming in short, uneven gasps. Then a faint, glad flicker of recognition lit up his eyes. "Travis," he murmured, "don't leave me. I don't wanna die."

Travis felt tears stinging his eyes.

The surgeon apologized for not being able to provide any laudanum or opium, but did hand Travis a half-full bottle of whiskey. Travis gently lifted Tommy's head and helped him to take a drink. Easing his head back down, Tommy reached for Travis's hand.

"Tell me a story, Travis."

Travis thought for a minute, wishing that he had paid more attention to the Cherokee stories that Grandpa had told him. Unable to think of anything other than the one about when possum got his tail, he decided to tell the one about why moles live underground.

Many ages ago there was a man who was in love with a young woman. But she disliked him and wanted nothing to do with this young man. He tried in every way to win her favor, but with no success. At last he grew discouraged and made himself sick thinking about it.

Then one day as the man sat alone in his despair, Mole came along, and finding the man so low in his mind, asked what the trouble was. The man told him the whole story of the woman he loved, and her dislike of him. When he had finished, Mole said, "I can help you. Not only will she like you, but she will come to you of her own free will."

That night, while the village slept, burrowing underground to the place where the girl was in bed asleep, Mole took out her Spirit Heart. He came back by the same way and gave her heart to the discouraged lover, who couldn't see it even when it was in his hands. "There," said Mole. "Swallow it, and she will be so drawn to you that she has to come to you."

The man swallowed her heart and felt a warmth in his soul as it went down, and in the morning when the girl woke up she somehow thought of him at once. She felt a strange desire to be with him, to go to him that minute. She couldn't understand it, because she had always disliked him, but the feeling grew so strong that she was compelled to find the man and tell him that she loved him and wanted to be his wife. And so they were married.

All the magicians who knew them both were surprised and wondered how it had come about. When they found that it was the work of Mole, whom they had always thought too insignificant to notice, they were jealous and threatened to kill him. That's why Mole hides under the ground and still doesn't dare to come up.

"I don't remember that story," Tommy said weakly. "It's a good one."

Travis smiled and held his friend's hand.

"Your grandpa tell you that story?"

Travis just nodded yes and continued to sit by Tommy.

Later, the doctor walked by and took Tommy's pulse. "He's gone," he said.

"We'll come and get him in a bit," Travis said, still holding onto his friend's hand.

The doctor nodded and then walked across the tent to sit at his desk to write Tommy's death in his log.

Travis stood for a moment and then went to get some of the other men to help him take care of Tommy's body. A few minutes later, they carefully wrapped the body in a wool blanket and carried it out of the tent.

Travis and the others stood silently by the grave they had dug as Tommy's body was lowered into the earth. There were no words. Travis and two others then filled the grave with dirt, patted it down and stepped back as Cedar began to sing a prayer song.

When the song was finished, the men turned and walked away, leaving Travis alone where during the course of the afternoon, the dead had been laid out in long rows, their clothes stiff with dried blood, and their features retaining in death the agony and pain with which they died.

Chapter Thirty-Seven

That evening, Travis, and his friends huddled in their blankets behind the church. Sawblade spoke quietly. "Look at the sky. The stars speak to us as they have from the beginning of time when the Creator made us."

"They're especially bright on a freezing night like this with no clouds to hold in the heat," Hunter said.

Remembering then, Travis said, "My grandpa always used to tell me a story about the stars."

"Tell us the story," Johnny said.

When the world was new, there were seven boys who used to spend all their time down by the council house playing the chunkey game where you roll a stone wheel along the ground and slide a curved stick after it to hit it. Their mothers scolded them, but it didn't do any good. One day the mothers collected some chunkey stones and boiled them in the pot with the corn for dinner.

When the boys came home their mothers dipped out the stones and said, "Since you like chunkey better than working, take the stones now for your dinner."

The boys were very angry, and went down to the council house, saying, "Since our mothers treat us this way, let's go where we will never trouble them anymore." They began a dance—some say it was the Feather dance and went round and round the council house, praying to the spirits to help them. At last their mothers were afraid something was wrong and went out to look for them. They saw the boys still dancing around the council house, and as they watched they noticed that their feet were off the ground and that with every round they went higher and higher in the air. The mothers ran to get their little boys, but it was too late, for then they were already above the roof of the council house—all but one, whose mother managed to pull him down with the chunky pole, but he struck the ground so hard that he sank into it and the earth closed over him.

The other six circled higher and higher until they went up to the sky, where we see them now as the Pleiades, which our people call The Boys.

The people grieved long after them, but the mother whose boy had gone into the ground came every morning and every evening to cry over the spot until the earth was wet with her tears. At last a little green shoot sprouted up and grew day by day until it became the tall tree that we call now the pine tree, and the pine is of the same nature as the stars and holds in itself the same bright light.

"That's a good story," Adahte said.

They all nodded. They all knew the story, probably better than Travis. They had all heard them many times. However, like most Cherokees they believed it was important to tell the stories repeatedly. That is how the Cherokee remained the Principle People.

Each was lost then in his own thoughts; the four of them wrapped their blankets tighter around themselves and lay looking up at the icy stars.

Travis did not sleep for a long time. He listened to the snores and coughs of the camp, heard the rush of a hunting owl's wings and thought about Grandpa. Then, Melody entered his mind. He smiled as he pictured her petite body, dark brown hair, and the way she had of tossing her head back when she laughed. He figured that she would be showing her pregnancy by then, and he pictured her sitting cross-legged on the bed, rubbing her belly with cocoa butter, and talking to the baby, perhaps telling it about him. Thinking such thoughts made him incredibly homesick and sad. Finally, he wrapped himself tighter in his blankets and slept a long fitful sleep filled with Melody, Allie, his parents, and Grandpa.

Chapter Thirty-Eight

The next night Travis was sitting around the campfire deep in thought. After the dream the night before, he was feeling low because of his longing for his wife and from being homesick. He was thinking about her and Allie and the little baby that was on the way.

"I think Travis is in love." Adahte teased.

"I miss my wife."

"Is she fat?"

"No."

"Too bad," Sawblade said. "I like 'em fat. Good to lay close to on a cold winter night."

"She's not fat," said Travis.

"Cuddly?" Someone else asked.

"She's nice to lay next to on a cold night." Throwing a rock into the bushes, he muttered, "On any night."

"I think it is time for a story," said George.

"A-ho," came the reply from the men.

After the Creator had created the Earth and all the plants and animals, he created a tall brown man with beautiful straight hair to help him on Earth. the Creator placed the strong, brown Cherokee man in the beautiful Smoky Mountains.

After a time the Creator remembered that although each man sometimes needs to be alone, each man would also need companionship to be his best. When the Cherokee man was sleeping, the Creator caused a green plant to grow up tall over the heart of the man.

The plant had long graceful leaves, an ear and golden tassel. As the plant grew, a beautiful, tall, brown woman began to appear at the top of the stalk. the man awoke and helped the beautiful woman down from the corn stalk.

Over a period of time, the man and woman built a home and planted the kernels from the corn. the turkey, a sacred bird of the Cherokee, showed the woman that the corn was ready to eat.

When the man came in for supper, she pulled an ear of roasted corn from the pot and offered it to him. He began to eat the first corn of Spring.

The first woman was called SELU or Corn Woman.

Chapter Thirty-Nine

For a while, the time near Bentonville had been dull. Travis had taken his turn on mounted guard. He had tended his gear and to Bolliver. For a while he had worked with the forage master, divvying out grain, mending harness, and tending the draft horses and mules that pulled the artillery and wagons. He also spent a few days cutting fire wood.

The weather had turned rough, with days of wet snow, freezing rain and high winds. After spending a few miserable and very long nights shivering away while cursing about the cold weather, Travis and the other men of his squad copied what some of the other fellows had done. They split logs and made rough little cabins and put in wooden floors of more split logs. The little cabins were squatty and only large enough to house four sleeping men, but they served well to reduce the mud and keep them warm on the freezing Arkansas nights.

The only pleasurable distractions during those cold dull days were ball games. The men carved and shaped ball sticks out of hickory with a webbed cup at one end and formed the ball out of deer hide and hair.

In spite of the frosty temperatures, the players were barefoot and wore only a breechcloth that barely covered their manhood. A few would fasten a strip of cloth around their head as a headband to keep their hair out of their eyes, but these were usually cast off in the first round of play as they served as a handhold for their opponents.

The game was rough and tumble and scores were made when the ball would strike a carved wooden fish on top of a tall pole, that earned seven points and two points were awarded if the ball simply struck the pole. A player first had to come into possession of the little deer hide ball by way of the stick, catch it in the webbed pocket of his stick or dig it from the ground. Then he could palm the ball or fling it at one of his pursuers, and run with all his might toward one of the goalposts before he would be knocked down in the most brutal way. There were no limitations on violence other than perhaps to scratch like a woman. When a player would bring another player down by pulling on his breechcloth, the man would be left naked as a jaybird, causing a great deal of laughter to ensue in both the crowd and among the players.

The teams walked toward each other from either end of the ball ground, yelling that their opponents were nothing more than timid rabbits and eunuchs. They whooped war cries and shook their ball sticks like they meant to kill one another, and when play would begin they nearly did. The ball was pitched in the air and everyone went for it with a great clash of upraised sticks, though the ball nearly always fell through them to the ground. Then they began raking for it in the dirt and grabbing the sticks of other players to snatch them away. It was a great confusing huddle of men, and the ball was no bigger than a walnut, so that Travis could hardly tell what was happening until a ball carrier broke free to run.

Then the players would slam into each other. They would wallow on the ground, struggling with each other even though the ball had since been passed on to another man, and he had also been knocked down so that at any one time there might be three or four wrestling matches going on, totally unrelated to the scoring of points.

When the game would finally be over, the men would be bleeding from wounds but grinning from ear to ear, no matter which side won or lost.

Travis enjoyed watching the games as the men played with a passion that reminded him of his high school football days.

The food was boring as well. Watie had discouraged foraging by that time and the Mounted Rifles had to depend on the supplies that they had brought with them. Corn pone was frequently substituted for bread and salt pork was substituted for the fresh beef they had enjoyed frequently in Indian Territory.

For the most part, however, the time spent was spent waiting. "Hurry up and wait" seemed to be the norm. Little did the men know that their boring days would soon be ending.

One crisp Ozark day, Watie's sentries came riding hard into camp.

"They're everywhere!"

"Who?" said Gabriel, dropping his cup and spilling hot coffee down his pants.

"Yankees!"

"You spot Yankees?" Travis asked.

"Spot some," one of the sentries shouted, "Looks like the whole Union army is headed right for us. They're all 'round us and coming fast."

Just then, two other scouts rode in, horses lathered and panting hard.

"Yankees. Looks like three sides," one said. "Blue coats all around."

"Get ready," snapped Sam. "Be back as soon as I tell Watie."

The Mounted Rifles hurriedly packed their gear, and just as Travis had Bolliver ready, he heard gunfire in the distance and knew that the Mounted Rifles were engaging men of the advancing forces. After Tommy and so many had been killed, the squads had been reformed and Travis was placed in the number four position - that of horse holder.

For thirty minutes, the Confederates resisted, but by four p.m., Watie, leaving artillery and other equipment behind along with one hundred and fifty casualties, was leading them in retreat. By the time Union troops fully arrived, the Mounted Rifles had withdrawn into the woods west of Bentonville a ways.

That night, after the battle, a half-inch of snow fell and the Mounted Rifles began to suffer. Travis and the rest huddled around small smoky fires thinking about the day's events and what the future might hold. As they sat quietly, eating cold rations, Yohola broke the silence with a story.

The old people tell us that once when the people were burning the woods in the fall, the blaze set fire to a poplar tree, which continued to burn until the fire went down into the roots and burned a great hole in the ground. It burned and burned, and the hole grew constantly larger, until the people became frightened and were afraid it would burn the whole world. They tried to put out the fire, but it had gone too deep, and they did not know what to do.

At last, someone said there was a man living in a house of ice far in the north who could put out the fire, so messengers were sent, and after traveling a long distance they came to the ice house and found the Ice Man at home. He was a little fellow with long hair hanging down to the ground in two plaits. the messengers told him their errand and he at once said, "Oh, yes, I can help you," and began to unplait his hair. When it was all unbraided he took it up in one hand and struck it once across the other, and the messengers felt a wind blow against their cheeks. A second time he struck his hair across his hand, and a light rain began to fall. the third time he struck his hair across his open hand there was sleet mixed with the raindrops, and when he struck the fourth time great hailstones fell upon the ground, as if they had come out from the ends of his hair. "Go back now," said the Ice Man, "and I shall be there tomorrow." So the messengers returned to their people, whom they found still gathered helplessly about the great burning pit.

The next day while they were all watching about the fire there came a wind from the north, and they were afraid, for they knew that it came from the Ice Man. But the wind only made the fire blaze up higher. Then a light rain began to fall, but the drops seemed only to make the fire hotter. Then the shower turned to a heavy rain, with sleet and hail that killed the blaze and made clouds of smoke and steam rise from the red coals. the people fled to their homes for shelter, and the storm rose to a whirlwind that drove the rain into every burning crevice and piled great hailstones over the embers, until the fire was dead and even the smoke ceased. When at last it was all over and the people returned they found a lake where the burning pit had been, and from below the water came a sound as of embers still crackling.

No one responded. They had barely escaped what could have been a tragic defeat that day. They knew they would sleep the rest of that night with a deep sense of good fortune in spite of their losses.

As Travis dozed off, he could hear the night bird calls of the signaling sentries blending in with the sounds of nature's own.

Chapter Fory
March 5, 1862

After the skirmish, things had quieted back down around the camp. And although hampered by freezing weather, early morning fogs, frequent rainstorms, and oceans of mud, Travis and the men of the Mounted Rifles probed the woods, patrolled the roads, and became a link in a defense line guarding the northern approaches to Little Rock. Meanwhile, things were happening behind the scenes that would culminate in the largest battle the Mounted Rifles would fight.

Back on Christmas Day, 1861, Major General Henry W. Halleck, Commander of the Department of the Missouri and the Department of the Mississippi, in charge of all military activities in the Western Theater, had appointed Brigadier General Samuel R. Curtis, a West Point graduate of 1831, and a veteran of the Mexican War, to be the new Federal commander of the Southwestern District of the Missouri.

On the next day Curtis left St. Louis by way of the South Pacific Railroad for Rolla, Missouri, headquarters of his new command, to fulfill the Union objective of driving the Confederates from the state of Missouri. This campaign came to be known as the Pea Ridge Campaign.

By February 16, Curtis's men had succeeded in driving the Confederates from Missouri: but, the Confederates had not been defeated. Realizing that fact and hoping to score a major victory over the Confederates, Curtis ordered his men to pursue them into Arkansas. As the month of February drew to a close, the nature of the war in Arkansas rambled on. Curtis, positive that he faced a larger force than he actually did, consolidated his approximately ten thousand troops around Elkhorn (Pea Ridge).

As a result, Jefferson Davis, President of the Confederate States of America, directed Major General Earl Van Dorn, to defeat General Curtis. In turn, General Curtis was determined to make up for Union General Fremont's recent failure in Missouri.

As a result, Colonel Stand Watie would receive orders to join the approximately 23,000 Confederates under Major General Earl Van Dorn's command that were gathering in the area near Pea Ridge, Arkansas.

In response to these and other orders, Watie and his Mounted Rifles were to abandon their Bentonville camp on March 5, and join other troops at Camp Stephens by Little Sugar Creek near Pea Ridge.

Travis and his messmates were happy to leave the Bentonville camp, since it no longer was fit for human habitation. After weeks of occupation, the site stank horribly. Pits dug for refuse were not adequate; seepage from latrines was an abomination, and in recent weeks there had arisen a serious question about the quality of the water. "We all have derangement of the bowels," Henry Watcher had complained, which the men all attributed to the water there.

Travis was in a little trance of astonishment. So they were at last going to fight again. Perhaps the next day even, there would be a battle at Pea Ridge, and he would be in it. He was having a hard time making himself believe it. He couldn't come to grips with the fact that he was about to mingle in one of the great affairs of United States history.

He had, of course, dreamed of battles all his life. As a child he had played with G.I. Joe and had scores of little green army men that had partaken in vague and bloody conflicts that had thrilled him with their sweep and fire. Contrary to Watie's army, his little army men had been equipped with a variety of weapons, mostly from World War II to the Vietnam era. They had include rifles, machine guns, submachine guns, sniper rifles, pistols, grenades, flame throwers, and bazookas. He also had radio men, minesweepers, and men armed with bayonets. His army men had also been equipped with tanks, jeeps, helmets, artillery, helicopters, jets, and fortifications. In visions he had seen himself a key player in their many battles. He had imagined civilians feeling secure in the shadow of his eagle-eyed prowess.

But once he had grown up, he had tended to regard battles as crimson blotches on the history book pages of the past. He had put them as things of the bygone with his thought-images of dragons and crowns and high castles. There was perhaps a portion of the United State's history which he had regarded as the time of wars, but it, he thought, had been long gone over the horizon and had disappeared forever.

* * *

After several chilly but pleasant days, the weather turned dismal as a late winter storm swept in. About noon on Tuesday, March 5, Stand Watie rode his horse into the middle of camp and the men were ordered to gather around. Travis was impressed with Colonel Watie and had had several opportunities to observe him in the performance of his duty and to listen to him speak to men from horseback. He thought that the commander of the Mounted Rifles looked and acted like the Confederacy's answer to Napoleon Bonaparte. Stand Watie possessed a contagious confidence and strong presence that impressed those around him.

All that Travis had remembered about Stand Watie was that he was the last general to surrender after the Civil War was over and that he had signed the Treaty of New Echota. He had since learned from Daniel that Stand Watie had practiced law and served as a sheriff in the Cherokee Nation. He had also served on the Tribal Council several years. He was a slave-owning planter that shared many values of the Old South. He had also learned more by listening to Daniel and Daniel Sr. talking during his furlough home with Daniel. Things such as, that when Albert Pike and Douglas Cooper had recruited Indian soldiers for the Confederacy in 1861, Watie had agreed to form his Cherokee Mounted Rifles cavalry unit.

To see Watie was to see his Mounted Rifles. His men trusted him, responded to his every command, and sought to acquire for themselves his grace and martial bearing. "My boys," he liked to say, as if they were his personal possessions. And somehow this pleased the men of the Mounted Rifles, for every one of them were proud brave members of Watie's command.

On that fateful day, Watie ordered his troops to leave all nonessential gear and prepare to move towards Pea Ridge to prove that they were worthwhile allies of the Confederacy. Most of Watie's cavalry did not have much stuff anyway; most carried their personal belongings in their blanket rolls with their oilcloth blanket wrapped around the roll to protect against the elements. Any other items were tied to their saddles or crammed into saddlebags. Other equipment such as cooking utensils were either lashed to wagons or to saddles and was the source of the jingling that accompanied the movement of mounted troops. An hour or so later, Travis and his comrades, forming a double column of about one thousand horsemen, moved into the woods heading in a northeasterly direction.

At the same time, Confederate Brigadier General Albert Pike was west of the Boston Mountains. He had headed his army of about 3,500 Choctaw and Chickasaw Indians towards Pea Ridge to join the other Confederates. Pike had been commissioned as a brigadier general on November 22, 1861, and given a command in the Indian Territory. With General Ben McCullough, Pike had trained three Confederate regiments of Indian cavalry.

Also headed to Pea Ridge were factions of Seminole and Creek, as well as a group of "Pin" Cherokees.

As the troops moved towards Pea Ridge, the temperature continued to drop. Sleet and snow covered the road. Progress was excruciating slow.

As he rode, Travis tried not to think too much about the upcoming battle. He forced himself to close his mind to conjecture, refusing to allow his mind to think about Yankees, waiting guns and cannon. If he allowed himself the slightest of such thoughts, it nearly froze his heart. During the battles and skirmishes he had been connected with, he had tried not to think at all. He had participated as if watching a movie, the roar of his own blood had consumed all thought and had driven him deep into the marrow dark, where he huddled in denial while another Travis loaded and fired the musket; another Travis rode Bolliver into the midst of Yankees, and waded through the resulting mess. Only afterward—when the terror was over and Travis had survived, did he dare to think again. He would look at his hands, or at Bolliver, or at the other men, and only then would he morph back into Travis Coker again. At that point, he could remember almost nothing of what he had done in the battle. The remembering came later, like a motion picture, as he was about to drift into sleep. Then he would watch as scene after scene unfolded, with himself in the staring role, and the terror and horror would return with perfect clarity and he was unable to force it to stop until the credits rolled at the end with Travis telling himself *That's not really me,* but knowing full well that it was.

So Travis went to great lengths not to think as he rode towards Pea Ridge. He recalled with clarity his drive around the Military Park on the morning of his accident. He knew that there would indeed be a battle so as he rode, he could not seem to keep from thinking about the ferocity of the impending battle no more than he could stop the beating of his heart. *I wish it was this time tomorrow or the next day or next week,* he thought.

Then a dreadful new thought entered his mind. He realized with a start that if the Civil War was going on in Arkansas, then it must be going on in Tennessee. What if everything everywhere had gone back in time? Would Melody be okay? For the first time, he wished that he had paid attention in history class about the civil war in Tennessee. Then his mind jumped back to Pea Ridge and he wished that he had read every marker on the circular drive around the Military Park. *What did I read about the Indian troops?* At the same time he was glad that he didn't remember.

Then he let a thought enter in about the Yankees that were waiting for him and immediately wished he hadn't. A line of trees blocked his immediate view for the most part, but he knew that there were homes in that area, homes with moms and dads, husbands and wives, boys and girls, innocent people like his Melody and Allie and the unborn baby. He also knew that somewhere close, very close, was the camps and rifles and sabers and cannon of the enemy. Watie had said that there was a field near the Elkhorn Tavern, and Travis knew that when the time came, there would be a good mile or more of trees and open field over which he and Bolliver would have to ride to get at the Yankees. Moreover, he knew that the Yankees had long since aimed their heavy artillery at every square inch of the field. Over there, too, were long bayonets and muskets soon to be aimed at him by men he did not know. Again, he thought about how absurd that they were men that had died over a hundred years earlier, men whose lives he could not imagine. Men, who would, if given the chance, send him straightway out of that Civil War hell to perhaps something even more terrible.

Then a new and unwelcome thought arrived in Travis's mind. There was really only one Yankee soldier that he needed to fear— the one whose every living moment since his birth had been moving him toward the moment when he would raise his musket or light the cannon or aim his pistol and drop death like a stone into the heart of Travis Joel Coker. But which one was it? For a moment, Travis stopped breathing. It was like being underwater in a lake or a dirty swimming pool, the real world was only a green circle of light too far above.

Look at you said a voice in his head, disapproving and cold, speaking from somewhere in his soul. It was a voice Travis had heard many times before; he believed that the voice belonged to the Hicks-Bahr Travis Coker with whom he had somehow swapped places and who rarely saw things as the Civil War Travis Coker did. *All worked up over something that hasn't happened yet, that might not happen at all. Get a grip on yourself. Remember, who you are, Travis. I won't have this, won't have it. Now, listen. Listen—*

Travis shut his eyes tight, *No, you don't* the other Travis demanded. *Listen.* So Travis set his heart against thoughts of his own death and of the impending battle and heard the murmur of the living, breathing men of Watie's Mounted Rifles, men he had become close to, men he had lived with and if need be, men he would die with.

Slowly, Travis began to pass out of the terror and his breathing settled into its regular rhythm. *All right,* he thought. *All right, I can stand it.* And he remembered at last the truth he'd had to remind himself of during college and at Hicks-Bahr time and again, he had always fought for what he wanted and he was strong. He had always thought that he could stand anything, even if he was uncertain about what was about to happen to him.

He touched the locket in his pocket and thought about Melody, Allie and his unborn child and knew that he would do whatever it took to enable him to survive. He decided that he would lift his musket or pistol, if and when the time came, and he would be a bold soldier for the Confederacy. He uncorked his canteen and took a long swallow, pushed the stopper back down, touched his rifle, and clicked to Bolliver to move along.

He realized that he had at last grown to appreciate the things that Grandpa had tried to teach him. He now appreciated nature and the animals that shared the earth with man. Now, instead of his mind busy with thoughts of presentations, meetings, appearances and mortgages and on and on, now his eyes happily took in the signs of the natural world. He had developed the ability to hear all of those things. He knew to be aware when the earth hushed, silencing all of its sounds, leaving him alone in the center of a wide silence with only the creak of the saddle and the clack of Bolliver's feet among the rocks.

He had learned how to give full attention to his surroundings. He was now able to read the trail as one might turn the pages of a book. He could tell how a rabbit had hurried along, running hard, for the prints of the hind feet planted far ahead of those on the front feet. He had learned to discern the reason for its rushing, for there might be signs of a coyote, his paw prints dug deeply into a bit of soft ground. Travis would continue to read the signs until both sets of prints veered suddenly into the brush.

He flicked his reins at Bolliver's ample hindquarters, feeling proud of himself. He had learned so much about so many things. Because of the war in which he was enmeshed, physically he was in the best condition of his life. He also realized that he had a whole different way of viewing things; his values had changed. Being in the war with those Cherokee men had rocked his core idea of himself. He was not the same man he was however long ago it was when he had driven his rental car out of the motel parking lot.

Huh, he thought to himself. He rarely thought about Hicks-Bahr at all anymore, and when he did, the whole corporate ladder climbing thing just didn't have the same grasp as it once did on him.

He was a changed man and he knew it. He had learned to endure amidst great odds, and he had survived. He had also learned to be a soldier; not just any soldier, but a Confederate soldier.

And more than that, Travis knew that he had become a Cherokee soldier.

As they pitched camp that evening at the place called Camp Stephens, scouts reported Curtis's army was only four miles distant. Without a doubt that meant "fighting tomorrow" to Watie's Mounted Rifles

Chapter Forty-One
March 6-7, 1862

Travis and the men of the Mounted Rifles spent only a few hours in camp that morning while Watie conferred with other Confederate commanders.

Travis wished that he could see Daniel and maybe find out what was going on. The mood around camp was quiet with a sense of preparation by the men. Many were praying, some were writing letters, and some were sleeping. At last, Colonel Watie came riding back into camp, flanked by Daniel and the other officers, bringing news that they would be facing a "boiling wasp's nest of Yankees."

"You boys get ready. Curtis's troops are dug into the bluffs further on this same creek in a field near the place called Elkhorn Tavern, where the stagecoach stops. That peavine covered ridge will be to Price's right flank, making it hard to counterattack. The Yankees will have to take the ridge to shoot down on either Price or Van Dorn. The Yankees will have Little Sugar Creek at their rear. With luck, the Federals'll be taken by surprise and not be able to get across the creek fast enough to keep from being slaughtered.

"We will ride with Colonel Sims to get on Pike's right flank between Drew and Pea Ridge."

"When do we move out?"

Colonel Watie scratched his face, then spat a black wad of tobacco. "Midnight," he said. "We're gonna move at midnight and take 'em at first light tomorrow."

The hours of the afternoon, evening and night, crawled by—leadenly, as far as the men were concerned. Travis felt a creeping chill which was not born of the snow that was falling or the wind. He had heard it said, "give a soldier enough to eat and he is satisfied." By and large during the time he had spent with the Mounted Rifles, he had had plenty to eat, but he had not been truly happy. He would think of his home, and loved ones, and of the comforts that he had enjoyed. That day, he made up his mind once and for all, that if he ever made it back somehow to the twenty-first century, he would look at things so differently. He decided that he would resign from Hicks-Bahr and figure out some other job to do so that he could work regular hours. He also confirmed to himself again that one thing he had learned for sure was that God, family and home was what he intended to stake his life and his family's lives on. That the good news of Jesus would hold the meaning and purpose of his life.

He also knew that if he ever got back, he would be going to pow wows with his grandpa, and take Allie to her first pow wow, *What a cute little jingle or shawl dancer she would be.* Those things would be first in his life. He wanted to fish and hike and kiss Melody and love her. He wanted to appreciate his parents while they were still in good health. He wanted to buy horses and ride and teach Allie and Melody to ride. He wanted to go to church every week and have Allie grow up loving Jesus.

During the past few months, he had become a changed man. Hungrily he had listened to the wisdom of Grandfather Richard and he knew that he was ready to listen to the wisdom of Grandpa.

I want to go home. I want another chance.

About ten o'clock, p.m., the order came to get ready. Throughout the cluttered sprawl of camp, men were beginning to rise stiffly to their feet as if some unseen herald had passed among them. Talk was growing thin, and there was little laughter. Some were already absorbed in the arrangement of their clothing, tugging at crotches and galluses, buttoning and unbuttoning and rebuttoning their coats. Some men painted their faces and were wearing turbans in the way of the early Cherokee as they had prepared for battle. After this came the drawing-on of accessories, accompanied by the clatter of cups and kettles and canteens and frying pans hung on blanket rolls that had wisely not been left behind, and no little cussing and grunting and tightening the saddles on the wooly horses. Travis, with his secret knowledge of the Battle of Pea Ridge, knew that there was nothing chivalric or grand about any of it, any more than the saddling of a horse was ever chivalric or grand—except that the men were preparing for battle, many of whom would soon be torn, eviscerated, or blown into a fine red mist before the muzzles of the Yankee guns. With that as a distinct possibility, he thought that even the buttoning of a man's fly assumed all the dignity of a final act.

Shortly before midnight the cavalry moved out, leaving their small cooking fires burning to deceive the Yankees. The road was filled with men, horses, mules and artillery, all slogging purposefully forward. They composed an army roused out without sleep, on the move toward another army holed in behind breastworks and waiting. And over all was the bitter cold and spitting snow of early March which served to bring about shivering and exhaustion in man and animal. The freezing column
"You men—over there—close up." Sam, hardly distinguished as an officer from the men he rode among, waved them to tighten the ranks. And so on they rode; knowing that less than three miles down the road they would ride into the teeth of a storm so fierce there would be no way out. Meanwhile, the Yankees had been felling trees to slow down the Confederate advance, in an effort to give General Curtis time to deploy his army and carry the fight to the Rebels. Two times, the Mounted Rifles encountered enormous tangles of felled trees. Without firing a single shot, the Yankees had struck a serious blow as the Rebels wasted precious time and energy in struggling to clear the road.
They made their way through the dark until the combined Confederate force emerged from the woods early the next morning, finding that they faced an entrenched Union position.
"We took too long getting here, may as well retreat." Sawblade said.
Just then Daniel rode up hard, his lathered horse steaming in the cold.
"We're not retreating," he snapped at Sawblade. "Listen up. Hear that? Gunfire." From the direction of the Elkhorn Tavern to the east came sporadic fire.
"That's where the real battle is. You men snap to and look sharp. We're gonna head for the Elkhorn Tavern. Gallop your men, Sam. We will succeed today!" Giving a quick "Be safe," and a wink and an affirming nod to Travis, Daniel turned and galloped off.
During the night the enemy had thrown together breastworks on the ridge, weaving together axed trees, timbers torn out of the abandoned houses of Leetown, anything the Union officers could commandeer for such use. And between that improvised

fortification and the cover in which Sam's men waited was a section of open ground. Where the Mounted Rifles were stationed, there must have stretched about three hundred yards of that open field, Travis estimated, and the woods bordering it on his side were so thin that any charge would take them into plain sight for five hundred yards of approach.

Fieldpieces, brought into line on the woods side, hidden above by the breastworks, opened up in a dull pom-pom duel. Travis saw a shell strike the earth not far away, bounce twice, still intact, and roll on toward the Confederate lines.

The whiz-whiz of the minies had not yet begun. And the waiting was the hardest part of all. Travis tried to pin all his powers of concentration on a study of the ground immediately before him, the slope up which they would have to win in order to have it out with the brush-hidden enemy. It was becoming daylight so that concealment was mostly gone.

Travis made himself calculate just which path to take when the orders to charge came. His pistol and his musket were loaded, and the pistol was in his hand. He glanced around. In the fields were Union batteries under Colonel Cyrus Bussey that would open fire when they spotted the galloping Confederate cavalry.

Then, slowly at first, the Mounted Rifles were on the move. The sun was then fully up, shining directly into their faces. But in spite of the glare, they could still see the Union works and the flash of guns along it. Then, under Sam's orders, they were moving faster, breaking out of a trot and into a lope.

Then came the Cherokee Rebel yell. Their lope quickened. Horses were running then, forming a great wave to get at the Yankees. The riders in Travis's line did not know—or care—that they were moving without the promised support of the other Confederates, they had no way of knowing that they were participants in a battle plan already too broken to mend. All they cared about was the galloping charge, the weapons in their hands, and the enemy waiting under the frozen morning sun.

Travis never remembered much afterward of that splendid useless charge except as confusion. He could not have told just when they were caught in a murderous crossfire which poured canister at their undefended flanks. A horse and man went down before him. Stumbling, Bolliver caught his foot against the writhing body, tripped and pitched head forward, knocking the breath out of Travis. For a moment or two the combination of trying to stay mounted and not being able to catch his breath caused Travis to panic as the world turned red and black.

Then Bolliver was up again, just in time for Travis to realize foggily that the Yankees were ripping at their flanks, that their charge was pocketed by lead and steel, being wiped out. He raised his pistol, tried to find some target, then fired feverishly without one, the gun's recoil sending shockwaves of fear through his whole being.

The first wave of riders had great gaps torn in its length. But those remaining still galloped ahead, screaming their defiance. Men faltered, the fire was breaking them, crumpling up the lines. All the Union might seemed concentrated in a lead-and-canister hail on the remnants of the brigade, turning the field into a holocaust in which nothing human or equine could continue to advance.

But Travis's group came on steadily from the trees, racing, yelling, steadfast in their determination to storm the Yankees. They were wild men, with no thought of personal safety. Travis caught a glimpse of Ihaveseen riding without stirrups, his right hand with a tight grip on the pole of the Cherokee Braves flag, its red and blue folds fluttering in the air.

Where is Watie? Travis wondered for a moment. *I thought Daniel said that Stand Watie never ordered a charge that he did not lead.* Where Watie or Pike or Van Dorn or any others of the Confederate contingent had vanished—he did not know. He jammed his now empty Colt into its holster, still not wholly aware that the breastworks were too far away for small arms fire to have any effect.

Just then the whole world was no larger than that stretch of open field and the breastworks on the ridge, the men in blue ahead of them. The Yankee fire still withered the galloping Mounted Rifles, curling them up as the freezing temperatures had withered and curled the leaves on the shrubs by Little Sugar Creek.

But they could not reach that ridge—except singly, or in twos and threes, then only to fall. And the waves of men no longer broke from the woods to lap up and recede sullenly down the slope. Out of nowhere, just as they fell back to the first fringe of trees, came Sam on his tall speckled horse. His sergeant's coat was gone, he rode in his shirt sleeves, and a bullet-torn tatter waved from one wide shoulder. Above his prominent cheekbones, his eyes were hot and bright, his jaw grimly set, his face was flushed, and his energy and will was like a cloud to engulf the disheartened men as he bore down upon them.

His galloped through the shattered groups of Mounted Rifles. The men were fast disintegrating into a mob as the realization of their failure in the field began to strike home. Sighting their Sergeant Sam, they followed his route with a rising wave of cheers—cheers which even though they came from dry throats rose in force and violence to that inarticulate Cherokee Rebel Yell which had earlier raised them past all fear into the field.

From his saddle, Ihaveseen whirled the Cherokee Braves flag aloft and around his head. Its scarlet length and blue field with white stars surrounding the red stars of the Five Civilized Tribes—the larger red star representing the Cherokees, made a tossing splotch of color, to hold and draw the men's eyes.

They were pulled together about Ihaveseen and his waving standard. Lines tightened, death-made gaps closed. They steadied, again a fighting cavalry and not a crowd of horsemen facing defeat. Yet Sam halted his men. He seemed furiously angry—not with them, Travis sensed—but with someone or something beyond the horsemen crowding about him.

With the Mounted Rifles halted, Sam took a minute to study the field, and reported that things didn't look good.

Travis's unit believed that Watie's main column of attack was moving up behind them at the proper interval and were expecting to see them ready for the grapple: but where were they?-- nowhere within sight or sound. Sam had the men dismount and hunker down close to the ground under the enemy's guns. As the sun rose higher, they began to shoot into the embrasures where the Yankees were working their guns. That distracted somewhat the fire of the enemy and diverted attention from the exposed unit. However, if it continued, they would be cut down by the Yankee artillery. There was only one hope for survival. Retreat. Retreat to the wooded area on the north side of the road.

"Retreat!" Sam bellowed, his voice faint in the roar of musket and cannon. His Cherokee Mounted Rifles readily obeyed, and mounted their horses, but Travis's heart leaped to his throat when he saw rank upon rank of men, both on foot and mounted, waiting in the trees where the Mounted Rifles were to seek refuge.

Too late. It was too late for Sam to issue any other command that would not get all his men killed. They charged, galloping headlong into the woods along the north side of the Bentonville Road.

Chapter Forty-Two
Martch 7, 1862

"Hold your fire," Stand Watie shouted to his men from the trees. "Don't fire." As Sam's men were retreating, they were firing at everyone having on a blue coat. This placed Watie and the other men in considerable danger because a number of the Rebel men without uniforms, including Van Dorn himself, were wearing blue.

Somehow, Travis and the rest of Sam's men had become separated from the remainder of the men when the Mounted Rifles had come through the woods and seen the Union batteries forming in the field. When the Mounted Rifles grouped for attack, there had been some confusion and Sam's men had cut away from the remainder. It had come as a complete surprise to Watie when he saw Sam's unit galloping down the road and past the deadly Yankee artillery.

"Watie!" cried Sam, recognizing friendly faces in the woods. From the field, Travis could hear the deadly musket balls and occasional cannon fire. The Yankees apparently had been as startled by Sam's charge as Watie.

"Get to cover or they'll shoot you in the back!" General Pike yelled. His brigade tramped past the Mounted Rifles, dropped to their bellies and prepared to fire across the field where Watie had intended to launch his attack. The general joined Sims, Watie, Sam and Daniel.

"What a complete disaster," Sam said. "We're lucky we didn't get killed."

"You are lucky," said Watie, angry that his men had become separated.

The men were confused as to the mystery of how the troops had become separated, and one of three things could be the only solution. The main column had either gone in another direction from Travis's own, or it had not started when the signal was given, or it had started, and when the enemy opened fire, had retreated. Sam's opinion was that it was more likely that some delay had occurred in the start and that the main column did not move up so rapidly as the storming party. The result was that the delay was seriously felt both by the advanced party and by the main column itself in the form of the shelling that had rained down from all the guns of the enemy, direct and cross fire, covering the entire field.

"We're in a real pucker." Pike barked. "We weren't expecting Curtis to be on us so quick-like."

Pike stuck a cigar in his mouth, lit it and continued to fume. "Watie, what do you think?"

"Well, they've got a three-gun battery. But I allow that we have to hold the road."

Albert Pike stamped his feet and placed his hands under his arms to warm them as he stared off into the distance. "Hmmm."

Watie continued, "If they take the road, Van Dorn's force'll be divided. We have to hold it."

"Hmmm. Let me think what in the Sam Hill we're gonna do." Pike studied the length of road, rubbed his eyes, and then began scrawling orders. He stabbed the paper into a soldier's hand, saying, "Give this to the brigade commander east of us. He's to divert the Yankees with a charge while we take the artillery battery."

The man hurried off while Watie and Pike conferred further out of Travis's earshot.

The troops hunkered down on their haunches; and as soldiers everywhere so often have to do, they waited.

They waited for the weather to get better, for the wind to die down, for something to happen so they didn't have to think about how miserable it was to live with the waiting.

At last Watie gave the orders. "We're gonna move out and capture that battery yonder and turn the cannon back on the Yankees down near Little Sugar Creek. If we are unable to do that, we will blow the cannon up and get out of there. I don't want any Cherokee blood shed because of any Yankee six-pounders."

Travis could see that the diversion was already moving into the field to the east.

Stand Watie called, "Sam, move 'em out now. For glory!"

The men galloped to the attack, and Watie immediately saw the trouble that posed. He had pulled the fire from the cannon down on his own men. Cannonballs slashing through his ranks, he found his attack blunted and drifting west, away from the support of Pike and the others in the brigade.

"Dismount. Take cover," Watie ordered when he saw his men being picked out of their saddles by Federal snipers. "If it's to be a fight, let us fight to the bitter end. Horse holders, let the animals go and assume a position on the line."

Travis jumped off of Bolliver, stumbled along, and finally skidded to a halt on his belly, letting Bolliver run free. His breath came fast, and he wondered if his heart might explode in his chest. He looked around for Bolliver, afraid that he would lose him, for there was no one in the world with more claim to the ugly gelding than Travis.

Looking around, he saw that many of his regiment had taken cover in the gully cut through the field. It was shallow groove, hardly more than surface erosion, but enough to provide some small cover. He drew his pistol and chanced a look over the rim of the gully.

"Attack, men, attack." shouted Watie. It might be the only way any of them left the field alive that day. Whooping like a brave on the warpath, Stand Watie led his men forward on foot, firing the best they could at the fortified positions to the south.

"Yahhhh-aww-wha—" There were no words in that, just the war cry which might have torn from any Indian warrior's throat, but which came instead from between Travis's lips: the famous Rebel yell done the Cherokee way with all its yip of victory as only a Cherokee could deliver it. Then they were rushing, yelping in an answering chorus, four and five abreast, through the field and under the dead limbs of the trees.

Ahead loomed the three cannon, belching forth their murderous devices, the very object of their attack. The enemy's fire grew hotter. The bullets began to come and Watie's men were falling, yet they pressed on, realizing that the nearer they could get the more likely were the shots of the enemy to pass over their heads. Reaching the outer margin of the field that fringed their cannon, Watie halted his party to take a breath before the final assault. The Yankee sharpshooters were very attentive and cut the brush away all around with bullets and tore up the ground some; but their range was long and their fire was not very accurate.

Watie's men then noticed an entire Federal company retreating across the battlefield. They sank down and shot down one Yankee soldier after another, routing the company and sending the enemy away in confusion as extreme as that which earlier had stalked their own ranks.

Somehow, through the tumult, Watie realized the diversion had worked. The Mounted Rifles and Sim's Texans had swarmed over the Union battlements. "The cannon!" Watie yelled. "Get those cannon, men!"

But just then Yankee bullets begin to fly. It was a Union counterattack of gigantic proportions. If Watie didn't order his men to retreat, the position would be overrun by the Yankees in a few minutes.

"Swing the guns around!" Watie called. "Aim 'em right on down their throats!" Travis put his hands on the carriage of the cannon, careful because the barrels were still hot from being fired. As soon as the guns were aimed in the direction of the advancing Yankee infantry, Watie himself grabbed a swab and applied it to the barrel to cool the metal. As he worked, so did three others of his cavalry who had some knowledge of the firing of cannon. Gunpowder and wadding and ball were rammed down the cannon barrel while another man prepared the lanyard that would fire the piece.

"Clear out," Watie yelled. Travis clapped his hands over his ears and turned from the cannon. The cord tautened and the cannon bucked hard and spewed out its load of death into the center of the Union infantry. "Keep firing" Watie yelled, as his men began readying the other two guns.

Watie wanted to order his men out of the artillery nest, but if he did so hundreds of Rebel soldiers would die. The Mounted Rifles were in a real fix. To stay tempted death. To leave meant death for even more Confederates.

Watie kept his men at their post long enough for Sims and Drew to get off the field. Ihaveseen was there with the Cherokee Braves flag. He had been shot through the muscles of his chest and shoulder. His last military service was to stick the flag pole into the ground beside the cannon. Travis could see dead men everywhere,—and blood-soaked brown, gray and yellow predominated in uniform color. But the three Yankee guns turned on their former masters had created confusion in the Union ranks long enough to give Albert Pike the chance to regroup and retreat northeast toward the Elkhorn Tavern.

At last, when Watie saw that Pike and his men were out of danger, Watie ordered the cannon blown up with the remaining powder.

"Back to the woods!" he bellowed, "Mount up and let's get outta here." It seemed like everybody was able to recapture their horses and get into the saddle. Many offered a stirrup to others to get on behind them, save Travis and Osprey, who ran to find their horses.

For some reason, Osprey went back towards the destroyed cannon while Travis turned and ran towards the trees, looking for Bolliver. Desperate to find his own mount, Travis walked further into the woods, his fear pushing him further and further away from the Mounted Rifles. *Bolliver*, he yelled in his mind, tears clouding his vision.

Somewhere among smoke and confusion and broken units and scrambled companies of survivors he must find Bolliver. He walked through the trees, fighting thirst, weariness, and the shaking reaction from the past few hours, afraid to allow himself to think what—or who—might still lie up on the peavine covered ridge under the frozen sky.

Boll-i-ver!

He paused near a dead hickory tree that had long-since been burned and split by lightning. He steadied himself against its peeling bark and turned his head with caution, fearing to be downed by the vertigo which seemed to strike in waves ever since he had retreated to the cover of the woods. He just wanted to find his horse and join up with the men. *Where are they?* He walked again, slowly, feeling oddly detached. His hand went clumsily to his mouth as he retched dryly. *Bolliver!* He soundlessly screamed.

He stumbled along, looking back to see only gray smoke drifting among the trees and hanging low to the ground. He turned in a circle; *which way are the men? Bolliver!* Shakily, he drew his pistol, praying that he could find Bolliver and mount before they both either got killed or captured. Bolliver had been loyal to him, and he wouldn't leave him.

At last Travis stopped beside a strong-running creek filled with round rocks. The woods rose black all around. He turned; heading up the creek, or was it down the creek? He had no idea; all he knew was that he was filled with fear. He was lost, lost in the damnable war and had no idea of what to do.

There, there ahead was the camp. Through the trees he could see a distant splotch of red and yellow—a fire. He could smell bacon frying. Travis shifted his feet forward, trying to walk faster. He felt as if he were striving to move a body as heavy and as inert as that of an unconscious man. It took so long even to raise his hand in greeting and he stepped carefully to keep his unsteadiness under control.

Travis started to jog to where the men were cooking in a pot hanging from an iron tripod. The men sprawled in their uniforms on ground cloths, their saddles and blankets serving as backrests.

"Well, well," one of them said, rising to his feet. He reached down and took a rifle from another man that also was starting to get up off the ground.

"Well, half-breed Rebel boy, are you lost?"

By the time Watie's regiment reached Cincinnati, Arkansas, guarding Albert Pike's rear the whole way, word came that Van Dorn's army had lost eleven hundred killed, twenty-five hundred wounded, and another sixteen hundred captured or missing.

But Stand Watie's Cherokee Mounted Rifles had gotten away—if not intact, then at least with most of its men still in the saddle.

One man, however, would be listed as missing ...

... Travis Joel Coker.

Chapter Forty-Three
March 7, 2002

Travis stopped, realizing that it was not Mounted Rifles cooking their supper, but Yankees. He stood frozen in time it seemed when suddenly something came hurtling down at him. It was the butt of a rifle swung by the soldier in the blue Yankee uniform. It struck him full on the head. Travis heard the crunch of bone splintering from that terrible blow that had hit him like a lightning bolt. His eyes blurred and filled with tears as he staggered back. Somehow, he did not fall, but continued on, his hands pressed to his face. Someone, Travis did not know who, reached out and supported him, keeping him from falling, until Travis was unable to stand any more and slumped to the ground as things started to spin around him.

As he fell, with both eyes open and as if in slow motion, Travis again saw the Yankee's face, saw him again lift his rifle, and felt the unbearable pain in his head. He felt like he was floating. He could feel his body beginning to tilt backward, yet he did not fall.

Soon he found himself in the lying down position and could suddenly feel something supporting his body. Sounds began to form in his ears and suddenly he recognized his wife's voice.

"Yeah, I've been feeling really good. Getting bigger."

He opened his eyes and he could see his wife talking on her cell phone.

"Yeah. Mm-mmm. Travis's parents left yesterday. They brought Allie to see me for her birthday. She's two now. Yeah. It was really nice having 'em here."

Travis blinked and looked around. He was in a bed...no a hospital bed in a hospital room.

Melody continued, "Oh, and my parents are flying out in a couple of weeks. Then, I think I am gonna go ahead and have Travis flown to a convalescent hospital in Chattanooga."

Melody? He tried to speak but something in his mouth made the words not come out.

"I want to have him all settled in Tennessee before the end of my pregnancy."

Desperate, he mouthed the words, *Is that you? What happened, where am I?*

Melody kept talking. Travis looked around at the nicely kept hospital room and noticed there were beautiful flowers on the table near his bed. Scrawled crayon drawings were hung here and there on the walls. Allie's favorite teddy bear sat on the shelf beside the television.

"Yeah." He could see his wife nodding as she listened to the person on the other end of the call. He tried to sit up, but something tugged at him. He looked down and could see an IV tube stuck in his arm.

From the corner of her eye, Melody saw movement and dropped her phone. "Travis?" Melody starting crying, rang for the nurse and grabbed her husband's hand.

He was home.

Chapter Forty-Four

Travis had emerged from his coma on Thursday, March 7, 2002, a hundred and forty years after the Battle of Pea Ridge. The doctor had questioned him by asking things such as "What year is it?" and "Who is the president of the United States?" to which Travis had replied "1862" and "Depends, it's either Jefferson Davis or Abraham Lincoln." The doctors had explained that away after Travis told them that before the car accident he had visited the Pea Ridge Military Park. They said that he had apparently dwelled on the Civil War during the coma.

The doctors had examined him from head to toe, surprised at how his muscles had not atrophied from lack of use. Travis was greatly frustrated that they didn't believe anything he had been trying to explain, so one morning he surprised them all, especially Melody, by answering all of the doctors' questions in Cherokee.

Melody had explained that Travis could not speak Cherokee. The doctors, always quick with an answer, had said that in Europe on at least two occasions, coma patients had awoken with the ability to speak a foreign language and were able to accurately describe the place they said they had visited.

The doctors had smiled and said that that too, with time and therapy, could be dealt with or explained.

Melody told Travis that Discount America had put $25,000.00 into a special bank account for him. In addition, the man in the yellow pickup truck's insurance had settled for five million dollars. She also said that Hicks-Bahr had continued to deposit his full salary into their joint account in Tennessee and that the company's accident insurance had paid the sum of $482,000.00. Their personal mortgage insurance had paid off the house. In other words, he was finally wealthy. His dream had been accomplished, although it didn't please him like he had thought it would.

Nights in the hospital he would dream about the war and wake up in a cold sweat. His biggest fear was waking up and being in the past again. He was so happy to be back home but was also pleased with his memories of Daniel and Richard and the visit to Cookson. Real or not, the memories seemed real.

Melody got a phone call from Travis's mom, after which she told Travis that Red Vernon's wife had been very ill and that Heavenly Red's would soon be closing. Immediately he told her to get hold of Red and tell him that he would buy the joint if Red and his staff would run it. He also told Melody that if Red was agreeable to such a deal, then to call his dad's office and have him buy the barbecue place.

While Melody was on the phone, he lay in his hospital bed and thought about all the times he had eaten at Heavenly Red's in his life. Cowan just would never be the same if it were to close. He thought about the time back in high school when his football team had lost the state championship. Two days later, the coach took the whole team to Heavenly Red's for specials and milkshakes. Red had even made a large cake in the team's honor for dessert. He then refused to let the coach pay for the meal, saying that the boys deserved the treat. Red had then gone around and shook each player's hand, telling them how proud he was of them.

Travis thought about the special and his mouth watered. A large barbecue beef sandwich, served with fries and coleslaw and topped off with two big homemade onion rings; he knew he had to get one just as soon as he got back to Tennessee.

Later, Melody came back and said that the deal was in the works at his dad's law office and that Red was very grateful. Then Travis told Melody that he planned on quitting his job with Hicks-Bahr and that he wanted to buy horses.

His parents had flown into Arkansas the day after he awoke and his dad told him that Grandpa had died a month or so before, and that he had left his farm and house to Travis. Travis said that he would keep it up so that Allie and the new baby could enjoy it as he had.

After ten days, Travis was dismissed from the hospital. Before they left for the airport, he had insisted and persisted against Melody's protests that they drive her rental car through downtown Bentonville and then out to the Pea Ridge Military Park. Melody had held his hand and cried as he walked around the park for over an hour, remembering.

As he read one of the commemorative markers at the battlefield, he thought about Watie, Daniel, Sawblade and Tommy. He thought about the Yankees and the sound of the cannon and the screams of dying horses and dying men. The marker was inadequate at telling the story, for what Travis saw was not a quiet field, but a battlefield filled with a chaotic mass of men and horses. Men choked by smoke and plagued by poor weapons.

Later, he had asked Melody to pull the car over by the side of the highway where Travis got out of the car and sat perched on the fence bordering a pasture in which a brown gelding calmly stood. Although the horse was smaller and better looking than Bolliver, Travis was deeply touched by the horse's choice to stand inches from him, periodically dipping his head down near Travis's leg and letting him scratch the tender spot between his ears. The serene and gentle image was not very different from the many that Travis had experienced with Bolliver. Travis had learned that having a horse can be one of the most rewarding blessings in life.

Travis was home and before he knew it, he was adjusting once more to the patterns of modern life. Gradually he became more or less accepting of the fact that perhaps during the coma he *had* dreamed the whole thing about being in the civil war.

He was up in the mornings with Melody and Allie, and after supper each night, as she had always done, Melody read the Bible aloud. To Travis, listening with an attention he had never given before, the stories were vividly remindful of his life before, during and after his coma. He understood the words in a way he never had before. Indeed, the hand of God was in it all. What he couldn't figure out though, was whether God's hand was there to guide, or was it there to witness with sadness the actions of the beings He had created? He also thought about how the crimes of man had never really changed. Throughout the Bible there were stories of murder and betrayal, of war and rumors of war. The Biblical times were not so different than the 1860's or 2002 after all.

He tried to talk to Melody about his experiences, and to her credit, she did listen, albeit with raised eyebrows. Sometimes it was obvious that she wanted to ask more, but Travis felt that she wouldn't be able to comprehend it all. Even so, he couldn't help uttering portions of the memories that plagued him, just as he couldn't help keeping other things hidden. He hoped that time would bring it all out. His story needed time to unfold, and Travis wished nothing more than a long lifetime to tell it slowly, to heal himself with his family.

Chapter Forty-Five

After he was home for a time, his mother called and had him come over. His dad was waiting for him in the study.

"I have a letter for you." He handed Travis an envelope. "I'll leave you alone now." His father kissed his forehead and closed the door.

Travis sniffed the cheap white envelope, breathing in the smell of tobacco, before he unsealed it.

My dear Travis,

When you read this letter, I know that deep down you'll be mad at me for playing this dirty trick on you. I am over 70 years old and they told me I have cancer. I write this letter because I don't think I will live until you are well again and come home from Arkansas. I write this to tell you a few things and tell you how much I love you, my grandson.

My soul has flown away, carried up high by the Creator. Life is good, Travis, but sometimes it's only when you step back from it that you see how wonderful it is. So you must remember to hold it close every day.

I have respected your decision to not be proud of your Cherokee blood. It makes me sad. When you were a boy, you were a Cherokee boy. You were not like other boys. I've seen you fall and get up with your teeth clenched, when other boys would have cried and given up. That courage is your strength, but it also can be your weakness. You must give in order to receive. Strength and courage can be turned against you if you don't make proper use of them. Perhaps you learned this during your long sleep in Arkansas.

I won't be around to guide you. The time has come for you to become the man that I always saw.

On the long journey ahead of you, never lose your Cherokee soul. Never forget your roots, because roots are what will perfume your existence; the memories of the past will be the scent that makes you want to get up and discover each new morning.

Remember the story of Sitting Bull, a bull buffalo sits on top of a hill, not because he is tired, not because he has given up, but because he looks where he has been. On top of the hill, he can look back on the past. Then, he can look forward to the future.

It is good to stop and take stock of our lives, to look back and ask, "What have I learned? How can I use this knowledge to go forward?" So like the buffalo, sit and see what surrounds you. I have watched you and see that you go in and out of your house every day. You don't notice that I watch you because you have been in a world of your own, anxious to get to work on time. You think about the traffic, you think about the day ahead. You think about what you will do when you get to your fancy office. Sit down, Travis. Sit down and see the world around you.

Now that you are back from Arkansas, you are at the top of the hill. Be the buffalo, my boy. The bull buffalo is the leader of his herd. He is strong. He is responsible for the safety of his herd. He looks back and he looks ahead. He looks to those that went before him. He follows the ancient paths to the best grazing. Travis, our lives become more meaningful when we remember those who went before us.

My precious grandson, I know that you remember the ways that I taught you. You know the stories of those that came before. Always trust your instincts, trust your conscience and your feelings. Live your life to the full. You are responsible for yourself and for those you love. Live up to that responsibility; never lose that look you had in your eyes when we greeted the dawn together when you were a boy. At night when I close my eyes, I remember you dancing in the pow wow. You must get that look in your eye again. Trust in the magic. The most important thing I gave you is your sense of wonder. Don't ever lose it.

I leave you my rattle and fan, and my gourd dance blanket. Dance, Travis. Only you know that you have fought in a war and you have won.

My sweet young man, I must leave you; hold on tight to this beautiful Mother Earth of ours. I love you, you were my everything, but I'm leaving with my mind at rest. I'm so proud of you.

Grandpa

Travis folded the letter and put it in his pocket.

He left the room with a firm step, as Grandpa had always taught him.

Chapter Forty-Six

Travis resigned from Hicks-Bahr and signed on to be a substitute teacher in the Franklin County School District. He also volunteered his time at a therapeutic riding center that offered a horseback riding program for children and adults with mental and physical disabilities. He enjoyed helping the students learn the fundamentals of riding a horse, as well as the basics of grooming and caring for the horse. He also spent some time each day by helping out down at Heavenly Reds, and by fishing and walking in the woods. He started having a barn built, intending to soon buy some horses of his own.

Melody was very happy. She had her husband back and she had the new baby, a boy that they named Ben Joseph Coker. Also, from his first week back home, Travis had started going to church, even on Wednesday nights. He went to pow wows and other Native American events and began teaching Allie about her heritage.

He was tortured by the discomfort of having to pretend that it had all been a dream, a horrible nightmare that had never happened. He had to pretend that perhaps Melody and the doctors were right, it had never happened. He had been in a coma and that was it. No one took him seriously; adamant that since he had visited the military park right before the accident, the Civil War had been what he had focused on during the entire coma.

But something in him resisted pretending. Otherwise, how could he know so many intimate details about Richard, Daniel, Sawblade, Watie, and all of the others? What about his new-found appreciation of his Cherokee heritage or for that matter, the fact that he could speak the language? At night, he could close his eyes and vividly recall the taste of dirty water from his canteen, the smell of horse sweat and the feel of his wool blanket against his cheek. He was familiar with the taste of jerky and foul coffee and hardtack. In his mind, he went through the steps necessary for loading, priming and firing a musket. He could hear the screams and moans of wounded and dying men. He then would think about the field hospital and be horrified at the possibility that he might "slip through" again into the past.

He was terrified on the day that Melody ran across the bag from the hospital that contained his belongings and the cut-up clothing he had been wearing the day of the car accident. She was going through the bag, throwing things away when she found the locket. She asked him if he had bought it at an antique shop in Arkansas. He thought he was going to pass out when she walked over and showed him the tin type photos of the woman and baby girl. He stammered an answer of something to the effect that he had indeed purchased the locket in Bentonville.

One evening after supper, after listening to Melody read a story to Allie, and after a time spent talking intimately with her, Travis went to bed, expecting to sink into sleep. Instead, he lay awake for endless hours; checking the clock at one a.m., at three a.m., and at four-thirty a.m., until the first light of the sun shined through the bedroom window.

He got out of bed early and drove into Winchester to the big library over there. The librarian helped him find the right book with the right records. Sitting alone at one of the smaller tables, he ran his finger down the page until he found what he was looking for under the heading of "Stand Watie's Cherokee Mounted Rifles:"

Private Travis Joel Coker, Tennessee, * Mustered in on *Unknown. * Missing in action at Pea Ridge, Arkansas on March 7, 1862.

Epilogue
June 6, 2002

After kissing Melody, Allie and Ben goodbye, Travis jumped into the Hummer and started driving into Cowan. Turning on the county road, he took a sip of coffee from his faded, red Hicks-Bahr insulated travel mug. There was no traffic.

Rounding a curve, he dropped the coffee at the sight of a large battered gelding calmly eating the tall grass by the road. Travis slammed on the brakes and swerved the Hummer into the ditch.

The horse was a homely creature. He was tall and bony, with a long face, a Roman nose, high withers with old scars dotting the landscape of his common brown hair. Big, football-like feet completed the package.

You're crazy, he told himself. He sat there, sweating and unable to move. The gelding eyed him and continued to munch the grass. The tall, ugly horse had an old leather halter which was attached to a short piece of rope.

Finally, he stepped out of the Hummer and approached the horse.

"Hey there."

The horse raised his head, eyed the man and continued to chew.

Travis held out his hand. "Come on, I, I ..."

Instead of touching the horse, he moved around to the horse's near side. There, on the left shoulder was a botched brand mark, "US."

The horse turned its head and butted Travis on the arm.

He stood stock still before reaching up and running a hand under the tangled mane. His other hand went into his pocket, opening and closing on an old gold locket, open, close, open, close ...

They stood there and Travis sometimes spoke to the horse in a low whisper, repeating a word in the Cherokee language, a word that the horse knew and was comforted by.

He then turned and started walking back down the road towards home. When he looked over his shoulder, he saw that the horse was following.

They moved through the warm sunlight, while the blue jays laughed in the woods.

Home ....

* * *

Additional information about Brigadier General Stand Watie, as well as photographs of the Pea Ridge Military Park, old photos of the Eagle Hotel, the Elkhorn Tavern and many others, are located on the author's website:

http://www.anniesbook.com

Author's Note

The preceding is fiction. With the exception of some of the Ratliff's, some of the Coker's, Stand Watie (his name is pronounced "weighty."), the Cherokee Mounted Rifles and the officers named in the story, all of the characters are fictitious. What is not fictional is the involvement of the Cherokee Nation in the Civil War.

Most Cherokees did not have slaves and lived simple lives caring less about the white man's war, while some of the wealthy, mixed-blood minority favored the South. Therefore, when Federal soldiers withdrew in the summer of 1861 and the Confederate army occupied Indian Territory, the Cherokee Nation voted to secede from the United States. A formal treaty, between the Cherokees and the new Confederate government would cost the Cherokees dearly at war's end. Some three thousand Cherokees enlisted in the Confederate army and about a thousand fought for the United States. They fought in a few battles in Missouri and Arkansas. The Cherokee Nation lost more than one third of its population. No state, north or south, came close to this.

In my research, I drew upon sources of the region around my home in Northwest Arkansas which is located on Little Sugar Creek. Camp Stephens was located at the turnoff of Sugar Creek Road and Highway 72. Our farm is located about five miles from the Pea Ridge Military Park and site of the actual battle. I am a Coker by blood and a distant cousin of Daniel Ratliff Jr., the grandson of Richard Ratliff and a great-grandson of Chlet Pathkiller.

The battle of Pea Ridge, fought March 6-8, 1862, is a seldom-publicized battle theater. However, it was one of the fiercest and decisive battles fought west of the Mississippi during the Civil War. Over 26,000 soldiers struggled for two days in Northwest Arkansas in the battle that would decide the fate of Missouri. But why was Missouri so important that so many men would risk their lives for it? Control of Missouri was the key to winning the war in the West. Military strategists, both North and South, were fully aware of this. Missouri provided an easy invasion route either north or south and controlled the Mississippi, Missouri, and Ohio Rivers. It had abundant natural resources, especially lead and iron ore, a large military-aged population and was the home of the Saint Louis Arsenal, with a stockpile of over 60,000 muskets.

This book was written to make the reader aware of the reality of soldier's life in the Civil War by presenting some of the little details of a Cherokee soldier's typical experiences, as well as provide a little education about Brigadier General Stand Watie and his Cherokee Mounted Rifles. It was my hope to portray the Confederate soldiers in this book as human beings making the best of often horrendous circumstances. Most importantly, I wanted to remind myself and my readers about our priorities. We all get so caught up sometimes in day-today life, our jobs, earning money, paying bills and the like, that we forget sometimes how precious our family, our heritage, our culture and most of all our Savior are to us.

From these pages emerges a portrait of a man being tested, developing skills of adaptation and endurance. Travis Coker was an unwitting participant, who evolved into a soldier and survived, and came away with a greater sense of himself and others, and a greater appreciation for the simple pleasures of life. As Travis learned these lessons, let us each take a moment to look at our own priorities. If just one person does so, then this book has succeeded.

Wado,
Kathy Lynn "Sonseeahray"

Research material used in writing this book.

- Confer, Clarissa, W., *The Cherokee Nation in the Civil War*, University of Oklahoma Press, 2007.
- Cottrell, Steve, *Civil War in the Indian Territory*, Pelican Publishing Company, 1998.
- Cunningham, Frank, *General Stand Watie's Confederate Indians*, University of Oklahoma Press, 1998
- Gaines, W. Craig, *The Confederate Cherokees, John Drew's Regiment of Mounted Rifles*, Louisiana State University Press, 1989.
- Hoig, Stanley, W., *The Cherokees and Their Chiefs*, The University of Arkansas Press, 1998.
- Hood, Charlotte Adams, *Jackson's White Plumes*, Lavender Publishing Company, 1995.
- Jordan, Elaine, *Indian Trail Trees*, Jordan Ink Publishing Company, 1997.
- Lardas, Mark, *Native American Mounted Rifleman, 1861-65*, Osprey Publishing Company, 2006.
- Marcy, Capt. Randolph B., *The Prairie Traveler*, Applewood Books, 1859.
- Mooney, James, *Cherokee History, Myths and Sacred Formulas*, Cherokee Publications, 2006.
- Shea, William L., *The Campaign for Pea Ridge*, Eastern National Park Civil War Series, 2001.
- Wiley, Bell Irvin, *The Life of Johnny Reb, The Common Soldier of the Confederacy*, Louisiana State University Press, 1943.

Printed in the United States
145367LV00001B/9/P